A SMALL WEEPING

A SMALL WEEPING

ALEX GRAY

Allison & Busby Limited
12 Fitzroy Mews
London W1T 6DW
www.allisonandbusby.com

Hardcover published in Great Britain in 2004.
Paperback edition first published in 2005.
This B format edition published in 2009.

'Lucifer Falling' from *Collected Poems*
by Norman MacCaig, published by Chatto and Windus.
Used by kind permission of The Random House Group Ltd.

A CIP catalogue record for this book is available from
the British Library.

15

ISBN 978-0-7490-8388-5

The paper used for this Allison & Busby publication
has been produced from trees that have been legally sourced
from well-managed and credibly certified forests.

Printed and bound by CPI Group
(UK) Ltd, Croydon, CR0 4YY

ALEX GRAY was born and educated in Glasgow. She has worked as a folk singer, a visiting officer for the Department of Social Security and an English teacher. She has been awarded the Scottish Association of Writers' Constable and Pitlochry trophies for her crime writing. Married with a son and daughter, she now writes full time.

This novel is dedicated to the memory of Cathrene Anderson 30.5.47 – 27.10.99

LUCIFER FALLING

The black radiance
was Lucifer falling.
Space grieved for him
shuddering at its own guilt
and moons were never the same
after passing through
the gauze of wings.
The crystal battlements shook
to hear him laughing;
and somewhere amid
the angelic jubilations
there was a small weeping,
forecast
of the time to come.

Norman MacCaig

Prologue

The feather wafted upwards, a fine wispy curve, and for seconds it sailed the air. Slowly, slowly it began its downward journey, tacking and spinning on the currents; slight, light, hovering and shimmering. The dust motes danced against the sunlight like a cloud of gnats as the white feather passed them by. It sank at last in a curtsey and settled on the bed, still as the body below the sheets.

Chapter One

There was something appropriate about the fog blotting out everything beyond the station, thought Lorimer as he made his way through George Square. It was as if the natural world was trying to obliterate whatever waited for him behind the swirling curtain of mist. The red surface below his feet was darkened to the colour of old blood, statues loomed out of the mist like silent sentinels and even the tops of buildings were obscured by the pall of dankness, giving an impression of walking through some subterranean chamber. He'd be doing that soon enough. The woman's body had been discovered in the lift between the upper and lower platforms of Queen Street station. Who she was and how she came to be there at all were the questions uppermost in the Detective Chief Inspector's mind.

Lorimer had been woken from a fitful sleep around three a.m. After the Transport Police had alerted the Area Control room in Cowcaddens, the call had filtered through to Lorimer as the on-duty DCI. Now he was rounding the corner of George Street, his eyes drawn to the striped scene-of-crime tape cordoning off the station's entrance. No taxis would be plying their trade up here for a while, that was for sure, he thought, seeing the line of official vehicles parked on North Hanover Street. He'd deliberately left his own car across the square, wishing to approach the railway station on foot as a stranger might have done. Perspective, that's what he'd wanted. But all he'd found was this Gothic landscape.

A spiteful little wind blew along the narrow,

cobbled lane across the road. It caught the back of his neck, reminding him, too late, of his wife Maggie's sleepy advice to put on a scarf. The uniformed officer standing outside was shifting from one foot to another, beating his gloved hands across his arms in an effort to keep himself warm.

"Sir?" The police constable came to immediate attention as he recognised Lorimer.

"Been here long, Constable?"

"About half an hour, sir. We were in the area," the PC explained, making a move to unlock the glass doors into the station. They opened with a sigh and Lorimer stepped into the light.

Inside was not much warmer, fog swirling along the tracks from the black hole beyond the length of a parked train. Lorimer stared out into the void, wondering.

"What about Transport? Wasn't there an officer on duty tonight?"

"Supposed to be, but they don't always stay in the station for the entire shift, sir," the constable replied, not meeting Lorimer's eye. Someone's head was going to roll for this all right, especially if the Press got hold of it. But the DCI didn't seem to be in a hurry to lay the blame at anyone's door. Instead he continued to stare down the track as if his vision could penetrate the tunnel's hidden gloom beyond platform 7.

His eyes wandered back along the length of the platform, coming to rest on blue painted plywood sheeting that surrounded the lift area.

"That was quick. Who rigged that lot up, then?"

"It was like that, sir. The lifts are being renovated at the moment."

"So how do we gain access?"

"It's downstairs, sir," the constable replied. "We've got the area sealed off at platform 8 on the lower level."

"The stairs are over by the other side, aren't they?" Lorimer murmured, looking round but making no immediate move across the forecourt of the station. He wasn't squeamish but part of him had wanted to see the station empty and open like this before the body downstairs took precedence in his immediate thoughts. He walked back along the platform towards the lifts then turned to face the building on the opposite side of the rails, the stationmaster's office. Even standing on tiptoe, Lorimer was unable to see the upper windows for the train parked beside him. He nodded to himself, wondering who could have had access to the lifts during the night. There'd be plenty of questions for the stationmaster to answer.

A scattering of traffic cones surrounded the entrance to the lift, a device on somebody's part, no doubt, to assist the Scene of Crime boys when they turned up. Lorimer approached the blue hoardings and peered in. The concertina doors had been pushed aside and he could see a single line of light from the shaft below. Voices murmured beneath his feet. Looking up into the empty socket of the lift mechanism, Lorimer saw only a tangle of cables. With a sigh he turned and headed for the stairs that would take him to the lower level platforms of Queen Street Station.

By contrast to the violet blue gloominess of the upper level, platforms 8 and 9 dazzled the eyes. The walls were wasp-yellow with a lip for seating and between the two platforms ran a central area supported by filthy, black pillars.

A huge bear of a man dressed in a British Rail donkey jacket emblazoned with orange fluorescent panels looked up as Lorimer approached the lift doors.

There was something like relief in the railwayman's expression; authority had arrived in the form of this tall figure whose hand took his in a reassuringly firm grip.

"This is Mr Gibson, sir."

"You're the stationmaster?"

"No, sir. But I was in charge tonight. I'm the supervisor," the man shook his head as if somehow he'd been responsible for the whole sorry mess within his station. "I, well…" he tailed off, raising a hand towards the lift. Then, dropping it with a sigh, he stepped back as if to introduce the main character in this early morning drama.

Lorimer gave the railwayman an understanding nod and turned towards the light flooding out from the lift.

The woman lay in one corner away from the door, her head resting against the wall. For an instant she looked like a rag doll that had been flung down by some petulant child, her legs splayed awkwardly. Long strands were escaping from a plastic clip that skewered her hair. Lorimer could see the gaping mouth that had opened in protest as her last breath was cut off. But it was her eyes that would disturb his sleep for weeks to come. Their expression of terror made his head resonate with her scream. He could hear it echoing around the damp walls of the station.

Lorimer would be glad when a police surgeon came on the scene to close those eyes.

His gaze dropped to the woman's neck. Two ends of a red chiffon scarf hung like banners either side of her chin. She'd been strangled. It was one of the commonest methods of killing that he'd seen in his career. Sometimes it was a domestic gone wrong, other times a crime of passion, but here? Just what had happened here?

He looked again at the red scarf and hoped to hell there'd be some traces for forensics. Lorimer stood back, taking in the dead woman's clothing in one glance; the soiled white jacket, skimpy top and short skirt were like a badge of her trade. She wasn't the first one on the game to be so brutally murdered in this city and she wouldn't be the last. Lorimer had long since learned to control the surge of pity and anger that threatened to overwhelm him in such cases but anyone observing that clenched jaw might see he wasn't yet inured to either emotion.

Lorimer walked to one side of the body, oblivious to the stares of the two men standing outside, then stopped. He hunkered down closer, considering the woman's hands. At first glance he'd thought they must be tied but now he saw that they had been deliberately arranged in a praying gesture, palm to palm, pointing towards her feet. Lorimer bent forward, his attention caught by the unnatural gesture. Was she holding something? Or was it just a shadow? Lorimer shifted his position so that the overhead light showed the woman's hands more clearly. Fearful of disturbing the corpse before the arrival of the on-duty pathologist and the SOCOs, the DCI peered at the space between the flattened palms. Yes, there was something there. Lorimer drew a pen out of his inside pocket and gently lifted one white cuff.

There, like a blossom of blood, lay a single carnation, its stem fixed between the dead woman's palms.

He let the sleeve of her jacket fall back into place, wondering what Dr Solomon Brightman might make of this murder. This looked like the hallmark of a ritualistic killing. Under his gaze the woman was being transformed from a flesh and blood creature to a victim whose death had to be solved. Lorimer had long ago learned the need to detach himself from the horror of a killing. The victim, whoever she was, would become real enough in the days to come, but for now he must force himself to see her objectively. He was looking at a new and complicated case and not just a case for forensics, either. They'd be mad not to use Solly's expertise as a criminal profiler.

Voices from the staircase made him look up. Two figures appeared out of the darkness carrying their kitbags. The cavalry had arrived in the shape of Dr Rosie Fergusson and Dr Roy Young, forensic pathologists. Between the two of them there should be some answers to the dead woman's silent cry for help.

Gibson, the railwayman, caught Lorimer's sleeve as he walked out to meet the two medics, "D'you need me for anything else?" The man's face took on a white glow under the fluorescent light making him look as sick as he probably felt.

"Yes," said Lorimer shortly, "but I wouldn't hover around here if I were you. Stay upstairs in the staffroom meantime." He glanced at the PC who had, until his arrival, been in charge. "Any chance of some hot drinks? It's freezing down here."

"We can rustle something up in the manager's

office," Gibson told them both. "I'll show you." He led the constable towards the stairs, his gait quickening. Lorimer smiled wryly. Even the biggest guys were still daunted by the sight of a corpse. Not so this pair, he thought, striding forward to greet them.

"You do pick them, don't you?" Rosie glared at him as if Lorimer had manufactured the murder all by himself. "Here I was all cosy, tucked up with a good book thinking nobody would be daft enough to end it all on a night like this." The diminutive blonde was already delving into her kitbag and pulling out white overalls.

"Don't listen to her," Roy Young laughed. "She'd be out of there like a whippet once the call came in." Lorimer grinned. Rosie's grumbles would stop the minute she set foot inside the locus. Her professionalism was total. Even though she was the senior pathologist she didn't pull rank and always took her fair share of duties. Looking at her now, pulling her hair back into a knot, Lorimer marvelled at how Rosie Fergusson revelled in the business of cadavers and their hidden secrets.

His thoughts were cut off by another voice commanding his attention.

"You beat us to it, then," Alistair Wilson strode across to join him. In the wake of the detective sergeant was a tall young man whose padded jacket made him look like the Michelin Man. Maggie had joked that the boy from Lewis was so new to his role as a detective constable that you could still see the shine. Niall Cameron nodded to Lorimer but immediately looked beyond him, his eyes drawn towards the figures huddled within the open lift.

"Want a look?" Lorimer asked. Both men stepped

forward and Lorimer heard Rosie's "tsk" of annoyance as she stood up to make room for the officers.

"Bloody hell, we've got a right one here," Wilson's voice echoed coldly over the deserted platform. "Put to sleep with a flower in its hand. What d'you think, young Niall? Is it Ophelia or what?"

Niall Cameron glowered down at the detective sergeant, his pale cheeks reddening, aware of everybody's scrutiny. Lorimer watched him, glad to note that the boy was wise enough not to rise to the bait.

"*She* hasn't got a name yet, Sergeant," Rosie snapped, "and if you don't mind we'll not find that or much else until you take yourself off!"

"That's me told, then," Alistair Wilson grinned at the pathologist, totally unabashed. He tried to catch Cameron's eye but the Lewisman had already backed out of the confined space and was looking expectantly at Lorimer.

"This your first murder case?" Lorimer murmured, steering Cameron away from the scene of crime, one hand lightly upon his shoulder.

The lad nodded, a frown creasing the space between his thick, straight eyebrows.

"Don't mind Sergeant Wilson. It's just his way."

"I don't mind. I just don't like to think of her as a *thing*, that's all."

Lorimer nodded. "I know, but sometimes it helps to keep a distance between the victim and the investigating team. A murder investigation is unlike any other. Emotions can run high."

Lorimer shrugged then added, "She probably will be named Ophelia just for the record, you know, now that DS Wilson has given her a soubriquet. At least until there is a positive I.D." Lorimer could see that Wilson's offhand approach had ruffled the lad but despite this Cameron was turning back towards the corpse as if he wanted another moment to see for himself.

"I know Dr Fergusson would be pleased if you attended the post mortem," he told the detective constable. "Only if you want to," he added, watching Cameron's jaw tighten.

"I don't mind," he replied with a diffidence that earned him some points with Lorimer. This one was cool under fire, all right.

"So," Alistair Wilson had caught them up now. "No handbag, no apparent identification. D'you think she was local?"

"Who knows?" Lorimer replied, thinking once more of the railway tracks that disappeared into the mist. "Depends what direction she came from, doesn't it?"

"Want me to ask about?" Wilson persisted. "Try Waterloo Street, maybe?" he suggested, mentioning one of the main haunts of Glasgow's prostitutes. He had thrust his hands deep into the pockets of his raincoat and pulled it tightly across his body against the bitter chill, but his eyes were alight with the desire to be off on the hunt for whoever had put an end to this poor wretch. His detective sergeant might seem flippant at times but Lorimer knew it was just a front. Under the surface Wilson was as angry and disgusted as any of them at the waste of a young life.

"Won't do any harm. If any of them are daft enough to be out in a night like this," he added.

"Oh, they'll be daft enough if they need a hit,"

Wilson laughed mirthlessly.

"Okay. It's worth a try. But make sure you've got an accurate description from Dr Fergusson. We'd certainly be wasting our time waiting for a missing person's report if she was on the game. Meantime, I think DC Cameron should take a statement from Mr Gibson. He was the one who found the body," Lorimer explained, pointing towards a door. "He's upstairs in the staff room," he added.

As if on cue, a constable descended the stairs bearing a tray of polystyrene cups, their contents steaming in the cold air like alchemists' potions. Lorimer retreated to the edge of the platform, observing the tableau around the open lift. An aura seemed to surround the group as though their breaths had clouded together. For an instant he thought about the dead woman's spirit. Then he turned and walked back to the stationmaster's office.

Lorimer was drinking his third hot chocolate of the night as he made his way back to the North Hanover Street entrance. The SOCOs had come and gone, the body was on its way to the mortuary and Frank Gibson had been driven home. His footsteps echoed across the stone floor of Platform 7. It was still as cold as the grave. He'd wandered around the perimeter of the station with DC Cameron, checking out the CCTV cameras. It was most likely the killer had come by car, parking in the car park at the back where no swivelling grey heads recorded the comings and goings of staff vehicles. There was so much to be done. CCTV footage from the area around George Square, North Hanover Street and Cathedral Street was being carefully checked by the night shift at Cowcaddens. The scene of crime people had gone over the area between the car park and Platform 7. It was the only logical way a stranger could have entered the station unseen. The black cab drivers were being contacted to find out about any late night drops or uplifts from the rank at the station door. And what would DS Wilson find from his questioning of the girls along in Waterloo Street?

Gibson's main concern had been for the minimum disruption to the trains. They'd keep the North Hanover Street entrance cordoned off from the public and Platform 7 was out of commission meantime, but the station would open for business as usual. Lorimer yawned. It wasn't yet daylight and he had hours of work still ahead of him. These nine-to-five commuters didn't know they were living.

Chapter Two

It had been a long day. Rosie stretched out with a yawn that made her jaw crack. It was good to be finished at last, she thought, sinking into the leather folds of her favourite chesterfield in the University staff club. The post mortem had shown death by strangulation and it looked like the ligature was the dead woman's own scarf. Forensic testing would verify that eventually, of course.

Lorimer had brought along his lanky Highlander to observe. Give the lad credit, thought Rosie, swirling the ice cubes at the bottom of her brandy glass, he'd not blanched at the sight of her opening up the cadaver. Some of them simply fainted away, usually the big macho ones that wouldn't flinch in a bar room brawl when glasses were flying. But DC Cameron had watched with an interested detachment as if he'd been one of her senior med. students.

The staff club was quiet tonight, just three elderly gentlemen discussing academic something-or-others over by the fireside. Rosie found the sound of their low voices soothing. She didn't want to make small talk or any other sort of talk until she had to. Despite her tiredness there was an underlying excitement. Solly would soon be here and then she could give him an account of the day's events.

Lorimer had assured her that the psychologist would be invited on board for this investigation. Although he was the Senior Investigating Officer, the Procurator Fiscal still had to be consulted. However, he hadn't shown any worries over Solly's involvement.

The queer sight of that carnation pressed between

the woman's hands still bothered Rosie. Straight-
forward murder was okay but weird stuff like that
gave her the willies. She considered the wording of her
draft report. She'd outlined the position of the praying
hands resting on the woman's vulva. It was a point
she'd already endowed with significance in her own
mind though the report afforded no room for sym-
bolic speculation. That was the area of expertise that
she expected from Solomon Brightman.

Solomon. She gave a tiny sigh. There was something otherworldly about him that she found both
attractive and exasperating, his timekeeping, for
instance. He was notoriously late for everything and
tonight he'd already kept Rosie waiting for the best
part of an hour. So why did she do it? Rosie asked herself. She was not a naturally patient person, just the
opposite, but since getting to know Solly she'd found
herself habitually waiting in the staff club where
they'd meet up after work. He didn't drive so Rosie
often dropped him off home even though his flat was
less than ten minutes' walk through Kelvingrove Park.

Rosie Fergusson was hooked and it surprised her.
Solly wasn't her type at all. He had no great interest in
socialising other than to sum up his fellow man, but he
seemed happy enough in her company even though
he'd been a bit shy to begin with. They'd met in the
most inauspicious of circumstances, the locus of a
grisly murder in Garnethill, and she'd taken an instant
liking to him.

The ice had melted in her glass. Rosie slurped the
watery dregs, considering whether to have another
and leave the car parked overnight. She could always
take a taxi home. If she didn't get a better offer, a bad

little voice murmured in her head. Rosie grinned at the delicious naughtiness of the thought then looked up to catch the barman's eye.

"Same again, please," she smiled at him, holding out the glass.

"Rosie." Suddenly Solomon was standing there looking down at her, his eyes twinkling gently behind those horn-rimmed spectacles.

"So sorry I'm late. Had to take another class for one of my colleagues. Fellow I told you about, remember? He's having a bad time of it, poor man." Solly unwound an enormous knitted scarf from his neck as he spoke, his expression somewhere between apologetic and glad to see her, as Rosie noted with delight. "There," he plonked himself down beside her and flung an arm around her shoulders, giving a friendly squeeze.

"Never mind that," Rosie told him. "You're here now and I've been dying to tell you what happened today. Lorimer's got a new murder case and he says you're going to be asked onto the team."

"In that case I'd better have a drink, don't you think?" Solly grinned at her. "Before you tell me the nastier bits."

Rosie waited impatiently as he sauntered over to the bar then returned with a pint glass of orange squash.

"That all you're having? I thought you'd be needing a double vodka at least," she joked.

"Really? Okay, let's hear it."

"Well, it started off this morning. Early. And I mean early. Something like four o' clock. Peter and I were called out to Queen Street Station. It was bloody freezing. Anyway. A woman's body had been discovered in the lift between the upper and lower levels. Strangled. Probably with her own scarf."

"Any idea who she is?"

Rosie shook her head. "Looks like a prostitute and there are plenty of traces of semen. No handbag, nothing in her pockets; young, probably early twenties. She'd been dead long enough for rigor to set in."

"Sounds pretty normal," Solly put in. "Sorry, I didn't mean that to sound callous, but why do they want me?"

"Ah, that's the interesting part. Whoever strangled her didn't just leave her lying there in a heap in the corner." Rosie paused for dramatic effect. "Wait till I tell you. They stuck a flower in her hands then put them together in a praying position. Like this," she added, placing her hands palm to palm, pointing down between her legs.

Solomon did not respond for a moment, gazing at Rosie's hands.

"What sort of flower?"

"A red carnation. One of the long-stemmed sort. Why? Could that have any significance?"

"Possibly. For the killer, at any rate."

"What about the praying hands? D'you think that might have some religious meaning?"

"How can I tell? I haven't even seen a report, let alone been asked officially to comment."

"Okay, let's look at this clinically. We'll say that God created Eve with the anatomical advantage of having arms that stretch towards the genitals; that might simply be the way they fell but I don't think so."

"Why not?"

"Wait till you see the photographs. It really looks like he's made a kind of ritual out of the flower and the hands. It's been done so carefully. But what I wanted to ask you is, why place the praying hands downwards like that? Why not fix them up so that they looked as if they were really praying?"

"You're hoping I'll make the leap between the genital area and a sexual motivation," Solomon gave her a half smile.

"Sort of. I don't know. She'd certainly been sexually active. There was semen in her mouth as well as in the vagina."

"Lorimer thinks it's a stranger killing, then? Just because of the flower?"

"I think so too, Solly. It wasn't like the killer was sneering at her. It was different. As if...oh, I don't know. As if he had some sort of remorse, maybe."

"A valedictory message, perhaps?"

Rosie squinted up at him. Her excitement had evaporated between waiting for Solly to arrive and his almost diffident response to her news.

"I thought you'd be pleased to be working on another case with us," she huffed.

The psychologist gave a sigh. "I'll be highly flattered to be asked, but my workload right now is pretty scary. With Tom's classes..."

"Solly, you don't mean that!"

"No, of course I don't."

"Then you'll come on board with us?"

"If you're sure I'll be asked. What about Superintendent Mitchison?"

Rosie made a face. The new superintendent was not

making himself popular with anybody. Rosie and Solly had met him at George Phillips' retirement dinner, never really expecting him to take over from the Divisional Commander. They'd all seen the Super's job as Lorimer's and it had been a shock when Mark Mitchison was appointed to the post.

"Mitchison would probably ask you to sign several forms in triplicate," Rosie snorted, "but he's not the SIO in this case. It's down to Lorimer. Anyway, I don't think Mitchison would oppose your involvement, especially if it gets the Press off his back. Having a celebrated profiler will give him all the kudos he wants."

"Well, we'll see," Solomon replied, nodding gravely into his orange squash. "We'll see."

"Yes!" Jimmy Greer punched the air and sat back down in front of his computer screen. It had paid off. A bit of chat here, a backhander there, ach, it was all in a good day's work. Tonight there'd be punters tut-tutting over the murder of some scummy wee whore but they'd be reading his byline. Jimmy's nicotine-stained teeth grinned out from his moustache as he typed in the copy. The Police Press Conference hadn't given that much away but Jimmy had his own methods of filling in the blanks left by tight-lipped senior officers. So far he'd avoided any brushes with the Press Complaints Commission, though he'd sailed pretty close to the wind a few times.

DCI Lorimer was in charge of this case and Jimmy knew he'd be lucky to get anything off him. Still, there were always hard up coppers who'd tip him the nod whenever there was something salacious enough to tempt the senior reporter.

Greer hunched his long, cadaverous frame over the desk, his reddened fingers tapping out the details he'd gleaned about the murdered woman. She'd still to be identified but from the description the man Gibson had given him, he could tell what she had been, all right. Anyway, no self-respecting woman should have been out in the station at that time of night.

Chapter Three

The case of Deirdre McCann was headline news for three days. By the end of the first week the political situation in the Scottish Parliament had taken precedence over the dwindling paragraphs concerning the prostitute's bizarre killing. Then there was nothing. Even Jimmy Greer couldn't manufacture a news item from thin air. Oh, yes, the case was certainly still a live one, he was assured, but damn all was happening, or that was how it seemed. He'd managed a piece on her mates for the Sunday supplement. There were lots of photos of the women lounging against walls and smoking. But his text had been padded up by the prostitutes' own stories. Not much was really known about the McCann woman. Twenty-three, originally from Airdrie, a known prostitute and heroin user, she'd been on the game since her mid-teens. There was no family in the background causing a ruckus, which was a pity. Both her parents were dead and her only sister didn't want to talk to the Press. Sometimes the family angle could keep copy going for weeks with protests about police incompetence thrown in for good measure.

DCI Lorimer hadn't forgotten Deirdre McCann though she'd been dead now for almost three months. Intensive police work had uncovered her identity and her manner of death but even with the help of Dr Solomon Brightman there had been no way forward in the case. Unless they were very lucky it would remain unsolved, adding yet another layer of discontent to Lorimer's present mood.

As he sat as his desk, scanning the latest memo from Mitchison, Lorimer wished for the hundredth time that George Phillips' taciturn face would appear round his door, demanding action, demanding results. But Lorimer only saw him whenever the former superintendent called round on some committee business for the Chief Constable. The new man in charge of the division was a different kettle of fish from old George. Fish was right, thought Lorimer. Mark Mitchison was a cold fish if ever there was one. He went by the book, didn't even take a drink or socialise with the lads. Lorimer had nursed some promotion hopes of his own, as everybody knew, so it looked too much like sour grapes to be other than polite to the new boss, but Lorimer groaned inwardly every time they met. Mitchison was a paper man. He generated forests of administration and memos on a weekly and daily basis. Lorimer was fed up to the back teeth with him and had even considered asking for a transfer.

There was a vacancy for a training officer at Tulliallan, the police college, and he had gone as far as writing for an application form. But he knew fine it would end up in the bin next to Mitchison's endless memos. Meantime it was put up and shut up. Maggie had been badly upset by his failure to secure the post of Superintendent. She'd seen it as a foregone conclusion, especially after the successful outcome of the St. Mungo's case. They all had.

Accepting the commiseration of his fellow officers had not been easy. It had been even harder to persuade them to transfer their loyalty to this new man whom so few of them knew. Lorimer had met him on various courses and at George Phillips' retiral dinner. He was a smooth, good-looking individual who curried favour with the Press boys. Anyway, it was done now, the man had been in the post for almost six months and if Maggie was disappointed by Lorimer's failure that was just too bad.

A knock on the door banished all these thoughts from his mind and he looked up to see the dark head of DC Cameron appear.

"A call from on high, sir," Cameron grinned. It was his oblique way of telling him that Mitchison required his presence. Why the blighter didn't simply phone through to his extension baffled the DCI. It was yet another of the man's annoying traits, using an officer to summon him to his office.

"Sit down, Lorimer," the Superintendent waved his hand in a sweeping gesture. Mitchison was full of this sort of little thing: mannerisms that only irritated. You'd think you were being invited into a Papal audience, Lorimer had remarked to Alistair Wilson the first time Mitchison had summoned them into what had been George's old room. Now, as he looked around him, Lorimer realised there was no trace of his old colleague whatsoever. The walls had been painted beige and there were mementoes from Mitchison's career hanging everywhere. Lorimer glanced at them. There was plenty to show that the Superintendent had been busy in various parts of the globe. It was, reflected Lorimer, like a kid's bedroom full of football pennants.

"I really don't know how to begin, Chief Inspector," Michison's frigid smile was directed at Lorimer.

"I understand that you have been contemplating a

move to Tulliallan." The nasal voice was not asking a question. Lorimer clenched his teeth. Someone at the training school had been gossiping. He cursed inwardly. It was becoming like the bloody Secret Service the way this man kept tabs on them all. Lorimer shot him a look but said nothing.

"Hm. Not too happy with detective work these days, perhaps. Too many cold cases?"

"On the contrary, sir," Lorimer forced himself to be icily polite. "Just keeping my options open."

"In that case you'll be pleased to increase your present knowledge of investigative procedures." Mitchison's smile never faltered and Lorimer had a sudden longing to wipe it off the man's face.

"Part of the Chief Constable's strategy for effective urban policing is to encourage you all to study methods used by police officers from overseas. This division is one hundred per cent behind him on this, naturally." The Superintendent rolled back and forth in his chair while Lorimer tried hard not to grit his teeth. Maggie was complaining that he even did it in his sleep these days. Mitchison's nasal voice expounded the virtues of his latest ploy.

"You may be interested to know that we have been chosen to play host to a most experienced officer from the State of Florida." Mitchison's smile became almost beatific but if he expected Lorimer to grin inanely he was much mistaken. This DCI wasn't giving the Chief Constable many brownie points for originality. It was only a few years back that there had been similar interest in comparative policing methods during the highly acclaimed *Operation Spotlight* campaign, when New York had supplied some specially trained officers to liaise with Strathclyde.

"Officer Lipinski will be arriving at Glasgow Airport at 10.30 a.m. next Thursday. I want you to be there to do the usual welcome-to-Glasgow on our behalf. Here's the dossier. I think you'll find it makes fascinating reading." Mitchison handed over a slim black file then raised his hand in another imperious gesture to show that the meeting was over. Lorimer stood up and dragged his chair over the thick new carpet pile.

"Sir," he gave a swift nod before turning away. It was all he could do to stop himself clicking his heels and saluting the man. Once out in the corridor Lorimer strode towards his own room then halted abruptly. He needed some fresh air after that. In a few minutes Lorimer was down the stairs and out of the building. He took a turn away from the main part of the city, out of reach of any close circuit television cameras that would show his whereabouts, and headed for the nearest park.

Glasgow wasn't short of wide green spaces. That was one of the things most visitors marvelled at. There were parks and gardens within walking distance of most parts of the city. And it wasn't just the tourists who wandered among the flowerbeds and fountains. Summer brought out the mini-skirted office girls clutching their lunches in paper bags. The first blink of sun and there they would be, basking in the warmth as if it were Lanzarote instead of the west coast of Scotland. They were as predictable a phenomenon as learner drivers in the spring.

Lorimer slowed his pace as a flurry of birds flew in front of him. The pigeons thrived on lunchtime crumbs. Lorimer screwed his eyes up against the sunshine, taking in the figures seated along the pathway. There were always some derelicts sunk over in the benches, biding their time to rake in the bins for scraps of their own. Lorimer knew them all by sight. Since some of them included his own touts, he liked to roll by the park when he could. However nobody was paying the detective any attention today and he came to a halt in front of an empty bench beneath a flowering cherry tree. Pink blossoms lay scattered on the newly cut grass and Lorimer flicked his hand over the seat where more of them had fallen.

If he closed his eyes for a moment he could pretend that he was back on holiday in Portugal. The heat gave that momentary illusion of continental sun. Even the noise of traffic didn't diminish the feeling. Lagos hadn't been far away from civilisation. For a few moments Lorimer indulged in the sights and sounds of Portugal in his imagination until the file slipped off his knee to the ground. As he bent to pick it up with a grunt he wondered briefly about the man he was about to meet. He'd be on his way pretty soon. Curious now, in spite of himself, Lorimer crossed one foot over his knee to balance the file and opened it. The officer's face looked up at him from the colour photograph. Lorimer grinned back. So this was Officer Lipinski, was it? Well, well. Maybe the Chief Constable's ideas about sharing policing methods wouldn't be too bad after all.

Chapter Four

The Grange was perched on a windy hill overlooking the terraces of Mount Florida and Cathcart. Like many of the old Victorian properties that had survived conversion into service flats after the war, it now served as a medical clinic. A wide strip of lawn curved around the chipped driveway then fell sharply away to a steep bank, ending at the path below in a mass of shrubbery. Tom Coutts noticed the huge buds of the rhododendrons tipped with scarlet. A few more weeks of sunshine and the whole lot would be a blaze of colour. As he approached the massive front door his eye rested on the ancient brass bell that pulled straight out of the stonework. There were still so many original features in this rambling place and Tom had sometimes wondered why they hadn't been swept away with all the other alterations to the old house. He heard the jangle of the bell and almost immediately footsteps came hurrying towards the frosted glass door.

Her smoky blue uniform appeared as an Impressionistic blob then the door was flung open and a young nurse stood there staring at him. Tom frowned at her then his brow cleared in recognition.

"Kirsty? Kirsty MacLeod?"

"Dr Coutts. Gosh. It's a while since I saw you. What brings you here?" The nurse ushered Tom into the darkened hallway where light from outside filtered through lozenges of stained glass flanking the main door, casting streaks of green and yellow across the pale emulsioned walls.

"I'm a patient," Tom grimaced but saw that his

half-smile had brought a look of curiosity to the young woman's eyes.

"Depression. Like most of the cases in here." Tom shrugged. "Just never got over her death, I suppose."

"Oh," the girl suddenly seemed embarrassed. "I'm sorry. Are you in for a therapy session, then?"

"Yes. I've been coming for a while now," Tom answered, directing his gaze at a spot on the floor. "Anyway, I didn't expect to see you here." He looked up then put out a hand, touching her sleeve.

"Community nursing wasn't…" she broke off as if stuck for an answer.

"Satisfying enough?" Tom suggested.

"Something like that. There was a post going here and I grabbed it. Not too many private clinics for nurses specialising in neural diseases, you know. I was lucky to get it."

"Nonsense," Tom chided. "Nan always said you were the best." He hesitated as if trying to find the right words. "We couldn't have survived without you, you know."

Kirsty looked away from him and he tried in vain to see her expression.

"Funny I've not seen you here before."

"I'm normally on nights. Just covering for some-one today," she replied. Kirsty turned back towards Tom but did not meet his eyes. "Your appointment," she reminded him, stepping towards the corridor that led to the therapy rooms.

Tom followed her, his heart thumping. It was the same every time. He had come to banish his demons but now the very act of entering this place had added to them. What tricks would they have in store for him today, he wondered, giving Kirsty MacLeod a little nod as he turned the door handle of a room marked "Patients' Lounge".

Inside there were several people seated in a circle. One metal chair was empty and as Tom entered all eyes turned towards the latecomer. His mind shifted briefly to the comforting familiarity of the lecture theatre where his students would meet his arrival with friendly enthusiasm. Now, as he faced this room full of people who were still strangers, all he could feel was a clutch of fear deep in his stomach.

"Tom, come on in," the psychotherapist beckoned him over to the only remaining chair set in the circle. On either side of the empty seat were the two men he least liked in the group. One was a young man whose shaved head bore strange Celtic tattoos. His faded black t-shirt was torn at the shoulders with another twisted design circling each pale, muscular upper arm. Bron had been in hospital for his depression, a fact that he flaunted to mere day patients like Tom.

On Tom's other side was Sam, a former shipyard worker who had been redundant for years. In the beginning they had told one another of their occupations and Sam had been openly contemptuous about Tom's profession.

"Psychologist, eh?" he had sneered. "How come ye cannae sort yourself out, then?"

Now as Tom sat down, he glared at the University lecturer as if he had no right to be there at all. Even the therapist came in for some verbal abuse but Tom knew this was part of his job. He probably expected it. How about the nurses, though? Were they trained to take that sort of crap, too?

As the therapist began his session Tom tried to concentrate on his words, using them as a mantra to focus on the topic. Anxiety. It was ironic that the very act of coming into this group situation should create anxieties for him, he thought. Being a psychologist didn't help in the least, in fact it had made him even more self-critical. Nan's death had been the trigger. But now he must move forward, he'd been told. Be positive. Affirmation was the key.

He would heal. He would be well again. Then there would be no need for him to sit with these patients whose anger reached out at him with invisible tentacles.

Chapter Five

Divine unclipped the belt that had pinioned her to the airline seat for considerably more hours than the scheduled flight should have taken. Her fellow passengers were rising now and pulling travel bags from the overhead bins. Divine waited. She was in the unenviable middle of the row of five that DC10 passengers strive to avoid, so she wasn't going anywhere fast. Besides, she was in no hurry now that they'd landed. The shuttle was leaving Heathrow in just under two hours. Plenty of time to ease herself out of this pigeon coop and find her connection.

The flight attendant smiled at her sympathetically. Not a hair of the young girl's head was out of place. It prompted Divine to return the smile and comment, "How come you girls look so fresh after a night like that?"

In an Irish accent that had charmed her American passengers the girl announced, "Oh, I'm bionic, me!" As if to prove her point she hopped up onto an armrest, revealing a tiny waist and a slim pair of legs as she reached towards another bin. Stretching her own long legs was something Divine was longing to do. Her sigh turned into a yawn.

At last the trail of passengers disappeared down the aisle and Divine ducked out of the seat and made her way onto British territory for the first time.

The flight to Glasgow was uneventful and a lot more comfortable than the larger aircraft that had ferried Divine across the Atlantic. She recognised several of her fellow travellers from the earlier flight. Some were obviously families and couples returning home to Scotland after their trip to the sun. There was a tall man with greying hair who had spent the entire journey deeply ensconced in paperwork. Divine glanced at his hawk-like profile several times. He was worth looking at and he intrigued her. Divine was a people person, her old mother used to say of her youngest daughter. If she couldn't work out what a person's occupation was, then she'd simply make it up. Like Paul Simon, she had always loved "playing games with the faces" of people she travelled with. Who was the guy? Expensive suit, thin tweedy coat folded on the spare seat beside him. (Another good thing about this flight were the empty spaces where folks could spread out.) A scientist, maybe? Looked the scholarly type.

Her gaze swept over the other travellers. There was that boy with the ponytail. He'd come across with them too. American down to the toes of his sneakers. But not such a boy either. His ponytail was thin and the sideburns showed grey curls. He could be anybody. Divine knew these things now. Anonymous looking guys might be bums or millionaires. She used her powers of observation these days instead of her imagination. After all, that's what had brought her so far in her varied career.

Lorimer looked at his watch then scanned the arrivals screen. Where the hell was Lipinski? At last the information on the screen rolled over and proclaimed that flight BA2964 had landed. Lipinski would have gone through customs at London so there wouldn't be too much longer to wait.

At last the figures of travellers began to emerge and Lorimer's blue eyes bore down the corridor. A thin fellow carrying a worn leather document case under one arm strode past the policeman without a glance, his long tweed coat flapping around his legs. There were several family groups, one of whom was an Asian couple and their little daughters. The two children were obviously exhausted, clinging to their parents' sides like colourful small limpets.

The stream of passengers dwindled and Lorimer began to look at his watch again with impatience. A tall figure strode into view, wheeling an enormous carry-on bag behind him. As the figure drew closer, Lorimer could see that it wasn't a man at all but a black woman, her shiny hair drawn back into a tight knot. There was something commanding about her that made Lorimer stare; that loping stride and the head held high. For a brief moment the woman's eyes flickered in his direction and he looked away. It was rude to stare, his mum used to scold him. From the corner of his eye Lorimer noticed the woman pausing to change the hand that dragged her baggage. But then he was aware that she had not moved on and was standing right beside him. For a moment Lorimer was confused as he cast a look over a face that was on a level with his own. Then she smiled that smile he'd seen in the photograph and Lorimer recognised her.

Divine thrust out her hand at the rugged-looking man before her. "Officer Lipinski. How are you?"

The introductions at Divisional HQ were over and Divine Lipinski from Florida State Police Department was ready to go. She'd made an immediate impression on the team, though at six-feet two that wouldn't be hard, Lorimer thought. A commanding figure she might be, but the woman was yawning now and Lorimer was suddenly glad that Maggie had insisted on him bringing the American home for her first evening in Scotland.

"Okay, you'll meet them again tomorrow." Lorimer was about to turn and escort Divine out to his waiting car when he noticed DC Cameron stiffen and look beyond them. He sensed rather than saw the Superintendent enter the room and there was an almost tangible shift in the atmosphere. Even Divine noticed that, he saw. She straightened up, feet together, and folded her large hands behind her back.

"Ms Lipinski, Superintendent Mitchison," Lorimer heard his own voice make the necessary introductions as the Superintendent came forward, a smile fixed to his thin face. Again Lorimer found himself irritated by Mitchison's body language; the fingers circling the air, that condescending head to one side. He watched Divine's face to see if she would succumb to the good-looking senior officer's overtures. Detached, Lorimer heard the small talk as Divine politely described her flight.

"I'm sure Chief Inspector Lorimer will take good care of you. We'll see you in the morning," and he swept a gracious hand in their direction. Lorimer glanced at Divine and was gratified to see her narrow her eyes at Mitchison's back as he left the muster room.

"Okay. Home-time. You're bound to be pretty tired, right?"

"Yeah. I could do with a nap." She waved briefly at the other officers who were beginning to drift back to their various duties, then followed Lorimer. He took her the quick way down the back stairs to the car park and opened the door of his ageing Lexus. Divine seemed to notice the car for the first time.

"Hm. Nice wheels. What kind of salary are you guys on?" she asked.

It was meant as a joke but somehow the question got under his skin. It was as if Divine Lipinski were suggesting that the Lexus was the fruit of some illicit backhanders. Lorimer shrugged and gave her his standard reply, "No kids." Even in its perennially unwashed state the car raised a few eyebrows.

He'd given his passenger plenty of legroom on the return from the airport and now she sank gratefully into the worn leather seats.

"A short guided tour on the way home?"

"Sure."

Lorimer took the car right into the heart of the city, drove slowly around George Square, pointing out the City Chambers, before heading for the new High Court building.

"That's the city mortuary, right there," he nodded, then glanced across at his companion. She was fast asleep. For a moment Lorimer took his eyes off the road and contemplated the woman beside him. In sleep her features had relaxed and she looked older and more vulnerable. Suddenly he was glad that Maggie would be at home waiting for them.

Chapter Six

Kirsty MacLeod stretched her arms above her head and yawned. God, she was weary. Never again, she chided herself. That extra shift three days ago had totally wiped her out. Never mind, it would soon be the weekend and she had the prospect of two whole days when she could lie in bed if she felt like it.

All the patients had settled down for the night. The ones on suicide watch were usually the last to drop off, despite their sleeping pills. Peter and the others were all in place, sitting near the opened doors of the winding corridor so she wouldn't have to worry about that part of the clinic. Upstairs the girls and women with eating disorders had long since turned in. Kirsty had checked on each patient, adjusting drips and turning the heaters up. It was a cold night and these poor souls really felt every draught in the old building. She only had to see to Phyllis and that would be that. Then she'd have supper with Brenda and a bit of a blether before writing up the evening's notes.

It had been hard working here at first after having been out and about in the community. She'd been accustomed to her housebound patients but that could have become a problem too. Kirsty wasn't the sentimental type but she had become close to a few terminally ill patients, and their deaths had been hard to take. Nan Coutts, for instance.

The woman's multiple sclerosis had worsened so rapidly that the pneumonia hadn't been too much of a surprise. And poor Dr Coutts. Now he was here as a day patient, suffering the aftermath of all that strain. Kirsty gave herself a shake. It didn't do to dwell on the past. She'd made her choice now and the clinic was a really interesting place to work, full of challenging patients. Her training in neural disorders had made Kirsty an ideal candidate for the post here, she thought with satisfaction. Not only was she experienced with MS patients but she had nursed psychiatric cases in the community too.

The Grange only housed one patient with multiple sclerosis, however, and that was Phyllis Logan. She was in a specially designed room near the back of the house, overlooking the gardens, away from the busyness of the clinic's everyday appointments and therapy sessions. It was peace and quiet that the woman needed now for the remainder of her days.

Kirsty closed the door to the nurses' rest room and made her way quietly down the back stairs. Dim light shone from the uplighters cupped against the wall as she descended into the gloom. Odd, she thought. Someone's put the downstairs light off. Kirsty fiddled with the switch at the bottom of the stair, hearing it click back and forwards. The corridor stretched into blackness and no light was visible from Phyllis's room. It must be a fuse. She felt her way along the wall slowly, hoping her eyes would become accustomed to the inky darkness before she reached the patient's bedroom.

Suddenly there was the noise of feet coming towards her and Kirsty felt herself relax.

"Thank goodness," she began, then her eyes widened as she saw the figure loom up out of the dark.

Her cry was stifled as gloved hands seized her throat, pressing into the jugular vein. Her heels slipped on the polished surface of the floor as she struggled. Then she felt herself falling backwards into a deeper darkness than she'd ever known.

Phyllis stared at the doorway. In the darkness she could make out a shape coming towards her. The figure moved closer and closer until she could see the eyes boring into her own. Then there was a smile that chilled her bones and a slight shake of the head that she couldn't understand. The figure leaned over her and she closed her eyes in terror, feeling the weight of this intruder across her bed. A cold wet drop of something fell against her hand as the pressure on the bed was released. When she opened her eyes she could see the figure looking back at her from the door. He put one finger to his lips and tiptoed out again.

Phyllis shuddered under the thick covers, wondering why he'd come in the dead of night to steal one of her flowers.

Chapter Seven

Maggie had surpassed herself. Lorimer wiped his lips on the pink damask napkin, thinking about why he'd never seen this table linen before. A wedding present unearthed for the occasion after all these years, perhaps? Their best crystal shone in the candlelight and it reminded Lorimer of Christmases long ago when they'd been to Maggie's parents for dinner. Then all the family silver had been specially polished for the celebratory meal. He could still remember the agony of trying to hold those tiny porcelain coffee cups without breaking off their handles. Maggie had understood his discomfiture and had never made that sort of fuss at home. Still, tonight he was impressed with her efforts for their visitor. Divine had slept the rest of the afternoon and into the evening.

"Great dinner, Maggie!" she enthused.

"Makes a change to have company," Maggie replied acidly, "and to have my husband at the table."

"Ouch!" Lorimer made a face at her but he knew fine she was right. He was hardly ever home to eat with her and as for guests, well, who'd accept an invitation when he was never there?

"How d'you put up with it? If it's anything like back home, the hours are hell," Divine remarked.

"Well, there are *supposed* to be working time regulations but…"

"But I don't keep to them," finished Lorimer. "We're meant to work no longer than an average of forty-eight hours but you know how it is," he shrugged, spearing a piece of asparagus with his fork.

"Sure do. But how do you feel about it, Maggie?

Doesn't it bother you?"

Maggie gave a half-smile and Lorimer could see the struggle on her face to appear nonchalant.

"Oh, I have my own work to keep me busy. And we do *sometimes* see each other."

"You teach school, right?"

"Yes. What you call high school."

"You were an English major, yeah?"

Maggie's eyes widened. "How did you know that?"

Divine gave a smile and raised one eyebrow knowingly. "They don't call me Sherlock Lipinski for nothing!" She took a sip from her wine glass and Lorimer gazed at the two women, fascinated to see their faces in the flickering candlelight. Divine's skin shone and her huge brown eyes glowed. Maggie's pallor was in sharp contrast. Lorimer felt a pang as he noticed the dark shadows under her eyes. Just how much did his job take its toll on her? He watched as she tilted her head back to drain her glass. That oval face and those high cheekbones still moved him. He knew her body so well. The slim tapering fingers that twirled the stem of her glass, the halo of dark curls caught in the light. He shifted his gaze and saw Divine staring straight at him. She wasn't smiling, and her expression was one of pity. For whom?

"Tell us all about Florida," Lorimer's tone was an affected heartiness, breaking the mood that threatened to make him poor company.

"Well. Tall order, Chief Inspector! Where do I start?" But once she'd started, Divine had no difficulty in talking. About Florida, about her home in the Everglades and the move she'd made to the Gulf Coast.

"Did you ever have any problems about being a woman in the police force?" Maggie wanted to know. Divine looked thoughtful for a moment then a hint of a smile animated her face as she recalled an incident.

"One time, not long after I joined the force, there was a woman who took exception to being arrested by a female officer. She was a kind of hippy type, you know, long-haired and dirty. But not the peaceful sort. Bit of a redneck, we thought. And my, was she feisty! My partner was a male officer, Rod Douglas. Biggish guy, almost my height," Divine smiled. "Well, this female, she keeps insisting in this little bitty voice that she wants a man to arrest her. Big Rod just shook his head and walked away. But she keeps on all the way down town that she *don't want to be handled by no woman cop*."

Maggie and Lorimer laughed together at the woman's exaggerated accent.

"Anyhow, when we finally brought her in she gets the once over in the cells and it turns out that she's not a female at all." Divine paused for dramatic effect. "She's a he!"

"Who got the biggest surprise?" Lorimer wanted to know.

Divine shook her head at the memory. "That guy was such a misogynist and there he was all dressed up fine and dandy in women's clothing!"

Lorimer looked across at Maggie, who was still laughing. It was nice of the American woman to have chosen an innocuous story like that. The night wore on with Divine recalling things from her past. She had them alternately laughing about the crazy things she'd encountered in some police cases and sobered by others that touched on the more bizarre side of human nature. She didn't elaborate, for Maggie's sake, he thought, but Lorimer found himself more and more intrigued by the way certain homicides were dealt with. The physical side to apprehensions wouldn't go down well on this side of the Atlantic, he knew, given the current legislation about human rights. But Divine seemed to relish that part of law enforcement. There was a lot more emphasis on getting results, too, he realised, remembering an item in the officer's file; Divine Lipinski held the highest total of successful cases in her own headquarters.

"The punishments meted out by your courts are a lot harsher than ours, aren't they?" Maggie observed.

Divine nodded her head but Lorimer couldn't tell if she was agreeing with his wife or with the severity of Florida's penal system.

The black woman raised her glass and looked at them both. "You guys let them off with murder, don't you?" The question was spoken softly and it made Lorimer feel distinctly uncomfortable. He wanted to defend his country's legal system but at the same time a number of his past cases screamed out at him. For a moment he looked at Divine in a new light. Just why was she here? Was it really just about comparative policing methods? Or was there a political agenda somewhere that he couldn't yet see? Lorimer wasn't ready to be drawn into an argument about the merits or demerits of their differing legal systems. Just how much might filter back to Mitchison, for a start?

He could feel Maggie's bare toe against his ankle, warning him off. She needn't have worried. Divine was good company but she was still a stranger in their midst.

"Tell me a bit about your education system," Maggie's change of subject was welcome, if rather obvious.

"You mean our high schools?"

"Yes." Maggie leaned forward on her elbows and Divine began a discourse on the state school system she'd experienced.

Lorimer let his mind wander as the two women discussed schools and students. It was really late now, well after one o'clock, and he had to have Divine back at HQ before nine this morning. Her body clock was probably all awry. He stifled a yawn as he let their conversation wash over him. He was vaguely aware that they were discussing scholarships of some kind when the phone rang in the hall.

"I'll get it," he was out of his seat and into the hall in three strides.

"Lorimer," his voice was crisp and formal.

"DC Cameron speaking, sir. We've got a big problem. I'm at the Grange near Mount Florida. It's a clinic of some kind. There's been an incident."

"One of the patients?"

"No, sir. Nothing like that. It's one of the nurses." Cameron paused. "Sir. It looks like she's been murdered."

Divine had made a move to join him but one look from Lorimer stopped her in her tracks. Besides, there was her hostess to consider.

For a moment Divine's expression showed her sympathy for anyone fool enough to take up with a cop. Lorimer was heaving on a dark jacket as he kissed the top of his wife's head.

"Don't wait up," he joked. Then he was gone, the pretty table and the candlelight forgotten as he closed the front door behind him.

The two women eyed each other in silence for a moment then Maggie reached for the Chardonnay. It was empty.

"Coffee?" she asked doubtfully, "or would you prefer something stronger?"

Divine flashed her a sudden conspiratorial smile. "Every time," she answered.

Chapter Eight

The big car leapt into the night and soon Lorimer was in the outside lane of the motorway. It should have taken him at least ten minutes to reach the Grange but the clinic came into view a whole lot sooner. As he walked up the drive, he wondered whether Cameron had alerted Mitchison. He would soon find out if the Superintendent had decided to make his presence felt.

"Okay, who's here?" Lorimer demanded as Cameron's rangy figure came up at him out of the dark.

"Dr Fergusson, Mr Boyd with the scene of crime officers and some local uniforms, sir."

"The Super?"

Cameron shook his head.

"Right, let's get on with it."

"Round the back, sir. The body's under the house in the basement. It's a sort of boiler room."

Lorimer was matching the Lewisman's long stride as he led the way round the side of the building. There were lights on upstairs, he noticed, and wondered which patients had been disturbed. He'd talk to them later. Find out if anyone had heard anything.

"A Mrs Duncan found the body. She's one of the ancillary nursing staff. Telephoned the local station and they contacted us." Cameron held up his hand in a warning. "Just watch the railing, sir, it's pretty shaky."

He wasn't joking. Lorimer felt flakes of rust come away on his bare hands as the railing sagged against the stone steps that led to the basement. It was obvious that this entrance wasn't used much. Why come in this way, then? Lorimer soon found out. The scene of crime boys had cordoned off the interior stairs of the basement. Lorimer stood at the back entrance of the Grange seeing the fluorescent lights that beamed down on the figures below. Rosie Fergusson was bent over the nurse's body. He could only see Rosie's back and the lower half of the corpse from this angle. Above them, on the other side of the grey room, Boyd's men were going about their painstaking work.

Lorimer moved towards the body, careful to avoid the area Boyd had sectioned off. Rosie glanced up at him quickly, gave a nod then shifted aside to let him see.

The nurse lay on her back, legs spread out under her uniform. Her arms had been pulled together, though, hands flat against one another, the tell tale carnation stuck between their stiffening fingers. Lorimer looked at her face. The soft dark hair had come loose from its hairband, he noticed, and was spilling over her cheeks. Hunkering down beside Rosie, Lorimer lifted a lock gently and then let it fall away from her pale skin. Her eyes were still wide open with fright. So was her mouth. Had she begun to cry out before he'd strangled her, he wondered? There was an expression of agonised disbelief that Lorimer had seen before on the faces of murder victims. He looked the length of her lifeless body. The pale blue uniform was crushed and there were rips in her black tights. That must have happened when someone dragged her down here, Lorimer surmised.

"From what I can see she's been attacked before entering the boiler room," Rosie told him. The footsteps of the scene of crime officers echoed against the concrete walls.

"And then given her flower," Lorimer muttered. The parallel was obvious. But would they find something here that would lead them to the killer of Deirdre McCann?

"Oh, no!"

Lorimer whirled round in time to see Cameron's white face, then the young detective was off up the stairs like a shot. Rosie shot Lorimer a look as they heard a sound of retching coming from the garden outside.

"Didn't put your man down as the squeamish sort," she commented. Lorimer frowned. She was right, but this was not the time to inquire about Niall Cameron's delicate disposition.

"Okay. Cause of death?"

"Manual strangulation," Rosie replied, tracing the curve of neck directly below the nurse's chin. "He came at her from in front, grabbed her with both hands, then did it." She looked across at Lorimer, eyebrows raised. "I think you'll find the compression was strong and swift. She died pretty quickly."

"But you'll know more in the morning," Lorimer added.

Rosie gave him a weak grin. "Yeah." She cradled the girl's head in both hands, shifting it gently to one side. "Hope you will, too."

"Don't bank on it. He hasn't even left a scarf this time."

Lorimer looked towards the girl's fingers, flattened in a gesture of prayer. The red carnation pointed downwards towards her thighs. "Just his calling card."

He stood up, still staring at the young nurse. Kirsty

MacLeod. Now who would break into this place and kill a nurse? Only a madman, a voice answered him. Lorimer gritted his teeth. He stepped away from the body and sidled around the area being dusted down before heading for the stairs to the clinic.

"May I?" he asked the nearest boilersuited officer.

"Just keep right against the wall, sir, would you?"

Lorimer made his way gingerly up the steps. There could be all sorts of traces here where she'd been dragged down. There was a handrail to one side. This one was painted with black Hammerite, unlike the one rusting outside. He hoped to hell there would be some fingerprints on it. The metal door at the top had been tied open with the orange binder twine that Boyd always used. Lorimer kept to the edge of the steps as he turned into the ground floor corridor. The floor was covered in grey-green vinyl, another good source for forensics to examine.

Was this where she'd been killed? The lights had been put out deliberately so it looked as though the killer had meant to waylay Kirsty MacLeod in this very corridor. Lorimer frowned; another suggestion that this was a crime committed by someone in the clinic. His eyes lit up. Could there be a patient here who'd been in Queen Street station three months ago? First thing in the morning he'd be back asking lots of questions. That was for sure.

There were swing-doors at the end of the corridor, hooked back against the walls on either side, and Lorimer could see that the main part of the building lay beyond this area. Large cupboard doors lined one side of the corridor walls. Lorimer opened them, only to discover shelves and shelves of hospital linen.

There were two doors opposite and Lorimer saw that one was ajar. He left it for the time being and tried the other. It was locked. Frowning, he pushed the other door, hearing it creak. Then he stood in the doorway.

Here was a patient and a very ill one at that. There were tubes protruding from the body and a machine that seemed to be pumping her mattress up and down. Was this where they nursed the terminally ill patients, perhaps? Lorimer had never seen anything like it. He was about to tiptoe away when a tiny movement caught his eye. The patient's head had moved the slightest bit and Lorimer found himself staring into a pair of bright eyes that were very much alive.

Phyllis had heard it all. The clang of a door in the distance, then nothing until the swing-doors had been swept open and that awful screaming had rent the air. During all the commotion, unseen hands had quietly closed Phyllis's door. The sounds were muffled after that but she'd been aware of voices and had heard enough to let her know something of what had taken place. Did they imagine she wouldn't hear them behind her closed door? They were wrong. This disease had robbed her of much, but her sense of hearing was heightened as never before. She knew when the police had arrived. She also knew that some unspeakable horror had taken place not far from her own room.

As she lay listening intently, she recalled the terror of that footfall. Her eyes had shut against the shadow entering her room. She didn't want to think about it any more. But now she found herself staring into a different pair of pale eyes. Were they blue? She couldn't make them out in this light. The man was staring back at her.

He was taller than average, built like a sportsman. Even though he stood quite still, Phyllis sensed a restless energy about him. His hair was dark against the outline of light from the corridor. She could see that much. He was the sort of man she'd once desired, she suddenly realised. Strong. Not the type to be indoors for long; always on the move. She'd always liked that in a man.

"I'm sorry. Didn't mean to disturb you," he said at last.

Phyllis liked the voice. It was a recognisable Glasgow accent but he spoke clearly and didn't mumble. How she wished she could reply. Carry on a conversation. A peculiar moan broke from her lips and she tried to move her head again. There was nothing she could do except widen her eyes to communicate her fear, her desperation. He looked at her harder and for a moment Phyllis thought he was going to step towards the bed. Just when she thought he was coming towards her, he seemed to change his mind and stepped back into the shadows once more.

"I'm sorry," he said again, but whether he meant he was sorry to disturb her in the middle of the night or that he was sorry for her, Phyllis couldn't tell. Then, as suddenly as he had appeared, he was gone.

Chapter Nine

Phyllis woke early every day. The night nurses always came to the laundry cupboard outside her room, pulling out the sheets, clattering the stiff doors and gossiping in their loud voices. Bored and wanting their shift to end so they could go home, they didn't give a thought to who might hear their raucous laughter. They always reminded Phyllis of the magpies outside her window, loud and rude. The cupboard door was banged shut at last and the voices disappeared down the corridor. Her door was deliberately left ajar and the wedge of light from the corridor shone dingy yellow through the gap. The venetian blinds shut out the daylight until other hands came to pull on the cord. Until then, Phyllis had to content herself with this half of her world. She thought of it as Inside now. Never as home any more. Inside was normally boring and predictable.

Her room lay swathed in darkness, only the corridor light picking out familiar shapes. The high bed dominated the room with its special mattress that moved in constant undulations to prevent bedsores. A hissing sigh from the pump mechanism below the bed repeated itself over and over, a sleepy rhythmic sound that Phyllis didn't notice any more. On her left was a chrome stand holding a plastic bottle that dripped fluids into her unresisting body.

The tubes disappeared below the white sheets. Other tubes led outwards and away, discreetly hidden by the folds of bedding. To the right of the bed a grey plastic chair gathered dust. It was for any visitors who might come at the appointed times. Phyllis no longer expected visitors from the outside world. Only the nursing staff attended her needs with monotonous regularity.

The window was on Phyllis's right. In the daytime she could see her lawns and flowerbeds, some shrubbery and the sky. Birds came pecking around the borders, friendly chaffinches or the robber magpies. Sometimes a robin trilled its distinctive note, and Phyllis tried to remember what cold, frosty days were like. The birds were highly satisfactory, but she liked the sky best of all. For hours she watched the cloud shapes slither and change; her imagination creating Gods and chariots, characters from mythology, maenads with streaming hair. She rarely saw the stars except in winter when Venus rose in late afternoon on a velvety blue sky. Then hands pulled the blind cord, shutting off her Outside with a sharp metallic snap. For now the sky was dark and shuttered from her sight.

In a corner of the room a small wardrobe held Phyllis's few clothes. They were all cotton for she never left the heat of this room any more. In earlier days when she could still move her arms and turn her head the nurses would heave her into a wheelchair and push her down the corridor to what they now called the day room. There she had been parked in her old lounge with its egg and dart plaster coving around the ceiling. The other residents had upset her with their staring or feeble attempts at one-sided conversation and she'd always preferred the relative peace and quiet of her own room.

Nowadays there were directives about lifting patients. It took two nurses to sit her upright. And they were always short of staff. So Phyllis was left with the television for company. She rarely permitted the staff to switch it on these days. They always asked first, thank God, and her tiny shake of the head allowed her room to stay silent. Once, long ago, she had watched the quiz shows, but nobody came to switch the thing off and she had tired of the interminable soaps that followed, invading her space. The programmes had been punctuated by advertisements reminding Phyllis of so many things she would never need again.

The yellow light flooded across the linoleum floor as the nurse pushed open the door. It wasn't Kirsty, her designated nurse, but one of the others whom she rarely saw.

"Morning, Phyllis. Time for your pills." The nurse barely made eye contact with Phyllis, turning her attention instead to the glass of yellow goo and the plastic phial of assorted tablets. Phyllis watched her face as the woman concentrated on tumbling all the pills onto a spoonful of the thickened liquid. The nurse's eyes never left the outstretched spoon on its journey to Phyllis's open mouth. She felt the metal spoon then the saliva began to ooze from beneath her tongue. One swallow and it was over.

"Right, then." The nurse flicked the residue from Phyllis's lips, leaving a smear behind that would feel sticky and uncomfortable until someone else came to wash her face. It was strange, she reflected, that she could still swallow a mouthful of medication like that in one gulp when a few drops of water would have set her choking. This disease had taken its toll on her throat muscles as well as so much of the rest. Speech was impossible now, and she rarely tried to communicate beyond a shake or nod of the head.

With a clack, the blinds were opened and weak daylight fell onto the objects in the room. Now the daily routine began. The first nurse was joined by a small, stout auxiliary with dark hair.

"Morning, Phyllis," she swept a practised eye over the bedclothes, resting for a moment on the patient's face. Phyllis was heaved into a sitting position to participate in the ritual of blood pressure, temperature and removal of her bodily wastes. She watched, detached, as if it was happening to someone else. She endured the harsh wet flannel on her face and body while the two women carried on an earlier conversation as if she wasn't there.

"Did you see her being carried away?"

"Sh!" the nurse frowned at her, nodding her head towards Phyllis, belatedly acknowledging her presence.

"Oh. Right. Och, she'll never know. Will you, darling?" she smiled a pasted-on smile in Phyllis's direction.

Phyllis closed her eyes as the hook pulled up the sling and raised her off the bed. Below her the two women pulled at the sheets, dashing the soiled linen onto the floor then smoothing on the fresh bedding with an expertise born of much practise. At last she was lowered back onto the cool sheet and the perpetually moving mattress. The ritual was completed by the auxiliary spraying the air with the scent of roses. For a while this would serve to mask the unpleasant smell of human urine. Left alone, Phyllis watched the spray, like mist catching the light as it fell. Her day could now begin. The sky with its ever-shifting shapes was there to see; and imagination, if not memory, would people her hours.

Now she could banish the memory of that nightmare in the dark. She closed her eyes but heard again the cry that had left her shivering. Had she really seen that shadow of malice falling against the cupboards outside her room? And those hands reaching to pluck a flower from her vase? No one would ever know what she had seen.

Chapter Ten

Lorimer stood outside the front entrance to the Grange, watching as Niall Cameron approached, recalling their conversation of the night before. He had found the detective constable leaning against the side of the building, head pressed against his arms. Lorimer had wondered at the sound in the dark until he realised the young man was sobbing quietly.

"I knew her, sir. She's a girl from back home," Cameron had told him, his face streaked with tears. "She's Kirsty MacLeod. We grew up together. She was in my wee sister's year at the Nicholson."

Lorimer had guided him towards the car where he'd heard the rest of the story. How Niall Cameron had left Lewis to join the police force against his family's wishes. How they'd wanted him to take over his late father's fishing boat but Niall hadn't seen a future there anymore. Now there was only his mother at home with the youngest one. All the others had left. Kirsty had come to the city too, but he'd never seen her. Until now.

"Should I come off the case, sir?" Cameron had wanted to know. But Lorimer had shaken his head. Some background knowledge would be useful.

Now the DC was closer Lorimer could see his bloodshot eyes, signs of a sleepless night. Well, it happened to them all in this profession. Young Niall Cameron had better get used to it.

"Okay?"

"Yes, sir."

"Talk to anyone from home yet?"

Cameron nodded. "There's only one next of kin,

the old auntie who lives in Harris. Kirsty's mother died of cancer when the lassie was twelve. Her dad was drowned some time back."

"Right. We'll probably find out more now from the director, Mrs Baillie. She lives on the premises. We only took a preliminary statement last night but there'll have to be proper interviews this morning. Alistair's here already, setting up an incident room."

Some things were better done in daylight, thought Lorimer. There was a team of uniformed officers doing a house-to-house inquiry along the road. It was a residential district with not a close circuit television camera in sight. They'd have to rely on the local insomniacs for any sighting of the killer. Last night had been thoroughly unpleasant. None of the staff had known much about the nurse's background or else they weren't letting on. The auxiliary who'd found her, Mrs Duncan, had been in a state of shock and could barely verbalise. Lorimer had been given a full list of all members of staff. It was a long list, given the staffing requirements for a twenty-four hour day to care for a number of vulnerable people. Still, records would be cross-checked on the computer and that might throw something up.

Those patients who'd emerged from their rooms last night had been surprisingly calm. Though perhaps some of them were sedated at night, anyway. They would all be interviewed at greater length this morning. Lorimer hadn't forgotten all those lights switched on upstairs.

Now, in the spring morning, it was hard to imagine that a murder had taken place in such a pleasant spot. The sky was clear and blue although there was still a chill in the air. Above him a blackbird was whistling unseen in the trees. Lorimer stepped back out onto the front lawn and walked as far as a curve of rhododendron bushes. Turning, he looked back at the house. It had a pleasing aspect from the front. Two enormous bay windows flanked the front entrance. The huge storm doors were fastened back and Lorimer could see shadowy shapes moving beyond the frosted glass. The clinic's employees were already having to go about the business of caring for their patients, after all. Some of the upstairs windows showed drawn curtains still, though it was past nine o' clock. Whose sleep had been disturbed during the night, he wondered?

Lorimer looked around him. The drive looped all round the grounds. To the rear were trees, more shrubbery and a high, stone wall. Beyond that was farmland. Could anyone have vaulted that wall and made off over the fields in darkness? Or, indeed, arrived from that very direction. An outsider. A nutter. That was the theory he was working on, anyway. Some creep who had a fetish about dead women and flowers. Brightman would surely have an opinion to offer. It was time he called him up.

The front drive gave on to an avenue of Victorian villas then a row of solid tenement houses on each side. There was a main road at right angles to the avenue, a mere hundred yards away.

One thing Lorimer had noticed as he'd turned the car into this narrow avenue: there was barely room to swing a cat because of the double-parking by residents. Maybe someone might have noticed a car in a hurry last night? That was just one of the questions his team of officers would be asking. Over the hill beyond the Langside Monument lay the Victoria Infirmary. Queen's Park stretched out the whole length of the main road right up to Shawlands. Another possible escape route for a killer. Lorimer grinned to himself, realising that he was already tuning into Solly's way of thinking. The psychologist liked to pore over maps relating to the locus of a crime as he began his search into the criminal mind.

Lorimer thought back to the long drawn-out investigation into the Saint Mungo's murders. That Glasgow park had been scoured from end to end. *The Dear Green Place*, folk liked to call their city. And so it was. He'd read somewhere that they had more parks than any other city in Europe. A source of pride to some, maybe, but a right bugger when you were trying to track a killer.

"Sir."

Lorimer's mind came back to the present. Detective Constable Cameron was standing in the porch and with him was the very lady that Lorimer wanted most to see. Mrs Baillie was the woman in charge here, her official designation being director of the Grange, a clinic that specialised in neural disorders.

As he walked towards the steps, he could see a tall, angular woman dressed in black shading her eyes from the morning sun.

"Good morning Mrs Baillie," Lorimer shook a hand that was damp with sweat.

As they turned away from the dazzle of light that bounced off the open glass door, Lorimer could see the director's face more clearly. Mrs Baillie would be somewhere in her early fifties, he surmised, though she'd looked a lot older last night.

Her dark hair showed not a hint of grey but this was belied by the network of tiny lines around her eyes and mouth, a mouth that was turned down as if in an expression of permanent disapproval.

"Come through to my office, please, gentlemen," she said and immediately turned right, opening a door set into the wood panelling. At once Lorimer noticed how the old house had been altered to form the present day clinic as vinyl floors gave way to thick patterned carpet. Light filtered from a landing window where a broad staircase swept upwards. An open door to the front showed them a huge bay-windowed lounge where uniformed officers were already setting out tables and chairs. Across the hall a curved desk wrapped itself around two angles of the walls, segmenting the corner into a reception area. A young woman in a dark suit and white shirt glanced up at them unsmilingly then continued with whatever she had been doing behind the desk, out of sight behind her computer screen.

"That's Cathy. You'll want to talk to her later, I suppose."

"We'll be talking to all the staff, ma'am," Cameron replied, glancing at Lorimer who had wandered towards the stair and was peering upwards.

"There are private rooms on that floor," Mrs Baillie snapped, making Lorimer turn back suddenly. "The patients are restricted to the west and south wing and use both upstairs and down. We have the administration down here." She strode ahead of them, ignoring the girl at the desk, and opened a door leading to the back of the building.

Lorimer and Cameron followed her down a set of four stairs that led into another corridor. Here windows to one side gave a view of shrubbery and an expanse of kitchen garden where a man in brown overalls was digging with a spade, his back to the house. A patient, Lorimer wondered, or one of the staff? Shadows thrown onto the garden made him press his head against the glass and look along the side, seeing angles of pebble-dashed walls masking the original contours of the house. A modern extension had been built onto this part of the Grange, he realised. Lorimer ran his hand along a grey painted radiator as Mrs Baillie unlocked a door opposite the window. It was cold to his touch.

"This is my office. Please sit down," Mrs Baillie had already taken her place behind an antique desk. Two upright chairs with carved backs sat at angles in front of her. The wood panelled ceiling of the office sloped into a deep coomb showing that the room was positioned immediately under the main stairs. There were no windows and so Lorimer left the door deliberately ajar. Claustrophobic at the best of times, he wasn't going to let his discomfort show in front of this woman.

"Who has access to this part of the house?" Lorimer asked.

"Oh, it's not kept locked, Chief Inspector, except my private office, of course. But only the staff would come through here. The patients have their own rooms."

"And is there any other way to reach this part of the building?"

"We have a back door that leads into the garden. It

can only be accessed from this side of the house."

"Not from the clinic?"

"No."

"And it's kept locked at night?"

"I do the lock-up myself. It's my home too, you know," Mrs Baillie gave a twisted smile and Lorimer found himself suddenly curious about the director. He inclined his head questioningly.

"My flat is upstairs. Part of my remit here is to act as a nursing director. Yes, I'm a fully qualified psychiatric nurse," she said, lifting her chin. "I run the clinic but I also have a say in the overall medical policy."

"I'm afraid we will have to interview the patients who were here last night," Lorimer told her.

Mrs Baillie hesitated then shuffled at some papers on her desk. Then she raised her head and regarded Lorimer steadily. "I'm afraid that won't be possible."

"This is a murder inquiry. The feelings of your patients simply don't come into the question."

"I hope you will respect their feelings, Chief Inspector. Many of our patients are seriously ill people and interrogation could do some of them untold damage."

"We quite understand."

"No, Chief Inspector, you don't. When I said it would be impossible to interview everybody, I meant just that," Mrs Baillie answered him defiantly. "You see, two of our patients left for respite care early this morning."

"But that's preposterous! You can't just let them walk out of here like that!"

"I didn't. In fact I took them to the airport myself."

"Where were they going?" Cameron asked.

The woman tilted her head and gave him the ghost of a smile. "Your part of the world, by the sound of it. A little place called Shawbost. It's on the Island of Lewis."

"But why on earth couldn't they stay here? And who are they anyway?" Lorimer protested.

"Sister Angelica and Samuel Fulton. Their plane tickets were paid for. And they were ready to go. I couldn't see any point in keeping them here."

For a moment Lorimer was speechless at the woman's audacity. And Lewis? Could there be some link between the victim and this respite centre?

"Give me the details of this place, please," he asked.

"Certainly," She pulled a card from a file on her desk and handed it to him.

"And, Mrs Baillie, no further patients will leave here without our knowledge. Do I make myself clear?"

"Perfectly, Chief Inspector," the woman folded her hands together meeting his angry glare with a cool gaze of her own.

Lorimer gave the card a perfunctory glance and pocketed it. It would be counter-productive to alienate Mrs Baillie, no matter what police time she had wasted. There was Kirsty's murder to solve and she was in a position to help them.

"Kirsty MacLeod. She was a psychiatric nurse, wasn't she?"

Mrs Baillie shook her head. "Kirsty had specialised in neural disorders, Chief Inspector. Her background was Care in the Community so she had worked with many patients who had illnesses of a psychiatric nature. However, the main reason for employing her was her experience with multiple sclerosis patients."

"Do you have many of those sorts of patients here?" Cameron asked.

"No, just the one. Phyllis Logan."

Lorimer nodded. Of course. That explained the woman down in that back room away from all the other patients. He recalled those bright eyes and that sepulchral moan. That was one resident who wouldn't be answering any questions.

"Isn't that rather unusual," Cameron persisted. "After all, this is a clinic specialising in psychiatric cases."

"We prefer to call them neural disorders. And MS is a neural disease," Mrs Baillie chided him. "But it's not unusual for Phyllis to be here. Not at all." She paused, glancing from one man to the other, a sudden twinkle in her eye. "You see, Phyllis Logan is the owner of the Grange. It really is her home."

Chapter Eleven

Lorimer had to hand it to them. They'd organised the interview schedule perfectly. Alistair Wilson had taken possession of the large lounge to the front of the house that was now their incident room. The minimum disruption to patients had been Mrs Baillie's priority. He wondered about that lady: a cool customer, but there had been something in her manner that the Chief Inspector had found disquieting. Maybe she'd been in denial, but he'd found the woman's detached, clinical manner rather off-putting. He thought over their recent conversation.

"She was a capable nurse. No problem to us at all." That was how she'd answered when Lorimer had tried to elicit information about the murder victim. Not "Poor girl" or, "I can't believe this is happening" which would have been understandable under the grim circumstances. Why might Nurse Kirsty MacLeod have been a problem to the clinic anyway? Or had there been staffing problems in the past? Lorimer picked up such nuances with his policeman's ear for detail. It wouldn't be a bad idea to investigate the staffing over the past twelve months. "All of our residential patients had retired for the night. Only the night staff were on duty. I was in bed myself."

In bed, mused Lorimer, but had she been asleep? And who else might have been lying awake staring at the ceiling, counting the hours till an uncertain dawn? He'd know soon enough.

The residents were to be made available to them after breakfast. That was exactly how Mrs Baillie had put it. And this morning she had shown no trace of sorrow for the sudden death of one of her staff. Her starched white collar and black jacket bore testimony to a careful toilette. There was nothing hasty or flung together about this lady. Lorimer had stared at her earlier, mentally contrasting her with the image of his wife flying out of the house that morning, hair tousled and jacket pushed anyhow into her bulging haversack.

Dark circles showed under Maggie's lovely eyes but Lorimer wasn't about to waste too much sympathy on a self-inflicted hangover.

He'd dropped officer Lipinski at HQ for her scheduled lecture before setting off for the Grange. That was one talk he'd be missing. He grinned to himself. What a pity! The squad at Pitt Street would just have to get on with it without him. All in all, Lorimer doubted if he'd had three full hours sleep himself. Mitchison would be banging on about Working Time Regulations before he was much older.

Lorimer was sitting at a table that had been pushed up near the huge bay window that overlooked the gardens. The morning light streaming in would show Lorimer and DS Wilson the full face of whoever came to sit on the other side of that table. Each person was going to be confronted by a pair of steely blue eyes that brooked no nonsense. It was just as well that Alistair Wilson was on duty. His sergeant's knack of showing deferential politeness would be especially soothing to the damaged souls in this place.

"Ready, sir?" Wilson had brought in the file of current residents' names.

"If they've all had their breakfasts," Lorimer growled.

He hadn't even had a cup of coffee and no one

seemed to be interested in offering him one. He looked at the annotated list. There were red asterisks against certain names. These belonged to residents whose rooms looked out to the front of the house. Mrs Baillie's was amongst them. Her bedroom was right above this lounge.

"Eric Fraser?" Lorimer read aloud, "Let's have him in first." The uniformed officer by the door disappeared.

"D'you want to start, Alistair?" Lorimer turned to his colleague. Wilson just smiled and shrugged. "Butter him up, you mean?" Detective Sergeant Alistair Wilson was no stranger to his superior's strategies.

The uniform returned. "Mr Fraser," he said, retreating immediately to his post by the lounge door.

Eric Fraser was a young man of medium height dressed in navy jogging pants and a matching hooded sweatshirt. As he approached, he ran one hand over his cropped bullet head and stared right at Lorimer with small, intense eyes. He hadn't shaved for days, by the look of him, and his clothes hung loosely over a thin frame.

"Mr Fraser, I'm Sergeant Wilson, and this is Chief Inspector Lorimer," Wilson had risen to his feet, come around the table and was shaking Fraser's hand. "Thank you for coming in to talk to us. Please sit down." Wilson's voice was all solicitousness. They didn't yet know the nature of these patients' illnesses. That was confidential, Mrs Baillie had insisted. "Meantime," had been Lorimer's terse reply.

"They told me about Kirsty," the young man began without any preamble. "She was nice. She listened to me. Not all of them take the time to listen," his voice held a querulous note and he looked accusingly at Lorimer although it was Wilson who'd begun the interview.

"We'd like to know if you heard anything unusual last night, Mr Fraser," Wilson spoke firmly, trying to draw the man's attention back.

Fraser made a derisory noise. "You mean all that screeching and carrying on?"

"What screeching was that, Mr Fraser?" Wilson put in. Lorimer pretended to scribble something on a pad in front of him, avoiding eye-contact.

If Wilson could capture his attention then he'd be free to observe the patient's body language. Right now he was sitting, hands clasped between his knees as if, despite the sun's heat through the glass, he was feeling cold.

"Mrs Duncan. She raised the roof with her racket. Came right up the stairs to fetch Mrs Baillie. I think anyone would've heard it through the partition walls. I certainly could."

"You don't have any sleeping medication, then, Mr Fraser?"

"Not at the moment," he replied, sitting up a bit straighter as he spoke.

Lorimer nodded to himself. A patient on his way to recovery, perhaps?

"How well did you know Nurse MacLeod?"

Fraser shrugged, crossing one leg over the other. "Not that well. She was nice. Nice-looking too. She always made sure we were comfortable at bedtime. She'd go to the bother of bringing me up a hot water bottle. That sort of thing."

"Did she ever talk about herself?"

"No. Not really. I'd asked where she was from. The accent made me curious. But she didn't really tell me much about herself." Fraser looked hard at Alistair Wilson. "We're a pretty self-absorbed lot in here, you know. Fragile psyches and all that," he sneered. Lorimer watched as his foot began to tap rapidly up and down, an involuntary movement, agitated. He wondered what the man's blood pressure would be if he had it taken right now. A worm-coloured vein on Fraser's temple stood out and Lorimer could imagine the beat of a pulse.

"Where were you last night, Mr Fraser, from midnight onwards?"

The foot tapping stopped abruptly and the man uncrossed his leg, looking towards Lorimer who had suddenly asked the question. For a moment he said nothing, simply stared at the Chief Inspector as if he had temporarily forgotten his presence.

"In bed. In my bed in my room. All night."

"And can anybody verify this?"

Fraser looked from one man to the other, bewildered at this sudden change of tack.

"I don't know. Kirsty and Mrs Duncan were the only two who would have been able to say I was in my room. They were the night staff on duty." He twisted his face into a frown. "But that's going to be the same for all of us. Except…"

He stopped, rubbing his hands up and down the thighs of his joggers.

"Except?" Lorimer prompted.

"Some patients are on suicide watch. They have nurses posted along the corridor who sit there all night just in case."

"And you'd have had to pass them to reach the back of the clinic, I take it?"

"Yes," Fraser replied, something like relief in his face. "Yes. Any of them would have seen me if I'd passed that way."

"Mr Fraser, you've been very helpful. I'm sorry we've had to disturb you but it is important that we have some sort of input from all the people who were here last night. Do you remember anything else, perhaps? A strange sound from outside?" Wilson asked.

"No. Nothing I can remember."

"Well, if there is anything at all, please get in touch with us. We'd be most grateful for anything you might recall later," DS Wilson rose to his feet and slid a card across the table.

"That's the number to ring. We'll be issuing this to all of the staff and patients," he smiled warmly and Fraser nodded, glancing warily at Lorimer before standing up again.

"I can go now?"

"Of course, sir, and thank you once more for your co-operation," Wilson's smile was positively beatific.

"Constable, would you ask Jennifer Townslie to come in, please?"

At last Lorimer was downing a cup of coffee. The morning had been reasonably productive. They had been able to eliminate most of the residents from their inquiries. Some, as Lorimer had suspected, had been dead to the world having been given sleeping pills. These included a few women with eating disorders who were on the upper floor. None of them were currently on suicide watch. Some of the residents were pretty frail and Lorimer knew it would have taken someone of considerable strength to attack and strangle the young nurse.

What most of them had heard amounted to very little other than the furore caused by the auxiliary, Mrs Duncan. It was time to wheel her in.

Lorimer wiped his mouth with the back of his hand. "Okay?"

Alistair Wilson gave a brief nod. They'd discussed this at some length. This was one witness whose statement would be crucial to the investigation. He just hoped she was in a better state than she'd been the previous night.

Brenda Duncan was a portly woman in her fifties. She rolled slightly as she entered the room, a thick winter coat folded clumsily over one arm, her handbag clutched in two ungloved fists. As she sank into the chair in front of him, Lorimer could see that her eyes were heavy. It didn't take much to guess that she'd been given some kind of medication after her trauma. She was smiling uncertainly and he wondered if she'd ever had to encounter the police before.

"Mrs Duncan," Wilson's voice was all concern, "thank you so much for coming back in. We realise how bad this has been for you." He gave his most encouraging smile as if to say there was nothing to worry about, they'd take care of it all. Lorimer could see the woman's shoulders visibly relax.

"Just take your time and tell us everything that happened yesterday evening."

"Well, when I found poor Kirsty…"

"No," Lorimer broke in, "before that, please. We'd

like you to tell us everything that happened from the time you arrived for your shift."

"Oh." The woman looked from one of them to the other. Her mouth was open and her eyes looked vacant for a moment. Lorimer wondered just how much medication she'd been given. And by whom? a little voice asked.

The mouth closed and the jaw became firmer. Her bosom heaved in a long sigh. "I start at ten so I was here at about twenty-to. The bus drops me off at the Monument and I walk the rest of the way. It only takes about five minutes or so. The patients are usually ready for their beds although there's no strict rule. We don't put out lights or anything like that. They can sit up and watch telly if they like. Some of them don't sleep too well, either. But most of them are early bedders.

"And which ones aren't, Mrs Duncan?" Lorimer wanted to know.

"Oh," the woman looked confused as if unsure whether by imparting this information she might be implicating a patient.

"Sometimes Leigh sits up late. He likes to watch the creepy programmes." She leaned forward, speaking in a whisper of confidentiality, "I don't think he should, mind you, but that kind of thing's not my decision."

"Leigh?" Lorimer was looking down the list of patients' names.

"Leigh Quinn," Mrs Duncan supplied.

"The Irishman," Wilson added.

Lorimer nodded. Leigh Quinn had been practically non-verbal during his interview, staring out of the window mostly. Afterwards they'd decided that a good look at his casenotes would be required. The man didn't seem quite on the same planet as the other patients.

"Did you notice anything unusual during the earlier part of your shift, Mrs, Duncan?" asked Wilson.

Brenda Duncan chewed her bottom lip for a moment or two, her eyes fixed on the bag on her lap. Then she shook her head, still gazing down as if struggling to see the events of the previous night in her mind.

"Nothing untoward, then. Just a normal night?"

The woman nodded her head.

"Where were you before you found Nurse MacLeod's body?" Wilson spoke in a matter-of-fact voice.

"Where was I?" Brenda Duncan looked flustered. "I, em, I would be..." her voice trailed off as she looked at the detective sergeant.

"Just take your time," he told her. "Try to remember your movements. What you were doing on the normal night shift."

"I suppose I'd been round the doors. They leave some doors open for the patients. The ones that need a bit of watching, you know," she whispered again. "I chatted with Peter, he's one of the nurses who sit with their patients at night. They all have designated nurses, you see," she explained, nodding to emphasise her point.

"Can you remember what you chatted about?" Wilson asked, an encouraging smile on his face.

"He was telling me about his holidays. He's just booked up a fortnight in Mallorca for himself and the family. I remember because it was such a windy night and I told him he was lucky to be getting away from all this horrible weather."

"And then?" Alistair Wilson let the question dangle in front of the woman like bait. Lorimer had been watching her face with interest. It had become more and more animated as she'd continued, almost as if she was relishing the build-up to her discovery of Kirsty's body. A dramatic event in a humdrum existence, perhaps? Sure enough there was a pause for effect and Brenda Duncan cast her eyes down. Lorimer watched her fumble in her handbag for a handkerchief. There was a loud blowing of her nose before the woman took up her story again.

"I went to make cocoa for Kirsty and me. There's a wee kitchen through the doors from where the patients' rooms are. I was surprised when I saw Kirsty wasn't there. She should've been down from checking the upstairs rooms by then. I thought maybe she'd gone to the bathroom, but I'd have seen her going past."

"It struck you as odd?" Lorimer asked quietly, confirming the tone in the woman's voice.

She nodded, "Aye. Odd. You could say that. Anyway she didn't come back and the cocoa was getting cold so I thought I'd better go and find her. She wasn't in the loo and she wasn't in either of the residents' lounges." Brenda Duncan bit her lip. "I don't know what made me go along the back corridor. Maybe it was when the light came on."

"What light?" Lorimer demanded.

Brenda Duncan frowned. "It was funny, now I come to think of it. The back corridor light just came on. I hadn't noticed it was off until I was through the swing-doors then it just came on."

Wilson scribbled something on his notepad.

"Go on, please," Lorimer pressed her.

"I didn't see anything at first. I just walked along the corridor. It was that quiet. Then I heard a noise. A kind of scraping sound. It was the door down to the basement. Someone had left it open and it was creaking in the wind. I pushed it open and switched on the light. And then I saw her."

This time the pause was for real. Lorimer could see fear loom large in the woman's widening eyes and he could easily imagine her screams. But now her voice sank to a whisper as she stared past them.

"She was lying on her back. I thought at first she'd fallen, so I hurried down the stairs." She swallowed hard. "Then I saw it. That flower. I knew then. I just knew she was dead."

"Did you feel for a pulse?" Wilson asked.

She shook her head and Lorimer saw her eyes staring into space, mesmerised by that image fixed in her brain.

"Kirsty was dead and all I could think of was that she hadn't had her cocoa!" Brenda Duncan suddenly burst into tears. The woman PC who had accompanied her into the lounge was by her side now and looking quizzically at Lorimer for instructions. No doubt she was expecting him to terminate the interview. Spare the poor woman any further suffering. Well, that wasn't always Lorimer's way. There were still things he needed to know.

"How long was it between the time you saw Nurse MacLeod alive and the discovery of the body?" The question brought a halt to the flow of tears. There was a wiping of eyes and the WPC retreated to her post by the lounge door. Brenda Duncan looked distractedly around her for a moment.

"I'm not sure, really. I remember it was after midnight on the alarm clock in one of the rooms. I'd seen Kirsty about quarter-past eleven, maybe. She'd been writing up some paperwork before she went upstairs. I went through the front to check the rooms. I put fresh loo rolls in, give the basins a wipe, that sort of thing." She looked nervously at Lorimer. "I don't know what time it was when I made the cocoa. Not long after."

"So that was the last time you saw her alive. At approximately eleven-fifteen?"

The woman's lip trembled. "I just made her cocoa. We'd always have a blether. But she never came. She never came." Brenda Duncan clutched herself with both arms rocking back and forwards, whimpering softly.

"Thank you, Mrs Duncan." Lorimer was finished with her for the moment. He nodded to Wilson who rose and helped the woman to her feet. "If you would just follow the officer out. We have a car to take you home," Lorimer's detective sergeant reassured her. "There will be a statement to sign later on but we'll let you know about that."

"Oh, just one more thing," Lorimer's voice stopped them in their tracks. "What about the patient whose room is at the back of the nursing home?"

Brenda Duncan looked nonplussed. Then she gave a small shake of the head. "Oh. You mean Phyllis? She's an MS patient. Totally paralysed. Can't speak.

Poor thing. Mrs Baillie can tell you more, I'm sure."
She looked uncertainly at Lorimer then added, "Can I
go now?"

"Of course. Thank you for your help."

Lorimer stood looking out as the police car drove
off. She hadn't mentioned seeing to Phyllis Logan that
night. Had anybody spoken to the owner of the
Grange? Was she even aware that a murder had taken
place under her own roof?

Chapter Twelve

Sometimes he let his mind wander back to the time when he'd been happiest. In his memory the days were always sunny, the cloisters full of friendly shadows. The work had been hard, especially all the studying, but the compensations of having his own vocation made up for everything. There were days like today when the wind blowing from the west reminded him of the gardens with their high walls clad with espaliers and creeping vines. If he closed his eyes he was back there once more, the mumbling sound of bees as they staggered from one lavender bush to the next making his head feel drowsy. The soil had been fine and black beneath his fingernails, a joy to cultivate. And they'd been so pleased with him, hadn't they?

A cold shadow crossed his face, making him look up as the sun disappeared for some moments. The nights, too, had been his. He'd plundered the hours of darkness, his footfall a bright echo on the stones of the chapel. A candle. He remembered there had been a candle, tall, the colour of honey, its flame bent sideways by the draught of his passing. The candle had stood for a sentinel on these special nights between midnight and dawn, flickering its pinpoint lights against the metal cross that lay within the coffin.

The bodies were always carefully dressed in white robes, the faces of the deceased facing skywards. Sometimes, watching them for long hours at a time, he wondered if their eyes would open and see him staring. In dreams he saw their dead eyes glaze like pale gobs of jelly, their heads turn accusingly in his direction. Perhaps that's why he had given them the flower, to appease them, stop their looks of disdain. They seemed to know everything, to understand his innermost thoughts. He'd decided that they were dangerous, these dead people, especially the very old ones with their wrinkled flesh hanging in folds, the candlelight magnifying each crease on the tallow skin.

The first time he had placed a red flower between the praying hands the wind had sighed outside the chapel door like a benediction. Then he knew it was all right. He had a blessing. The priests had sounded their delight. Bells had rung in his honour and the clever boys had lifted him shoulder-high through the college gates. He'd been feather-light, a wisp on the air, able to float down into the coffin and embrace the cold figures lying there so stiff, so stately. Death was sweet. Couldn't they understand that? Death released them all. He released them now, these women, from their hateful lives. Better to be dead and in a clean white coffin. Clean and cool with the flicker of candle-flame.

He groaned as the pain filled his thighs. Would they never leave him alone, these waking dead? Was he burdened with this task for all eternity?

Chapter Thirteen

Number twenty-eight Murray Street was one in a row of faded red sandstone tenements, once the glory of the tobacco merchants who had helped the city to prosper, but now split into a mismatch of bedsits and small flats. Kirsty MacLeod had rented one of the basement rooms.

Lorimer had spoken to the landlady briefly on the telephone. Now their feet thudded on the uncarpeted wooden stairs that led them in a spiral down to the lower level. Lorimer took in the landlady's scuffed leather shoes and much-washed cardigan as she turned the stairs below him. Her clothes were covered in an old-fashioned overall, the kind his granny had worn to the steamie to wash the household linen, but he noticed the hem of her skirt was unravelling at the edge. Whatever rent her tenants were paying, it didn't seem to make a fortune for the woman.

"How long had Miss MacLeod been renting from you?"

"Well, let me see," the woman turned her head towards Lorimer. "She's been here about eighteen months." Lorimer caught a glimpse of tears start in her eyes. They had reached the bottom of the stairs and stopped outside a door marked 3B.

"I can't believe she's dead," her words fell in a whisper and she looked away, suddenly embarrassed at her own emotion. She fiddled with the key in the lock. Lorimer cast his eyes over the green painted walls. The place reminded him of an institution rather than a warren of bedsits, although the faint smell of joss sticks lingering in the corridor spoke of a student life he remembered well. Lorimer stood on the threshold of the room. The dark green curtains were still drawn and his eyes took a few blinks to adjust to the dim light.

"Have you been into this room since Miss MacLeod left for work on Thursday?"

The landlady looked fearfully at him, shaking her frizzed grey hair.

"Oh, no, Chief Inspector. I didn't like... Well. You know. It didn't seem decent," she trailed off, her hands wringing the flowered cotton overall. She hovered in the doorway, uncertain.

"You don't need to stay if you have other things to get on with. I'll bring the keys when I'm done. All right?" His face creased into the reassuring smile that he brought out of his stock expressions for the old and vulnerable. The woman nodded and disappeared along the corridor. He waited a moment until he could hear the sound of doors banging and pots being clattered before turning into the room once more.

Kirsty MacLeod would have kept the curtains shut whenever she'd had a night shift, he told himself. Security-conscious. Even when the windows looked out onto a brick wall, he mused, leaning over a wide desk and drawing the heavy folds aside to let in the daylight. He stood with his back to the desk taking in the contents of her room.

The neatly made up bed was up against one wall, a scattering of soft toys over the pillow. Lorimer recognised a rabbit with floppy ears and a stupid grin embroidered onto its face. It was a Disney character but he couldn't remember which one. There was the usual tired-looking furniture that every city bedsit seemed to afford: dark varnished wardrobe, chest of drawers, bedside cabinet. At least they matched, he thought. A stereo system had been rigged up in one corner on top of a steel cabin trunk. Lorimer looked at the walls, expecting to see the usual wallpapering of pop posters but there was only one of a Runrig concert dating from several years back and a travel poster depicting the standing stones of Callanish.

Lorimer flicked on an angle-poise lamp that stood on the desk and gazed at the picture. The stones seemed to heave out of the Lewis earth as if they'd grown there from ancient roots. So, Kirsty had reminders of home. That was hardly surprising. Lorimer's gaze continued along the line of photo frames on the mantelpiece. There was one of a laughing girl with her arms around an older, white-haired woman. It took him a moment to realise that it was Kirsty. Images of her body sprawled across that concrete floor flicked through his brain. He'd only seen her once, dead at the Grange. This was a younger, carefree teenager and the old lady might be a relative, the aunt, he thought, taking in the background of hills and sea. The other photos included one of her graduation, a close up of a collie dog, its tongue lolling, and an old black and white photograph of a man and woman outside a cottage. Her parents, probably. No young men were included in the line-up. A surprise, really, given that she'd been such a pretty girl.

An empty coat hanger swung from a discoloured brass hook on the back of the door. Her personal clothing had been taken from the nursing home to forensics for examination. Lorimer turned suddenly at the noise of a bluebottle buzzing at the closed window. It heightened his awareness of the silence in the room. No hands would come to switch on the stereo. Nobody would sing a Gaelic song as they tidied or made up the single bed. There was a feeling of utter emptiness, as if the room itself knew that Kirsty was never coming back. Remembering the landlady, Lorimer supposed that another tenant would eventually move in. He sighed, shoving his hands into his pockets. Life went on. It had to. Someone would come to take the girl's personal effects away later in the day. More forensics. More grief for the relatives, wherever they were. For now Lorimer had to gauge the sort of girl Kirsty had been and hopefully find some helpful documentation. A neat, tidy person; from the look of the room, she would have her paperwork somewhere to hand, collated and sorted.

The desk drawer was the obvious place and Lorimer was not disappointed. A red leather five-year diary sat on top of a sheaf of papers. He rustled through them. Payslips were clipped together, a plastic bag contained a pile of receipts and a guarantee for the stereo. Bank statements lay in order in a blue ring binder. Lorimer flicked through them. Nothing obviously wrong there. A floral paper file held letters with a Lewis postmark. It would all have to be taken away for close perusal. Suddenly it all seemed so intrusive to Lorimer. It didn't stop with the killing. Even after death, the girl's private life had to be dissected as thoroughly as her cold corpse.

His fingertips brushed against a small, metal object in a corner of the drawer and Lorimer pushed it into sight. It was a tiny key. Lorimer picked it up. Her key to the diary, surely? He fitted it into the lock and turned. The red book sprung open as if someone had breathed life into its pages. Flicking from the back, Lorimer noticed that the diary had spanned all of the last five years, its tightly written pages giving details of Kirsty's life.

The final entry had been 31 December last year. Starting at the top of that page he read of five different sorts of Hogmanays.

1999 Ceilidh at the Halls. Didn't get in till after two. What a night!!!!

2000 Working tonight. Watched the Rev. I. M. Jolly on TV. A good laugh. Wish Aunty Mhairi had the phone.

2001 George Square for the bells. Millions of mad folk but it was great fun. Bitter cold. Went to someone's party in Hyndland afterwards.

2002 Great to be home. Chrissie and I stayed in with Mhairi as she had a bad cold. Loads of neighbours came in after the bells. Malcolm's black bun went down a treat.

2003 Last New Year in Glasgow. Hope next year brings better luck.

Lorimer gritted his teeth. What bloody irony. All this year had brought her was a grisly death at the hands of some lunatic. He glanced over the five entries again, turning back to confirm his first impressions. Yes, she'd been back to Harris twice in those five years. Had she intended to go back for good? *Last year in Glasgow.* What had her plans been for the future? And with whom? Who was Malcolm?

He flicked back through the pages until the diary

fell open of its own accord. Lorimer frowned. Cut neatly out of the centre of the little book were several pages, the remaining thatch of paper left to prevent the diary falling apart at its stitched seam. What had taken place to make Kirsty MacLeod obliterate several weeks out of a record of her life? And in which year had this event happened? A love affair gone wrong? Something so embarrassing that she couldn't bear to re-read it in the following years? Lorimer closed the diary, weighing it in his hand. He'd have to read the whole thing. Then ask even more questions. Slipping the diary into his pocket, Lorimer let his eyes rove around the room once more.

He'd had enough. The place gave him an impression of girlish innocence, of a Kirsty MacLeod who was doing her best to survive in this alien environment. As he looked again at the picture of the standing stones, Lorimer couldn't help feeling that the nurse would have gone back to the islands eventually.

He turned on his heel. The boys would be back later to strip the place. For now, all Lorimer wanted was to leave the airless room to the fly trapped against the dusty windowpane.

Chapter Fourteen

Glasgow University sat high above the west end of the city on Gilmour Hill, its spiked spire a landmark for miles around. To the south it overlooked the Art Galleries and the river Clyde beyond. That particular morning Tom Coutts felt real pleasure in the view.

"Makes you feel good, doesn't it?" he smiled at Solomon. They were sitting on a wooden bench by a strip of grass, warmed by unexpected sunshine.

Solly smiled back. Tom hadn't looked as relaxed as this for a long time. He nodded at his companion.

"Coming back into work soon, then?"

Tom sighed. "I hope so. They tell me I've done well, whatever that means. Thought I knew all the psychobabble but it's different when you're on the receiving end," he grinned wryly. "But I can't fault them. Okay, it's taken a while and you must be fed up with all the extra marking. Sorry about that," he added. "Still, I feel better than I've felt in ages. And this helps," he spread a hand over the banks of primulas spreading down towards Kelvin Way.

"I wanted to ask you something, Tom. About the clinic."

"They using you as their profiler, are they? Good. I'm glad," Tom Coutts nodded approvingly.

"I know DCI Lorimer's spoken to you about the victim. Must have been hard when she was Nan's nurse."

"One of Nan's nurses," Tom corrected him gently. "Yes. It was a shock. I'd only seen her a few days before the murder. Hadn't even realised she worked there. But then I didn't keep in touch with any of them after the funeral."

"I wondered if you would help me. Give me some information about the clinic. From an insider's viewpoint, as it were."

"Listen, I'd be glad to. You've no idea how grateful I've been for all your help, Solly. Anything I can tell you, anything at all that might help build up a decent picture for you." Tom laid a hand on Solly's arm as he spoke. "Mind you, I can't fault the clinic. The therapists were very professional. I thought the place seemed well run."

"How about the other patients?"

Tom grinned. "Aha! Run into a problem over patient confidentiality, have you?"

"Something like that," Solly replied blandly. Mrs Baillie had not been pleased at having to give her patient files to the police. She would be even less inclined to co-operate with a civilian, he thought.

"Want to give me a grilling before I go up to Lewis?"

"Lewis?"

Tom inclined his head. "Didn't you know? They've got a respite centre on the island. Most of the longer term patients have a chance to go up there for a break at the end of their treatment. I was offered the chance and I thought, well, why not. A few days with some clean air can only help. Then I'll be ready for work again."

Solomon shook his head. A respite centre. On Lewis? He wondered if Lorimer had any inkling of this. Kirsty MacLeod came from Lewis. This was an element that kept coming into the equation. A coincidence? Or was there something more sinister going on that they'd all missed?

"Tell me a bit about the patients you met during your therapy sessions."

"What's there to tell? These are folk who are part of a system, Solly. They're more a danger to themselves than to anyone else. It's the loose cannon you're looking for. The one who's never seen his G.P. The one everyone sees as normal. *You* know that." Tom drew him a disapproving look.

Solly nodded and shrugged. "Perhaps. But just indulge me for a little. Tell me about the patients who were in your group."

Tom took a deep breath. "Well. They weren't the same for a start. I can remember one or two who came after I started, but to be honest I don't have a lot of memory about who was there at the beginning of my treatment. Except the long termers, the residents."

Solomon crossed one leg over the other, listening but not interrupting.

"The Irish chap, Leigh, he's been there all along. Eric came a couple of months back. Then there was an older man called Sam something. He'd been a shipyard worker. And the nun, of course. She's been there for ages. How she can afford it, goodness knows. I thought they took a vow of poverty and that place doesn't come cheap. Even with medical insurance."

"The nun. What was her name?"

"Sister Angelica. Poor soul. She'd been displaced from her last convent when it was closed down. Had lived there all her professional life, I believe. She simply couldn't come to terms with any change." Tom turned to Solly, his eyes suddenly hard. "Bereaved, really. Like me," he added. "People tell you to pull yourself together, you know. Think time will help, as if grieving should be contained in a respectable amount of time: so many months and no longer. It's not like that, though. Not for some of us. Sister Angelica suffered from manic depression. She'd come into the Grange after an attempted suicide."

"When was this?"

Tom shrugged. "Don't know. She was there when I started the sessions and she's still there, as far as I know."

"Do you remember any of the patients who were given the chance to go to Lewis?"

"No. You see, the make-up of the group changes so much from week to week. There were the ones, like me, who came in as out-patients and then there were the residents."

"But some of the residents would continue as out-patients for a while, surely?"

Tom frowned. "Yes, I suppose so, but you'd really need to check with the Baillie woman. She'll have all that sort of thing in her files. Cathy, the girl on reception might be a better bet, mind you," he grinned conspiratorially at Solly.

"Thanks, Tom. Would you do me another favour?"

"Surely. Anything I can."

"Would you mind writing down everything you can remember about the residents in your therapy group? It might help me."

"Of course," Tom patted his arm. "In fact I'll get on with that right away." He rose from the bench and flexed his shoulders. "Getting too old for sitting on park benches," he laughed. "Good hunting, Solly."

Solomon stood on the platform of the bus, gripping the rail as it braked to a halt. The bus had taken him from University Avenue all the way over to the south side of the city. Now, according to his A to Z, there was only a short walk to the Grange. His mind was still buzzing with last night's marking load. Final year exams were a headache for all the staff at this time of year and Solly found it one of the few times when he had to struggle to clear his mind and focus on other things. They were such a vulnerable lot, his students, under their guise of bravado. One girl in particular, bright, feisty and chasing a First for all her worth, seemed to have cracked under the strain. The psychologist had been saddened to read her scripts full of generalisations and glossed-over statistics. Hannah was so much better than her results would suggest. The girl was one of a group who had failed to come to his exam preparation classes earlier in their course, he remembered now. Solly always made it his duty to give every student a chance to find out about the psychology of exam preparation. It had so much more to do with strategies and mental attitude than sitting up burning the midnight oil. Still, there were some kids, like Hannah, who would never be convinced.

Dismissing students from his mind, Solomon recalled the file on Kirsty MacLeod. His present remit was to the dead rather than to the living.

The road to the clinic ran slightly uphill and the pavements were narrow on either side of the road where, as Lorimer had told him, there was extensive double parking. Even during the day, thought Solly. Perhaps a fair proportion of the residents were retired? An interesting thought. Would there be more eyes to see during the daytime? The psychologist had a list of local people who had been interviewed in the house-to-house enquiries following Kirsty MacLeod's murder. These were so time-consuming for the police whose resources were often stretched to breaking point anyway.

Solomon stopped at the brow of the hill. The red sandstone tenements petered out here, giving way to a few solid Victorian villas at the end of the cul-de-sac. The Grange was just one of those that had undergone extensive renovation. Most had been divided into residential flats, a more marketable proposition these days, and certainly a saving on Community Charges. Opposite the Grange two houses had been given quite different makeovers, however. What at first appeared to be a large family home was in fact a dental surgery. Next door to that was a pub, the sort that could be found in any town the length and breadth of Britain. There was a poster outside advertising the weekly events along with its chips-with-everything bar menu. The psychologist crossed the road towards the surgery, noting the house name, Palmyra, still engraved in faded gold over the glass lintel. Standing back, he could see several cars nosing around the back of the building. The front gateway was only wide enough to admit pedestrians so there must be another entrance to the driveway, Solly thought, his feet taking him round the side of the old house.

There were four cars parked: two were BMWs with this year's registration and one was a classic Jaguar, its racing green bodywork sleek and polished. Dentistry was paying well in this part of the world, if appearances were to be believed, Solly smiled to himself. The

fourth car was a Vauxhall, K656 BLS. He made a note
of all their numbers, telling himself that Lorimer's
team had probably covered just such details already.
He was aware of the need to tread carefully. There was
no reason to fracture the relationship between the
DCI and himself. What really interested him, though,
was how the cars had come into the parking area. Sure
enough there was a double wooden gate that had been
fixed into the high stone walls. No moss was clinging
to the stone posts either side of the gate, unlike the
furred surface along the older section of the wall, suggesting that the entrance had been constructed in
recent years. On closer inspection Solly could see
trails of purple toadflax growing out of the crevices
between the pitted stonework. The gate itself was a
solid affair of thick timber, dark with creosote that
had not yet weathered. He gave the latch a push and
found himself in a cobbled lane running down the
length of the street.

Solly shut the gate behind him. There was no sign
of a padlock although there was a hasp attached to the
left gate. He fingered the metal loop, checking for
fresh scratches that might show if a padlock had been
taken off recently. There were none that he could see.
Did that suggest a laxity in the dentists' security? Or
was this a fairly low risk area? Solomon decided to
walk back down the lane rather than retrace his steps
through the grounds of the surgery.

Looking up and down he could see the black shapes
of wheelie bins all along one side of the lane. A bin
lorry could manoeuvre its way up here, then. The lane
wasn't as narrow as it seemed. Solomon looked again
at the wooden gates. Had the killer opened them and

simply parked his car in the empty driveway, leaving quietly from the back lane? Was that a possibility Lorimer had considered? The wall ran all the way back down to the main road so Solomon headed towards the last building on the street.

At one time it may have resembled its neighbour but now several ramshackle extensions had transformed the house into a mock Tudor pub. The roof still had the same grey Welsh slate but there the similarity ended, the building having spawned a series of flat-topped, concrete extensions that almost reached the perimeter wall. Here, too, there was a back entrance, but this was a high narrow green door. Solomon tried turning the round handle but it was locked fast. There was no other exit that he could see. With a small sigh, he headed back to the surgery gate and slipped into the grounds. There was nothing to be gained from walking all the way back down the lane and up the road again.

As he made for the front gate, the door to the surgery opened and a woman appeared, buttoning her raincoat as she emerged. Solomon gave her his usual benign smile but she merely stared for a moment at him before crossing the road to the Grange. He watched her walk up the driveway until she was hidden from sight by the rhododendron bushes.

Solomon stood for a few minutes just outside the gate. From here the upper windows of the clinic were visible. Anyone standing at those windows could see into the grounds of the dental surgery, Solomon's logical voice reasoned. It was time to have a look around the Grange itself. He rubbed his hands together. The residents might prove to be quite fascinating.

Rosie washed her hands, noting where the sweat from her surgical gloves had left pink tinges along the palms. She dried them thoroughly on the paper towel then pressed the lever on the industrial-sized hand cream dispenser that sat over the basin. It was a routine she followed religiously after a PM. Your hands are your primary tools, she often told her students. The girls were the ones who usually followed her advice. It wasn't a very macho thing for the boys to rub hand cream into their fingers. Body-piercing, dreadlocks, they were quite the thing, but hand cream?

Rosie smiled as she thought of her conversation with Solly on the subject. He'd made her laugh with his acute perception of their attention-grabbing strategies, showing her, even as he gently mocked their outward appearances, how sensitive he was to the students' underlying vulnerability. At the time Rosie had found herself thinking what a great father Solomon Brightman would make. She had been immediately appalled at herself for the thought. Was she becoming broody or what?

Solomon was going to see the people at the Grange today, he'd told her. She'd likely see him in the staff club just around teatime. Sometimes she'd have a quick orange juice as she scanned the room for her dark, bearded friend. Other times he'd be there ahead of her reading the papers in what had become their favourite corner. Funny how he was a creature of habit in some ways when he was so unpredictable most of the time. They'd discussed the two murders, Rosie offering her professional opinion but sparing him the grislier pathological details when she remembered.

Solly had a delicate stomach for such things. The pathologist usually delighted in tormenting lay people with the finer points of her post mortems but she'd made an exception with Solly.

Lorimer had teased her about their relationship. She was fairly sure Solly found her attractive. He had invited her down to London for his sister's wedding, hadn't he? They'd had a great time. He'd been so attentive, showing her all the traditions surrounding a Jewish wedding to make her feel at ease. And afterwards they'd danced and laughed all night. Lorimer was no fool. She fancied Solly like crazy. It had taken all her powers of concentration to keep her hands on the steering wheel as they'd driven back up north. But Solly? Just how did he really feel about her?

Rosie looked in the mirror above the basin. She pushed her fingers through her blonde hair. There were a few wee laughter lines around the eyes but it wasn't a bad face, she told herself. No need for the Botox just yet. Maggie Lorimer always joked that Rosie was the other woman in her husband's life. That was just Maggie's way, though. The older woman was given to flattery. Rosie stuck out her tongue at the face in the mirror and turned away. Poor Maggie. She didn't have much fun with Lorimer working all the hours that his job demanded. Maybe she could suggest a night out. A foursome. Cheered by the idea, Rosie whistled to herself as she came out into the corridor of the mortuary. A shelf full of white skulls grinned down from above as if sharing in her good humour.

Alice paused from cleaning the bathroom windows as she looked down on the figure below. From her vantage point high above the grounds of the clinic she could see him wandering slowly towards the back of the building as if he was looking for something. She gave the window a push outwards so that her cloth could reach the fixed pane in the middle. But she couldn't take her eyes off the stranger.

"Hey, Nellie," she called back into the room. "C'mere an' see this. This one doesnae look like polis, does he?" she asked as a thickset woman in green overalls pushed her way towards the open bathroom window. Together they stared at the figure below them. As if sensing he was being watched, the man turned and looked up at the two cleaners.

"Naw, he isnae polis," Nellie decided. "Looks mair like a foreigner tae me, hen."

"Whit's he doin' moochin aroon' here, well?"

Nellie shrugged. It was none of her business. She hadn't liked being questioned by that wee slip of a polis wumman. But still an' all, there wis a murderer on the loose.

"Ach, I suppose we'd better tell Mrs Baillie," she decided.

Alice screwed her face up. "Gonnae you go, eh, Nellie? Ah don't like."

Nellie grinned. "Feart of her are ye?" Seeing Alice's weak grin, the older cleaner stuffed her cloth into the pocket of her overalls and turned to leave. "Ach, a'right. But keep an eye on whatshisface, okay?"

"Aye. Thanks, Nellie. Yer a pal."

Down below, aware of the slight interest he had created, Solomon turned back towards the front door. He would have to request permission now to walk about the grounds. A pity. He'd liked to have wandered around the back of the building free from any prying eyes. He looked up at the name carved out of the keystone above the main door. *The Grange* were the only visible words, there was no brass plate to intimidate the patients with the idea of a clinic for neural disorders. In fact, it was more like coming to a private residence. That was probably the whole idea, he told himself.

Solomon stood on a tiled porch beyond the open storm doors trying to peer through the frosted glass. The security panel to the right of the door showed five buttons. Five numbers to be memorised. Solomon wondered how often they were altered, how they were chosen and by whom. He heard the sound of feet approaching, then a blurred shadow opened the door to him.

"Dr Brightman? We were expecting you. I'm Mrs Baillie. Won't you come in." As the director of the clinic held open the door, Solomon's first impression was of a woman who'd had too little sleep for too long. She looked as if she were holding herself together by sheer strength of will.

"Actually I'd like to look around the grounds. Especially at the back of the building," Solly explained in his gentlest voice. "Would that be all right, Mrs Baillie?" He could see the relief in the woman's body as she nodded.

"Will you need me after that, Dr Brightman?" she asked, then seemed to hesitate before adding, "I have an appointment in town."

"If I might just have your permission to stroll around? It helps to form an impression of what may have happened that night."

"Of course. Ellie Pearson will be here to show you the layout of the Grange. She's our most senior member of staff."

The woman's voice had become more brisk, as if she resented Solly's deference. As the door closed behind her Solly wondered what sort of a strain it must be to run a clinic of this sort where one of your staff had been murdered.

At the back of the building a high wall ran the length of the grounds. Thick rhododendrons divided the Grange's gardens from those properties on either side. Solomon imagined the closed-in aspect of the grounds had been simply to maintain privacy whenever the house had been a private dwelling. Now it took on another aspect. As he gazed around he could see that there was little chance of escape for anyone who wanted to make a secret getaway. And that included the residential patients themselves. They had to have a certain amount of security, Solly told himself, remembering the panel on the front door. There was a responsibility to care for fragile people here, some of whom were being protected from themselves. How, then, had the killer made his way in and out of the house when there were such watchful eyes among the staff? The only conclusion he could come to was that the killer had been inside the clinic from the start. That's what Lorimer had suggested. One of the patients might be the self-same killer that had strangled Deirdre McCann. They were trying to obtain permission to take forensic samples right now. Adhering to Human Rights legislation held up the process considerably, he knew, making officers like DCI Lorimer champ at the bit.

So far medical staff, auxiliaries, cleaners and odd-job men had all been questioned along with the more lucid patients. Even their friends and families were coming under Lorimer's scrutiny. There was nothing to indicate an escape route for a killer coming out of this area unless he had been a pole-vaulter. The wall behind him was easily twelve feet high and the bushes seemed quite impenetrable. No, the killer must have taken the route across the road, possibly through the dentists' car park and out into that back lane. Or, a little voice reasoned, he'd simply stayed inside the clinic, going about his normal night-time activities. His or hers.

Nothing was even clear about that, although Rosie had voiced her opinion that it probably had been a man who'd taken the lives of the two women. Strangulation had been exacted with considerable force. But, Solly had argued, many of the nursing staff were females used to hard manual work. Nursing was a pretty physical occupation after all, even in a private clinic like this one.

As he stood looking at the basement door he knew there would have to be much more data before he could create any sort of profile. The signature of the praying hands with the flower conjured up a picture of a person who had remorse for his actions. Was the killing a compulsion motivated by some deep-seated problem in his past? Something that therapy had failed to resolve? Solly looked from the basement door back towards the street. Opportunity might be a starting point but it only led him back to the clinic itself. Clasping his hands behind his back, Solomon walked thoughtfully round the far side of the building. His shoes crunched on the pale golden gravel that served as a pathway. Was that another form of security? Did the staff listen for wayward feet outside the walls of the clinic? The killer had opened the basement door and left it swinging in the wind that night. But where had he gone afterwards? That was a puzzle indeed.

"Dr Brightman? Mrs Baillie's gone out but she said you could stay as long as you needed," Ellie Pearson told him.

She looked at him uncertainly as if this exotic-looking man were not to be trusted and that the director was slightly crazy in letting him loose among their patients. Her white slacks and short-sleeved tunic gave the woman an extra air of briskness. Round her neck dangled a pair of half-moon spectacles. The woman was probably about his own age, Solly guessed.

There was something intimidating about medical personnel in uniform, Solly mused. Not that he could be easily intimidated. Such observations impinged on his consciousness without making him react to them in the slightest.

"Thank you. I have a note of the clinic's layout somewhere." He searched in several pockets before drawing out a much-folded piece of paper.

"Here we are. So I won't need to keep you from your duties, Sister," he added, nodding wisely at the name badge on the woman's chest. He turned slightly away from her and opened the makeshift map. There were red highlights showing the basement and related areas. To reach these he would have to pass the residents' main lounge and the long corridor where their downstairs rooms were located. Through an open door to his right he saw Sister Pearson making for a staircase. He looked back at the plan. That led to Mrs Baillie's own apartment. What else might be up there? Anyhow, she seemed to be satisfied that the psychologist could be left to his own devices. Perhaps they'd become inured to strangers crawling all over the place since Kirsty MacLeod's murder. Just as the thought came to him, Solomon was aware of an emaciated figure shuffling out of a nearby room on his left, pushing a zimmer frame in front of her. His heart sank as he took in the woman's face with its cadaverous hollows. She wasn't old at all, but wracked with whatever eating disorder had ruined her body. She stopped and looked up at him as Solomon drew level with her.

"Good morning," he smiled politely, giving a nod in her direction. The woman smiled back at him showing red exposed gums. At least her hair showed some signs of care, a shiny grip held its wispy strands back tidily from her brow. China blue eyes regarded him hopefully for a moment then looked away as if failing to find the face that they sought.

As Solomon passed her by, he noticed her hands clutching the zimmer's metal rail. Despite the blue veins standing up on her hands, the fingernails were trimmed and polished. There were some signs of care here, at any rate, thought Solly. Some attractive prints on the wall, bright pastel scenes of Tuscany depicting gardens and arbours. Restful, he mused, good choices for a place like this. Somebody had put plenty of thought into the details and Solomon was impressed.

The corridor came to an end with double doors that swung away from him automatically and Solomon stepped into an area that had the unmistakeable smell of a hospital. His map wasn't needed here. There were signs on the walls indicating an upper level of residents' accommodation and another door marked Staff Only. There was no window on either side of the corridor, the only light coming from overhead strips that glared down on the pale linoleum flooring. A door to one side was slightly ajar. Remembering Lorimer's description of the multiple sclerosis patient, Solly paused. Whoever had killed Kirsty MacLeod had passed by just here. There was a faint mechanical sound from within but nothing more. Not wishing to disturb the patient, Solly crept past quietly. Beyond the stairs was the door leading to the basement. He pushed it open.

Rosie had described exactly where the murder had taken place. The floor was clean now, but there was a red cross on the paper that showed the spot where they thought Kirsty MacLeod had been killed. Solomon stood looking back down the corridor. The swing doors would have muffled any sound the girl might have made. Only one person could have heard her had she cried out. Once more he looked towards the room where a woman lay wasting away with that awful disease. She was completely paralysed, Lorimer had told him, and had no power of speech. No threat to a killer, then.

The basement door creaked as Solly turned the handle. Darkness met his gaze and he fumbled for the light switch as his eyes adjusted to the gloom. Only the first few steps were visible. His hand felt the switch yet he resisted the instinct to flood the place with light, trying instead to see through the shadows;

trying indeed to imagine what the killer would have seen. Had he thrust the young nurse's body down the steep flight of steps? There would have been a thud as her corpse hit the concrete floor below. Or had he dragged her step by painstaking step into the boiler room?

Solomon tried each idea on for size. The victim's tights had been ripped, suggesting she'd been pulled rather than pushed. But if she'd been dead, the weight would have been considerable even to drag downwards. As his eyes became accustomed to the dark, Solly counted the seventeen metal steps that separated the boiler room from the upper floors of the Grange. Perhaps he'd pulled her down the first few steps where definite traces of fabric had been found. The door opened outwards so there would not have been so much effort needed to manoeuvre a body through in the first place. Had he given up after the first few steps before sending her corpse tumbling down? Had something panicked him? He must have made sure she was dead.

Forensics found nothing to suggest that he had interfered with the body. His only need had been to pull her hands flat together and then add his final touch, the red carnation.

Solly switched on the light and the room below was suddenly visible. It was smaller than he had thought it would be with its fluorescent strip hanging on a long wire suspended from a fitting on the ceiling. The wire had been looped and fastened to one side, presumably as an aid to changing the light fitting.

"How many psychologists does it take to change a lightbulb?" Rosie had teased him. Her voice came unbidden into his mind. He was suddenly very aware of her presence there in that basement room where she had examined the young nurse's body. Solly had seen her at scenes of crime before and marvelled at her clinical, detached manner. He stared down into the basement room. Had the killer walked calmly out of the back door, stepping over the girl's dead body? Had there been a quickening of his pulse as he'd climbed the stairs out into the back gardens, escaping from the sight behind him? Or was there another explanation altogether that involved someone staying behind in the Grange? And Brenda Duncan had come on the scene so soon after that, hadn't she?

Solly stroked his beard thoughtfully. Whatever scenario he came up with, one thing stood out clearly: it had taken a very cool and determined person to carry out this attack. Whoever had planned this had expected to get away with it. They'd known the layout of the clinic and had knowledge of where the nurses would be on duty. Or had they? Was this just a random stranger killing after all? Solomon closed his eyes. Had the killer known about the MS patient, too? Try as he might his vision of this killer was of a figure that had disappeared back into the labyrinth of doors and corridors, a killer who had brought a red carnation for a pretty lady.

He would have to seek plenty more information before the vision took on flesh and bones but for now he had the sense that creating this profile was going to take all his time and energy.

Chapter Fifteen

The boat from Uig was always on time, the man at the pier assured them. Lorimer, wrapped in his winter jacket, hoped fervently that he was right. Solly stood near the edge of the metal ramp looking out over the choppy grey water, his long black coat flapping round his legs. Even his beard had lifted in the wind, making the psychologist look like one of the ancient patriarchs.

They had travelled up early that morning, Lorimer doing all the driving. Solly didn't drive, never had and claimed it was something he could happily do without. He'd certainly enjoyed the trip though, gazing out of the window and commenting on all that he saw on the way up. It had been Lorimer's idea for them to make the journey together. Almost a week had passed since Kirsty MacLeod's body had been found in that dingy basement. Forensic reports showed that strangulation had probably taken place in the clinic's corridor. The body had been dragged through the clinic to the basement door then halfway down the stairs. It appeared that the killer had then flung Kirsty away from him, making her land flat on her back on the cold concrete. That much they did know. What had happened next was a matter of conjecture, though Solomon had been inclined to think the killer might have remained inside, despite the open door.

A huge file of statements from staff, residents and anyone who had known the young nurse had accumulated back at the Division. Yet Lorimer was troubled by how few people there seemed to be who had known the girl intimately. It was almost as if she'd deliberately kept a low profile. Or perhaps her friends just weren't willing to talk for some reason.

The landlady hadn't had much to offer apart from the fact that the rent was always paid on time and she'd been a quiet girl. No one in the neighbouring bedsits had offered more than that. It was Dr Tom Coutts who had been most helpful. He'd seen Kirsty MacLeod a few days prior to the killing and gave the police a fair amount of background information. She'd been one of the community nurses who'd cared for his wife up until her death last year and Tom had only charitable things to say about the young woman from Harris. She'd been a caring, compassionate person, he'd told them. Had the knack of making Nan feel better just by being there beside her. They'd followed this up with visits to the other community nurses and heard the same story of a nurse who'd had a proper vocation. All the residents at the Grange had liked her. She'd been a good listener, Eric Fraser had told them.

There was an old aunt, Kirsty's only living relative, whom they would interview, but the main spur behind this journey was the revelation about the respite centre, Failte. Mrs Baillie had been strangely reticent about its existence and quite unrepentant about letting her two patients be transferred there the day after Kirsty's death. One was Sister Angelica, the nun, and the other was a man called Sam Fulton. Both patients had been in Tom Coutts' cognitive therapy classes. DC Cameron had raised an eyebrow when he'd been told that the DCI was heading for Lewis and Harris.

He could have dispatched one of his junior officers but there was something that he wanted to see for himself up here. This respite home was a sanctuary of sorts. And right now it was sheltering two people who had suddenly disappeared following Kirsty's murder. Samuel Fulton's name had come up on the police computer. His record showed an involvement in two domestic incidents. There had been more, according to the file but previous charges had been dropped until he'd broken his wife's arm. A man with a record of violence being quietly shipped up to the Hebrides at the outset of a murder inquiry did not rest easily with Lorimer. The significance of the other patient being a nun was not lost on him either. Those praying hands on each of the two victims might have emanated from some twisted religious brain. And Harris and Lewis were famous for religious piety. Looking into the water, Lorimer wondered what these islands were like. He would be there soon enough.

The journey up from Glasgow had taken more than six hours. Lorimer had pushed on through Rannoch Moor, a strange, bleak landscape that never failed to conjure up the blasted heath of *Macbeth*'s three witches, he told Solly, who'd nodded wisely. Glencoe had shown its usual dark brooding shadows but the sun had appeared briefly on the Commando Memorial at Spean Bridge as Ben Nevis lowered through a covering of cloud, snow still visible on its higher slopes.

"I'm ashamed to say I've never been further north than Loch Lomond," Solly had told him as they drove past loch after loch on the way to Skye. Lorimer had slowed down at Eilean Donan, letting Solly have an eyeful of the well-photographed castle out on its peninsula. Lorimer had been polite about it but that was all. There were some tourist spots for which he couldn't muster up much enthusiasm. The quiet and lonesome places like Rannoch and Glencoe held more real magic for him. He'd hoped to show Solly the Cuillin but the journey from the Skye bridge north to Uig was a disappointment. Mist had covered the mountains and there was hardly anything to see save the hunched, damp shapes of sheep at the roadside.

They'd driven through Broadford on the road north and now here they were at Uig, waiting for the boat that would take them across to Harris. At least the rain was off, thought Lorimer, clapping his hands against the arms of his jacket to keep warm.

Solly had given up his post by the water's edge and was slowly walking towards him.

"Any sign of it yet?" Lorimer asked him.

"Just coming in, now."

Lorimer walked further down the pier, glancing over the concrete wall. There it was, Caledonia MacBrayne's ferry. *The Hebrides*, the man at the ticket office had told them. The car ferry cut a swathe of white foam from her bows as she neared them. She was making good speed and Lorimer wondered if she'd overshoot the pier. Solly and he quickened their pace as they walked the length of the pier back towards the parked cars. In a matter of minutes the boat had moored, disgorged its passengers and Lorimer was driving into the bowels of the car deck. By the time they'd collected jackets and locked the vehicle, *The Hebrides* was sliding through the waves once more.

"Look, I know it's cold, but how about coming up on deck?" Lorimer asked. Solly nodded cheerfully enough but pulled up his collar as they ascended the narrow metal staircase. The wind hit them full on the face as Lorimer opened the door to the upper deck. But the DCI didn't care. There was an hour and a half of sailing before they reached their destination and he wasn't about to spend it sitting in a smoke-filled bar.

"Is that your famous Cuillin, then?" Solly asked, pointing to the flat-topped hills rising above the mist.

"No. They're MacLeod's Tables. We couldn't see the Cuillin from here anyway, even if the weather had been any good," Lorimer told him, watching as the huge hills reared their heads above Skye, as if mocking their departure.

"Still, you've seen some of Skye's mountains."

"They're amazing!" Solly stared as the hills receded from them.

Lorimer was gratified as Solly exclaimed his delight. There was something childlike about his enthusiasm. They stood huddled together on the top deck, the sea breeze whipping across their faces, watching as Skye faded into the distance, a tumble of clouds obscuring its contours.

For a while there was only a large expanse of moving water, then a group of islands came into view.

"What are they?" Solomon wanted to know.

"Think that's the Sheant Isles," Lorimer replied, trying to recall the OS map he'd pored over the previous night.

A smoky green horizon unfolded as the light played over the contours and curves of the landscape. Then the shadows deepened and became the hills of South Harris.

A lighthouse stood bravely amongst a cluster of black rocks, dazzling in the spring sunlight. Somewhere, Lorimer had read, these southerly shores boasted miles of deserted, white sandy beaches. Now he could make out a rocky shore with dots of white here and there along the coastline. As they drew nearer the dots became small houses.

"What's that?" Solly asked, pointing into the waters ahead. Lorimer followed his gaze. Orange marker buoys bobbed up and down quite far from the shore; too far for an anchorage.

"Creels, I think," Lorimer answered. "They're probably floats to show where the lobster creels are kept."

The boat rounded the rocks and suddenly they were coming inshore to what appeared to be a tiny hamlet. This couldn't be Tarbert, the largest town in Harris, surely? Lorimer looked over the harbour. The colours seemed to have been washed with a different sort of rain from the slate grey stuff that fell on his city. Or was it the light? It was as though everything was being magnified. Details were sharper, like the cluster of men in orange jackets who were working on the pier; uncoiling the thick mooring ropes, pulling the gangway into position, standing by the few motorists who were about to leave those shores. A knot of people stood around the edge of the pier waiting for the boat, but not passengers. He could see that. Waiting for the mail, perhaps?

There were women whose heads were wrapped in scarves and men in flat tweed caps. Bunnets. His dad had worn a bunnet, Lorimer remembered. He had a sudden vision of that tall, spare figure doffing his tweed cap to any ladies passing by; a gesture from a bygone age. Would Harris have retained any of the dignity of yesteryear or would it be just like everywhere else, in pursuit of the latest trends?

Lorimer's reminiscing came to an abrupt halt as a voice called over the loudspeaker system.

"We are approaching Tarbert. Would all drivers please return to their vehicles. Thank you." The voice was taped, of that Lorimer had no doubt, but it had a soft melodious quality that he recognised. It sounded just like Niall Cameron.

They made their way down the very steep staircase leading to the car deck and located the Lexus wedged between a British telecom van and an ancient Ford Transit. Two men in overalls and thicksoled boots were squeezing their way amongst the vehicles.

As they passed, one of them nodded briefly, saying, "Aye, aye. Grand day," as if he were exchanging pleasantries with old friends, instead of total strangers. Solomon gave Lorimer a meaningful look. This was certainly a world away from their city streets.

Then they were inside the car and all around them engines were roaring into life in the bowels of *The Hebrides*. There was the unmistakeable sound of wood against steel as the boat docked and Lorimer waited impatiently for the moment when he could surface again. If there was one thing that made him uneasy it was being locked in below water level like this. Maggie even teased him for his dislike of war films depicting life in a sub.

At last it was his turn. As Lorimer accelerated off the metal ramp and onto the safety of the Tarbert streets he glanced at Solly and smiled indulgently, noticing how he twisted around to catch a glimpse of the tiny shops and houses as they passed out of town. The gesture reminded him of his wife and her zest for anything new and unfamiliar. Suddenly Lorimer wished that he, too, could recapture Maggie's vast capacity to enjoy life. He'd lost that feeling long ago, somewhere between the back streets and the City Mortuary.

Kirsty MacLeod's last known Harris address was c/o Mhairi MacLeod at Borve Cottage in Rodel. There had been no telephone number. Rodel was not so far away in terms of mileage but it took Lorimer the best part of an hour before the road sign proclaimed that they had reached the village. Several times he'd had to swing into the curve of a lay-by to let another car pass. Lorimer hadn't minded. They weren't running to a time schedule after all, and had booked into the Rodel Hotel for one night, so all the stopping and starting had given him the opportunity to look over the coastline. The day was still fine, although he'd noticed more clouds gathering overhead. The blues and greys of sky were reflected in the water but it was the green that really struck him; everything from a dark bottle green where rocks undoubtedly lurked, to a dazzling emerald reflecting light above the white shores. The brochures hadn't exaggerated.

These beaches were endless swathes of white sand licked by curling waves; and not a soul to be seen.

"We could be on another planet," Solly had murmured, gazing round from the shore to the hills crouching around them. He'd been pretty impressed by this Hebridean island and Lorimer was gratified. Okay, so it was his first visit to these parts too, but he still felt proprietorial. Scotland was *his* country.

Rodel, or *Roghadal* as the Gaelic sign proclaimed, appeared to them suddenly around yet another winding corner between the hills. A quick glance told Lorimer that he was below the infamous site of the quarry that had caused so much public dissension amongst the islanders. As they drove past a lone cottage a man rounded the side of his shed, stopped and caught their eye. Suddenly he waved and smiled. Lorimer was struck by the expression of open friendliness on the man's face. It was as if he were welcoming them home rather than saluting a pair of strangers to his island.

Lorimer had only moments to absorb the man's working dungarees and shock of weather-bleached hair as they drove by. Looking in the rear view mirror, he could see the man leaning on the cottage gate, following them with his eyes. It was a small thing, maybe, but it impressed itself on Lorimer. Suddenly the city seemed light years away.

"The natives are friendly," quipped Solly, nodding into his beard as if the incident were being filed away for future reference.

"Looks like we've arrived," Lorimer replied, indicating a sign for the Rodel Hotel.

"Not exactly a metropolis, is it?" Solly joked. There had been very few houses along the road and now they were passing an old church.

"That looks interesting."

"It is," replied Lorimer. "That's not just any old church. What you have here is the ancient cathedral of Saint Clements. I fancy having a look around it while we're here," he added to himself. But business would have to come first.

The road took them on a loop and soon he was driving through a courtyard to a large edifice whose grey stones rubbed shoulders with the harbour walls. So this was Rodel; one hotel and a scattering of houses strung out along a windswept stretch of land.

"Hardly surprising that Kirsty came away to the city," he told Solly.

"Interesting, though," replied the psychologist. "I expect it's a close-knit community. The sort of place where it's well nigh impossible to keep things to yourself." Solly gazed over the harbour wall at the stretch of ocean.

"This is the sort of place where people would know each others' secrets," he added, turning to raise his eyebrows at Lorimer.

"See you in the bar," Lorimer gave Solomon a nod and made his way up the narrow stairway. He pushed open the unlocked door of his bedroom and shivered as an icy blast came from the open window. They were a hardy lot up here, then. Telling himself that he'd had enough fresh air during the crossing to last a good while, Lorimer pulled down the sash window. For a moment he looked out at the waves beating against the harbour wall. Had Kirsty MacLeod stood on that very pier watching for a boat that never came home, he wondered. He'd ask a few questions downstairs. Bars the world over were a perennial source of information.

There was no one behind the bar although the brass clock on the wall made it after five. A faint rolling sound came from the floor beneath his feet and Lorimer guessed that a new beer cask was being brought up from the cellar. The noise grew louder and then a slim figure appeared from a door behind the bar. He was about nineteen with that fresh complexion and shock of dark hair that defines the Celt. The green t-shirt sporting a brewer's logo showed that he was one of the staff.

"Oh, hallo there. Didn't realise there was anyone in yet. What'll it be?" The words came out in a breathless rush.

"Vodka and tonic, please." Lorimer had already considered the possibility of an interview with an old Hebridean lady and he didn't want to be smelling of drink.

"Just come in, have you?" the young barman inquired.

"That's right."

"Holiday?"

"Not exactly, though I'd like to do a bit of sight-seeing," Lorimer fenced the question.

"Oh, you'll see some grand sights over here. Never seen beaches like ours, I'll bet!" The pride in the lad's tone was unmistakeable. "Or the standing stones."

"You mean the ones at Callanish?" Lorimer knew a bit about these ancient rivals to Stonehenge.

"Och, no. Not just those. We've our own down here. There's MacLeod's stone just along the road. You'll have passed it by, no doubt, not knowing what to look for." The boy smiled and Lorimer had the sense that he was indulging this visitor from Glasgow. He'd have cultivated a pleasant manner for the tourists, no doubt.

"Is this your first time on the island?"

"Yes, it is, but I was hoping to look someone up while I'm here," Lorimer fixed his gaze on the barman. "A Miss MacLeod."

The boy gave a short laugh. "Oh, there are lots of

MacLeods in these parts. Which one would it be that you're after, now?"

"Mhairi. A Miss Mhairi MacLeod. An elderly lady."

The boy's smile dropped like a stone. He narrowed his eyes at Lorimer, trying to sum up his visitor. "You mean Kirsty's Aunty Mhairi?"

"That's the one," Lorimer said cheerfully, taking a swig of vodka. His expression never betrayed the vision inside his head, of that lonely little figure in blue dumped in the basement of a Glasgow clinic.

"You Press, or what?" The lad's voice was devoid of any semblance of courtesy now and he placed both hands on the edge of the bar defiantly.

"Or what, I'm afraid," Lorimer replied, taking out his warrant card and laying it open on the polished surface of the bar. He watched the boy's face relax a fraction.

"Chief Inspector Lorimer," he read aloud.

Lorimer pocketed the card again. "Miss Mhairi MacLeod?" He let the name hang in the air.

"Aye, she's at home, just along the road past the cathedral. The two white houses joined together. Miss MacLeod's is the first one. You can't miss it."

Chapter Sixteen

Borve Cottage was a five-minute walk from the hotel. They must have passed it on their way into the village, thought Lorimer as he and Solly reached the long white house. It might have been a single dwelling house in days gone by but was now split into two semi-detached cottages. Deep-set windows told of thick walls that had withstood centuries of Atlantic gales but, despite its age, the stone seemed freshly painted and both gardens to the front showed signs of recent care. As Lorimer reached out a hand to the brass knocker, his sleeve caught on a tendril of clematis trailing down beside the door. He looked up to see fat buds along the new shoots, promising a froth of pink to come.

Solly stood to one side, whether out of deference to the DCI or simply to see how the old lady would react, Lorimer couldn't tell.

When the door opened a diminutive, grey-haired woman stood before them. Her lilac twin-set topped a heathery coloured tweed skirt and her leather lacing shoes looked as if they'd walked for miles over the rough island terrain.

"Miss MacLeod?"

"No. She's through the house. Who shall I say is calling?"

"Detective Chief Inspector Lorimer, Strathclyde CID and Dr Solomon Brightman," Lorimer held out his warrant card and the woman peered short-sightedly at it.

"You'll be here about Kirsty, I suppose?" her tone was disapproving but she opened the door wider to let them in.

"That's right," Lorimer answered and was on the point of asking the woman's name when she fixed them with a gimlet stare and said, "Follow me, please."

The woman closed the door behind them and stepped into a darkened hallway.

"She's through here." Lorimer and Solly followed her into a light, airy room facing the water. An old lady was sitting with her back to them in a huge wing chair that faced the bay window.

"Mhairi, it's folk from Glasgow to see you. A Mr Lorimer from the police and his Doctor friend." Lorimer was struck by the change in the woman's voice. It was the tone one would use with a child, soothing and whispery. He stepped forward just as the old woman turned her head towards the voice. For a moment he was speechless. Mhairi MacLeod might be over eighty, but she was one of the most beautiful women he'd ever seen. Her face was smooth and brown with not a sign of a wrinkle except where fine spider's web laughter lines spread from her mouth and eyes. The snow-white hair was wispy and caught back in a net but he could see its abundance of plaited coils and wondered if it had ever been cut. The eyes regarding him were blue, but faded.

"Mr Lorimer, Dr...?" she turned to Solomon and gave him a sweet smile.

"Brightman. How do you do, Miss MacLeod," Solly came forward, gave a stiff little bow then took the old woman's hand.

"Would you like a cup of tea, gentlemen?"

"Thank you. That would be most welcome," Solomon replied before Lorimer had time to think.

"Make us all a pot of tea, would you, Chrissie. And could we have some of those lovely scones you brought in? Thank you, dear."

Mhairi MacLeod waved her hand at the two men. "Bring a couple of chairs over and sit beside me. The view's too good to miss." There was a twinkle in her eye as she addressed Lorimer. He looked around, found two small wooden chairs, each with plump embroidered cushions, then lifted them over and set them down on either side of the wing chair.

"I don't know what I'd do without Chrissie. She's been so good to me since Kirsty's passing."

"She's your home help?" asked Lorimer.

"Oh, don't let her hear you say that! No, no. Chrissie's my next-door neighbour, which makes life easier for us both. Home help? Dear me, we don't have such luxuries in this part of the world unless we're really poor old souls with nobody to care for us." She glanced as Lorimer turned his chair slightly inwards. "Did you have a good journey up?"

"Yes, indeed," Solomon answered.

"You're not with Strathclyde Police, are you, my dear?" Mhairi MacLeod looked at Solomon with interest.

The psychologist shook his head and turned his large brown eyes upon the old lady. "No, I'm helping the police with their case. I may be able to construct a profile of Kirsty's killer which would assist the investigation," he explained.

"Ah, like *Cracker* on the TV?" she smiled at them. "Oh, we're not entirely in the backwoods here, we do have the television. Don't know what Chrissie would do without *Coronation Street*," she added. "You're not from this part of the country, then Dr Brightman?"

"No. I was born in London, but Glasgow's my home now," Solly replied.

She nodded. "Aye. And it was poor wee Kirsty's home for a while." Lorimer noticed her lip tremble for a second but then Chrissie came bustling into the room bearing a tray laden with what looked like the best china and a huge plate of buttered scones. She set it down on the table in front of the old lady.

"Right, I'm away ben. Just give me a knock when you want me through," Chrissie told her and marched out of the room. They heard the front door close behind her.

"She said to give her a knock?" Solomon asked, puzzled.

Mhairi MacLeod smiled at him. "Aye, with my stick." She picked up a walking stick that lay at her feet and motioned with it towards the partition wall. "I don't have the telephone, you see. A couple of raps and Chrissie knows I need her."

The old woman leaned forward and grasped the teapot with both hands then concentrated on pouring out three cups of tea. Lorimer's instinct was to offer to do it for her but a glance from Solly warned him off. Mhairi MacLeod might be old and infirm but she was still the hostess in her own home. Lormer watched her frail hand shaking as she passed him a cup. She saw his expression and pursed her lips together in a gesture of determination. Chrissie might have to make the tea but she was the one who would serve her guests.

She took a few sips of tea then placed her cup back on the tray, rattling the saucer. Her shoulders sagged as she leaned back into the deep armchair and patiently folded her hands.

Mhairi MacLeod gave a short sigh. "Right, now. You've come to see me about Kirsty, haven't you?"

Lorimer looked straight at her, returning her directness. He nodded. "I'm afraid so."

"Don't be afraid, Chief Inspector." Her hand was suddenly covering his own and he felt the warmth of its light touch. "May I ask you something first?"

"Go ahead."

"Kirsty," she paused to let the name roll off her tongue as if she'd become unused to saying it. "Did she suffer much? I never asked before."

Lorimer saw her bite her lip to stop it trembling. "No. Not at all. She'd hardly have known what was happening. The Doctor said it was over very quickly. There were no signs of a struggle," he added gently.

For a moment Mhairi MacLeod stared at him, those faded eyes trying to outmatch his own blue gaze. Then she nodded, apparently satisfied that Lorimer was telling her the truth.

"There are several things we'd like to ask you about Kirsty, your niece."

"Great-niece, Mister Lorimer." There was a faint smile around her mouth as she corrected him. He smiled back.

"Did you know of any men friends that she'd made in Glasgow, anybody she might have written to you about? A particular boyfriend perhaps?"

"No. Nobody special. She used to say she was waiting for Mr Right. But I don't think he ever came into Kirsty's life." She gave a sigh. "She wrote regularly and would have told me if she'd met a young man. Always started her letters, *Dear Aunty Mhairi, I'm fine, how are you?*" Suddenly the old woman's face crumpled and she groped into the depth of a cushion behind her back for a handkerchief.

"Here," Solomon was immediately hunkering down by her side, offering a large white linen hanky. There was silence except for the blowing of her nose and a muffled sobbing from the folds of the handkerchief until Mhairi MacLeod shook her head at them. "So sorry. I'm just a silly old woman."

"No, you're not." Solomon was holding her hand now and stroking it with some concern, his eyes fixed on the old lady's face. She straightened up again and wiped her eyes.

"What was I saying? Yes. Kirsty had nobody special down in Glasgow. She'd had a nice boyfriend up here, Calum, but he went away down to university and they only kept in touch occasionally; birthdays, Christmas cards, that sort of thing."

"Did she ever mention anything about her work in the letters?"

"What sort of thing?" The faded eyes were alert again.

"Did she say if she was happy? Did she like the staff? Was she was coping with the patients, that sort of thing."

Mhairi MacLeod frowned. Was she remembering something? Lorimer asked himself.

"I sometimes wondered if Kirsty was suited to the nursing," she began slowly. "She took everything so much to heart. Became involved with her patients. Grieved terribly whenever one of them passed over. Oh, I know it's a grand thing to be concerned about those who are sick, whether in mind or body," she said, waving a hand at them. "But you need to be a bit hard to be a good nurse, don't you think? It's the same in the police, I suppose," she directed her question to Lorimer who nodded silently. Her voice was quiet when she added, "Kirsty wasn't hard enough, I'm thinking."

They waited for the old lady to elaborate on that statement but apparently that was all she had to offer on the subject.

"Did Kirsty ever talk to you about anything that was worrying her?" Solomon asked.

The old lady looked at him, troubled, as if such questions had never occurred to her before. Her eyes drifted away from them and looked out over the view of the water beyond the shore. Solomon and Lorimer watched her intently. Was there something she recalled? They waited.

"I don't know. Maybe there was something. I felt a sort of sadness in her a while back. I thought maybe she was homesick. She was so good to me, you know. Always wrote cheery letters. Kirsty wouldn't have wanted to burden me with her troubles."

"She kept a diary," Lorimer began.

"Ah, yes. Her five-year diary. I gave it to her one Christmas." Mhairi MacLeod narrowed her eyes. "You've been reading Kirsty's diary?" she asked, affronted.

"This is a murder inquiry," Lorimer reminded her quietly.

"Of course. It's just…" she bit her lip.

"Just that we seem to be invading your great-niece's privacy," Lorimer finished for her.

Mhairi MacLeod nodded slowly. "Just that,

Chief Inspector."

Lorimer drew the red diary from his pocket. He'd read and re-read the entries till the wee small hours but had found nothing enlightening in its pages.

"She mentions someone named Malcolm. On the Hogmanay before last," Lorimer suggested.

"Aye, she would. That'll be Malcolm Munro from the store. He always brings the black bun. They were all here then, all the folks from Rodel."

"This Malcolm, he's not an old boyfriend, then?"

Mhairi MacLeod's eyes twinkled for a moment. "He's sixty if he's a day, Chief Inspector. Kirsty's known Malcolm-at-the-store since she was a wee girl spending her pennies on sherbet dabs."

Solomon smiled and caught Lorimer's eye. The picture of Kirsty MacLeod was beginning to take shape. Solly warmed to this island girl who had become a victim for no apparent reason.

"There are several weeks missing," Lorimer opened the diary and showed her. "From May to late June."

The old woman took the book from his hands and turned its thin pages, her gnarled fingers tracing the dead girl's writing.

"Why would she do that?" Mhairi MacLeod asked, her eyes troubled.

"I was hoping you might be able to tell us," he replied. "I thought something might have happened that she didn't want to remember."

"Or let anybody else see," Solly put in.

"Kirsty never did anything she'd be ashamed of," she said firmly. "And there were no affairs of the heart," she added, looking down at the diary. Solomon watched her stroke the pages as if she were giving comfort to a troubled mind. She wasn't so certain of that, though, was she? What young woman was going to confide her most intimate secrets to an old lady? One she loved too much to burden with her own troubles, he thought, echoing the old woman's words.

"So there's nothing you know that would have upset Kirsty to the extent of cutting up her diary?" Lorimer asked.

Mhairi MacLeod shook her head slowly.

"We think we know so much, don't we? And all the time we really know nothing at all." She spoke softly to herself as if she'd forgotten their presence in the room. Then she turned and Lorimer could see tears in her eyes. "It's not right, is it?" she whispered. "Her mammy and daddy and now wee Kirsty. I should have been away long before them all." She lifted her hand as if in protest. "And here I am. An old, done woman taking up space."

Lorimer didn't reply. For how could he be expected to comment on the unfairness of life? That was what his job was about most of the time. Solomon's eye caught his as Lorimer looked up and the psychologist inclined his head towards the door. Lorimer gave a brief nod in reply. It was time to go.

The early evening sun was glowing against the hillside as they stepped out of Borve Cottage.

"Do you mind if we pay a short visit?" Lorimer asked, indicating Saint Clement's Church.

"Why not," agreed Solly. The two men made their way over to the entrance, Lorimer stooping slightly as he ducked through the doorway. It was the smallest cathedral he'd ever seen, Lorimer thought, blinking as the gloom enfolded them. The stone flags that were polished from centuries of use gave a dull echo as they walked out of the light and into the shadows.

Neither of them spoke a word. It was as if these grey walls hadn't noticed the passing of time. Lorimer had felt like this before. Sometimes standing by a mortuary slab he had that sense of being a tiny speck of dust in a swirling, meaningless universe.

Now here, as his footfall sounded on the worn stones, the Chief Inspector wondered at those Saints who had risked everything to try to bring their beliefs to these parts. What had it all been for? Was the so-called Christian West more law-abiding than in those far off pagan times? Perhaps, just perhaps. He looked over to where Solomon stood poring over a leaflet that he'd picked up from a small wooden table. Did Solly have any religious beliefs? Judaism was so old and venerable. In all his dealings with human behaviour had Solomon retained something extra to sustain him against cynicism? Somehow Lorimer knew that was a question he'd be unable to ask.

As if aware of his companion's scrutiny, Solly turned around, waving the leaflet in his hand.

Lorimer joined him, noticing that there were postcards for sale. An honesty box lay beyond them, fixed to the wall.

"Listen to this," said Solly. "Tradition has it that Saint Clement of Rome was banished to the Crimea where he was put to death by being thrown into the sea with an anchor around his neck. The Church was built by MacLeod of Harris in the thirteenth century as Saint Clement was the patron saint of the MacLeods. Within the church is the tomb of

Alexander Macclod, domino de Dunvegan 1528."

As Solly picked up a few postcards and rattled in his pocket for change, Lorimer took a lingering look at the interior of the tiny, ancient cathedral. He tried to imagine all the folk who had come to worship here over the years. Then another thought came to him. Kirsty would have come here. And her old Aunty Mhairi. Lorimer chewed on a raggled nail. The MacLeods had been here for centuries. That meant that there would be a whole load of them outside. In the graveyard.

For a moment Lorimer stood with his face up to the last warmth of the setting sun. Heedless of his presence, a sheep cropped at the grass. Overhead a gull mewed. He took a deep breath and smelled something fragrant in the soft air. All his weariness seemed to fall away like a cloak being shed. He could so easily forget everything in this quiet corner away from the world. The sky and sea merged into one blur of blue. Somewhere beyond lay a world of offices, streets, computers, files, telephones...all the paraphernalia of his working life.

Lorimer gave himself a shake. He was in danger of being beguiled by the quiet of this island. It was a place like any other, he persuaded himself, inhabited by people as culpable as any in the city.

He stepped in among the lichened gravestones, looking at the names. He was right. There were lots of MacLeods. Some were so old that their inscriptions had faded into decay. He moved among them, shaking his head at all the infant deaths centuries before. Lorimer bent to read the carving on a stone that had leaned over with years of westerly gales. The words were still clearly marked:

> Be Ye Also Ready
> The Small & Great Are Here

Lorimer gave a rueful nod of acknowledgement and passed on down the line.

There was another MacLeod, a Donald MacLeod who had fought in the '45 rebellion. Several lines of inscription told any passer-by that here lay a man who'd been preceded by three wives, who had borne him nine children. Lorimer gave a twisted smile. He was barely in his forties himself, but he'd long ago given up any hope of producing any kids to carry on his own name. He read on. The old man had died in his ninetieth year, it said.

"Incredible, isn't it?" Solly was suddenly by his side. "What accounted for their longevity, do you think?"

"The whisky?" Lorimer joked.

"I wonder. Did they have a healthier way of life, perhaps?"

Lorimer shrugged. The world that he and Solly came from wasn't particularly healthy any more. The Sunday supplements were forever carrying a story about someone who had changed their city life for one in a remote part of Scotland. Taking another lungful of Hebridean air, Lorimer could understand why.

There were more modern headstones on the far side of the graveyard. The detective's feet left soft imprints on the springy turf as he walked amongst them.

At last Lorimer found the one he'd expected to see.

It was inscribed to another Donald MacLeod. Lost at Sea, told the deeply cut words. The wife's name had been added not long after. Kirsty Grace. There was space below for another inscription. When would this grave be opened to lay their daughter to rest? That was the question emanating from the blank grey patch of marble.

"When I find her killer," Lorimer spoke softly to the gravestone.

Chapter Seventeen

"Okay, be with you in half an hour."

Maggie put the phone down. She was really far too busy with marking these junior exams to go out for the evening but maybe she could catch up in her spare periods tomorrow. The seniors were off on exam leave, after all, she argued with herself, and it was Divine Lipinski's last evening in Scotland.

The papers were neatly piled up by her armchair, red marking pen on top, as Maggie glanced guiltily at them. Someone had once teased her that all teachers were programmed to serve. It was true. She found it hard to switch off from work. There was always pressure, always new demands, new directives. In recent years she and her colleagues had hardly time to learn one set of assessment techniques when some wise guy supplanted them with something different. The wise guys had never been teachers, or if they had, they'd long forgotten what the inside of a classroom looked like or, more to the point, what kids really needed for the big, bad world after school was out for good.

Maggie suddenly found herself longing for a change. Surely other countries' systems couldn't be as restrictive as the current Scottish curriculum? She day-dreamed her way to the bathroom and started to wipe away the day's make-up.

She'd dress up tonight. It was a lot warmer and it was staying lighter for longer now. The face in the oval mirror stared back at her, pale skin with fine lines etched around a discontented mouth. She faked a smile then made a face at her reflection. Time for war paint, she told herself.

Thirty minutes later Maggie alighted from a taxi outside the Corinthian. The effort of dressing up in a shorter skirt and slim-heeled shoes was well rewarded when she caught sight of all the lovely young things parading their designer gear at the bar. As usual, Maggie's eyes were drawn towards the gorgeous gold painted ornamentation that gave The Corinthian its name. Her gaze lingered on the fabulous dome with its subtly shifting colours, then she looked around and saw Divine sitting by the hearth. The fire wasn't lit tonight but it still looked the cosiest part of the enormous room.

"Well, what d'you know. Mrs Lorimer. Fashion statement herself!"

Maggie stuck her tongue out and both women laughed.

"What're you drinking tonight, ma'am?" Divine asked in mock flattering tones.

Maggie rolled her eyes to heaven, "I don't mind so long as there's lots of it. I came by taxi and I intend to go home that way. *Happy*." She emphasised the word. But when the waiter came for their order she found herself about to ask for the usual white wine spritzer.

"Two Harvey Wallbangers," Divine drawled before Maggie had time to speak and suddenly that was exactly what she wanted. Something different that fitted her mood of rebelliousness. She leaned back, crossing her legs over silky stockings, not caring if she showed a bit too much thigh.

"Well, Divine. This suit you for your last night in Glasgow?"

"It's neat. Pretty. Reminds me of some of our old buildings back home. What did it used to be before?"

"Oh, it's an old building all right. I can remember when it was the High Court but before that it was the Union Bank of Scotland. Long before my time. I think I read somewhere that it was originally a family house." Maggie scanned the Classical mouldings around the ceiling. "The present owner made sure that all the original architectural features were kept."

"Wish more people were like him," replied Divine. "If you ever come over to Florida I'll show you something. It's called the Ca'de Zan. Built right on the water to look like an Italian Palace. You'd like it."

Maggie bent over her drink, considering. Should she confide in this woman?

"You might be able to show me round sooner than you think," she replied.

"Oh? Why's that?"

"Listen, I know you'll not be here after tomorrow, but I'd still like you to keep this confidential," Maggie began.

Divine nodded, her dark eyes solemn.

"I've applied for a transfer to America. Just for a year. It's an exchange programme that's run between Scottish and American schools."

"And how does the Chief Inspector feel about that?"

Maggie didn't answer and in the silence that followed Divine's eyebrows rose in surprise. "You mean you haven't told him?"

"No. Not yet. I wanted time to think about it."

"So why tell me?"

"Oh, I don't know. Maybe because you're a policewoman. You travel." Maggie hesitated. "I just thought you might understand."

Divine gave a sigh. "Honey, I do, believe me. Being in the police force takes over your whole life, whether it's here or back home. I've seen lots of folks split up because of the pressure."

"Oh, but we're not, I mean…" she tailed off, confused.

"Just need a bit of time out?"

"Something like that. I've always wanted to travel but the years just seem to have slipped by and I've got into this rut. We both have. Then I saw the poster about the exchange." She shrugged her shoulders. "It was like something telling me to grab the chance with both hands."

"And how d'you think your husband will react?"

Maggie looked away. "I'm not sure. I really don't want to hurt him. But lately I wonder if he even thinks about what my life is like."

"Hey. Want my advice? Go for it. It's only a year and if you hate it you can always come back. I mean," she grinned at Maggie encouragingly, "nothing's set in stone, is it?"

"No. I suppose you're right."

"Of course I am. Now let's drink to the future."

Divine raised the tall glass and gave a wink.

Suddenly Maggie felt a lot better. Was it such a big deal after all? Surely people went abroad all the time with their work and without their partners?

"The future," she agreed and took a long cool drink. The cocktail tasted sweet and different, a portent of good things to come.

Chapter Eighteen

Lorimer's mouth felt like someone had made him chew on sandpaper. He groaned and rolled over, reaching out for Maggie's warm body. He came to, feeling the sudden edge of the bed. Maggie? Then he remembered where he was. He opened his eyes to the light. Someone had drawn the curtains closed and the room was flooded with deep pink reflected light. Lorimer closed his eyes again. What was it that was flickering at the edge of his mind?

Dougie, the youngster behind the bar. He'd sat there drinking malts and quizzing the boy for hours. Solomon had listened to their questions and answers, sipping his orange squash and nodding as he absorbed the information. Had Dougie known Kirsty? That was what Lorimer had really been after. At first he thought he'd hit pay dirt. Everyone had known her and her business, it seemed. From birth to death there didn't seem to be a way of keeping secrets on this island. What was it the lad had said? *It's not gossip. Folks just share their lives with one another. That's the way it is.* And Kirsty MacLeod's life had seemed just the same as any other young islander's. She'd left home to board in Stornoway and attend the Nicholson Institute, like all the teenagers from these parts. And, like many of them, she'd made her way to the big city. For what was to keep her here? Unemployment was just as bad up here as anywhere else, Dougie had pointed out. That was why so many folk had wanted the quarry to go ahead. He'd been okay, his dad owned the hotel. That's what he wanted, to stay here and live in Rodel. Kirsty had been no different from the young folk who had left the islands to work in Glasgow, Lorimer conceded. It was her death that made her stand apart from them. But there was still too much missing from what Dougie could tell him. There were no hidden depths, nothing to distinguish Kirsty from any other young island girl leaving home to train as a nurse.

He heaved himself out of the narrow bed and felt the floor cold beneath his feet. Today would bring him into contact with other nurses who cared for the Grange's patients, and, of course, the patients themselves. Lorimer found himself speculating about the two who had been in Glasgow at the time of Kirsty's murder; Sister Angelica and Samuel Fulton. They'd caught an early morning flight from Glasow to Stornoway. Mrs Baillie had not been prepared to make any cancellations. The clinic would have lost money, she had claimed. Lorimer shook his head. Call him a suspicious beggar, but there was more to all this than met the eye.

"This came for you, sir." Lorimer looked up from his bacon and eggs to see young Dougie holding out a long white envelope. He waited until the boy had gone then ripped it open. Solly glanced up inquiringly as Lorimer studied the message. It was a fax from Alistair Wilson. Suddenly South Harris was back in the twenty-first century, mused Lorimer. He scanned the opening paragraph quickly.

The Grange was trying to forge links with another expanding group of clinics, he read, and there had been a report ordered by their bankers into this group's financial stability. Lorimer's eyes travelled down the rows of facts and figures. There were sections on the group's business profile, accounting systems, profit and loss forecasts and future strategies, one of which included the absorption of the Grange. The directors had borrowed heavily in order to expand and modernise their existing clinics. The report's advice was that the bank would continue its level of lending meantime but wanted to know a definite date for the acquisition of the Grange. But how could that be? Phyllis Logan was the legal owner. Had the paralysed woman some legal representative who would advise her on such matters?

Lorimer frowned, remembering the woman's argument that the clinic could not afford to waste her patients' plane tickets. Mrs Baillie seemed to be more concerned with saving money than an investigation into the death of one of her staff. She'd not even told them about the existence of the respite home until then, this other part of the MS patient's estate. Failte, it was called. The word was Gaelic for welcome, Lorimer knew. What sort of welcome would they have for a Glasgow policeman and a criminal profiler?

His car wasn't built for roads like these, Lorimer realised as he pulled into a lay-by for the sixth time in five minutes. They had obviously met the ferry traffic coming from Tarbert. He paused to look out over the wide sweep of sands below them, then his eye travelled inland. The road was clear again and he turned back onto the grey strip that wound down towards sea level, glancing every now and then at the changing colours of the water.

"Look out!" Solly's shout made Lorimer yank the

wheel sideways as something white bounded towards them. There was a thud as the car hit the verge. He pressed the window button, cursing the object of their sudden stop.

"Bloody sheep!" Lorimer looked down at the offending beast that was now grazing frantically on the other side of the narrow road. He glanced across at Solly, who was trying to hide a grin, then he eased the big car off the grass verge and back onto the road. He'd have to be more attentive to these sheep meandering across his path.

The rest of the journey passed without incident though Lorimer had to keep his wits about him negotiating the twists and turns, especially among the rocky landscapes as they climbed into the hills north of Tarbert. The treeless wastes were bleaker to Lorimer's eyes than even Rannoch Moor. No wonder so much of the population had left over the decades. Yet there would always be a core of islanders who stayed at home. There were signs of recent resurfacing to the road and Lorimer reminded himself that tourism kept many local folk in employment. He had to admit that there was a wild beauty about the coastline. And these slabs of black rock striped with silver crystals were amongst the oldest known rocks on earth. Lorimer passed a sign for Callanish. He'd love to bring Maggie here to see these legendary standing stones.

"Who exactly runs this respite centre?" Solomon asked suddenly.

"A couple by the name of Evans. He's a psychiatric nurse and she does the housekeeping and suchlike, I believe. They're not locals. Came up in answer to an advert, in fact."

"What do you know about them?"

"Not a lot. But I think we'll soon find out," replied Lorimer. Roadside cottages were no longer solitary dots on the landscape but were now like joined up writing. "Civilisation," he muttered under his breath as he read the sign, *Steornabhagh*, though he wasn't at all sure that he meant it.

"Do you mind if we don't go straight to the clinic? I'd like to pay a courtesy call to the local nick," Lorimer asked. "I feel the need to rally the troops, if you know what I mean."

"Do you think the troops will be on our side?"

Lorimer grunted. Solly had a point. Nobody liked officers from another division, let alone another region, encroaching on their patch. He'd just have to hope the natives were as friendly here as they'd been in Harris.

Stornoway came as a surprise. Fishing boats swung gently on their moorings along the harbour's edge as Lorimer drove slowly towards the centre of town. He rolled down the window and breathed in the salty, fishy tang.

"Fancy a walk?" Solomon asked.

"Okay. I could do with stretching my legs," Lorimer replied. He parked away from the harbour in a designated area. For a small place there were plenty of double yellow lines and he wasn't about to get on the wrong side of the local lads.

"This is where she came to school," Solomon spoke half to himself as Lorimer locked the car.

"Yes. The Nicholson Institute. One of Maggie's

friends came up here to teach languages years ago."

He tried to visualise Kirsty as a teenager, giggling on her way from the hostel to the famous high school, then breathed a long sigh. The Stornoway air stinging his eyes had a purity that was suddenly at odds with his vision of the nurse, her hair scattered over that lifeless young face.

The local police station was in Church Street. From the pavement in front of it Lorimer spotted three steeples close by, a reminder that these parts were supposed to be full of God-fearing folks. Well, that remained to be seen.

"Chief Inspector Lorimer, Strathclyde CID," Lorimer held out his warrant card carefully for the duty sergeant to see. The officer, a huge bear of a man whose grizzled hair still held a hint of red, raised his eyebrows but looked past Lorimer to the Jewish psychologist, who stood smiling his knowing little smile. Following the man's questioning gaze, Lorimer stepped aside.

"This is Dr Brightman from Glasgow University."

Solly held out his hand to the sergeant who gave it an abrupt once up-and-down.

"Dr Brightman is assisting Strathclyde with our double murder inquiry," Lorimer explained.

"Aye, the MacLeod girl. Terrible thing, that," replied the sergeant. "How can we help you, sir?" he said to Lorimer.

"We're here to visit a place called Failte. It's some sort of respite home for recovered mental patients." Beside him Lorimer could feel Solly wince at the description.

"Isn't it for patients who have suffered some sort of neural disorder?" the sergeant replied, frowning. "That's what we were told." He sidled along behind the desk and tapped at the keyboard of his computer.

"There, see." He swivelled the screen around for the two men to read.

Failte: Centre for holistic care and recuperation. Specialising in the after care of patients who are recovering from neural disorders. Patients are often disorientated when they arrive and may take some time to integrate with staff and nearby residents. It is hoped that the local police officers will do their best to be discreet and understanding while those patients are part of the community.

"That's community policing for you," the big policeman said proudly. "We take care of people up here, respect their needs, you know."

"There isn't a big crime scene here, then," Lorimer joked.

The sergeant bristled, obviously disliking Lorimer's flippancy. "We may not have the kind of crimes you boys have down in Glasgow, but there are still law breaking elements about. Especially with drugs," he shook his head wearily.

"But there's been no trouble of that sort at Failte?" Solomon inquired politely.

"Oh, no. They keep themselves pretty much to themselves. We see them wandering along the roads, out for fresh air, poor souls. No, we've never had any bother with them at all," he replied, adding, "Are you staying long, Chief Inspector?"

"I shouldn't think so," Lorimer replied to him. "Although I'd quite like to see it from a visitor's point of view some day."

"Aye, there's nowhere like it. They can say what they like about their fancy Benidorms and Lanzarotes but we've a better place than any of them," the sergeant stated emphatically.

"Well, maybe I'll manage to come up here again. Thanks for your time." Lorimer shook the sergeant's hand and turned to go.

"Do you know where this place is?" Solomon asked as they walked back along the street.

"Yes. According to my AA map it's further out along the north coast," Lorimer replied. "Near a place called Shawbost. Shouldn't take us too long to find it. And we certainly won't get lost. There is only one road from Stornoway."

Lorimer was right, the road from the main town in Lewis cut directly across the land towards the further coast. Apart from the ubiquitous sheep, there were few signs of habitation along their route. Gazing out of the window, Solomon marvelled at the landscape of windswept grasses and gently sloping hills. Small birds swooped past the windscreen and away, their identities a mystery. Despite a lack of trees the landscape was pleasing and, as the clouds raced across the sky, the psychologist smiled to himself, enjoying the shifting scenery as if it were a gift.

Chapter Nineteen

The sign for Shawbost was accompanied by another giving the mileage to Callanish, Carloway and Stornoway. There was nothing to indicate the where-abouts of Failte. Lorimer drove slowly along past the houses scattered on either side of the road until even those petered out.

"Maybe it's further on?" suggested Solly.

"We'll see."

Turning a bend on the road, Lorimer saw a long driveway that ended slightly uphill at a large, grey two-storey house. There was no sign at the road end.

"Bet you that's it," he said and swung the car along the rutted path that led to the house.

To one side of the old house was a pebbled area with a red pick-up truck, so Lorimer parked nearby and signalled to Solomon to come with him.

"You're right," said Solly, pointing to the word cut into grey slate by the doorway. Failte.

"My great detecting skills," Lorimer smiled, raising his eyebrows. So far, so good, he thought, but what would their reception be now that they had arrived?

They hadn't long to find out. In answer to the shrill bell, footsteps came thudding downstairs towards the door. It swung open to reveal a young woman dressed in jeans and sweater.

"Hallo. Can I help you?" she looked curiously at Lorimer then shifted her gaze to Solomon. Lorimer saw the smile spread across her face and watched as she flicked back her long fair hair. He made a mental note to tease the psychologist about his fatal attraction to blondes.

As always, Lorimer held out his warrant card. "I understood Mr and Mrs Evans were in charge here," he ventured.

"Yeah, that's right," she turned and yelled up the stairs. "Mu-um! There's a policeman to see you."

The sound of a door slamming and a toilet flushing was followed by a voice calling out, "Just coming!" then a woman appeared at the top of the stairs, wiping her hands on the apron tied around her waist.

"Frances Evans. You must be the men who phoned me from Glasgow, right?" she spoke breathlessly taking Lorimer's hand in a damp grasp. "This is my daughter, Rowena," she added, indicating the girl who still continued to smirk in Solly's direction. "Finish off those bedrooms for me, will you, lass?" she said, giving the girl a friendly pat on the shoulder.

"See you later, maybe," Rowena grinned then raced up the stairs and out of sight.

"Come on into the lounge, will you. Would you like a cup of tea or coffee? Or can I offer you both a spot of lunch? We're just having soup and sandwiches, but you're welcome to join us."

Frances Evans spoke in a rush, making Lorimer wonder if she were always so garrulous. Or was it the presence of a police officer that provoked this nervous chatter? Lorimer had witnessed this effect countless times. It didn't mean a person had anything to hide; sometimes it was simply the awkwardness of unfamiliarity.

"Thank you, but no. We'd really like to speak to your two residents as soon as possible."

"Ah," the woman dropped her hands by her sides.

"Of course. That's why you're here, isn't it, to see Sam and Angelica. Well, Sam's out with my husband at the moment and Angelica's gone for a walk. Oh, Just a minute," she broke off and crossed to a window that overlooked the road. "That's them now," she said, turning back to Lorimer.

"They had to go into Stornoway to the chemist's. Sam's on special medication, you know," she confided, stepping past them and bustling out into the hall once more. The rattle of a car braking against the stony drive set off a dog barking.

Following the woman out of the front door, Lorimer saw a black and white collie racing towards the car, a distant figure following.

Standing in the doorway, Lorimer saw two men emerge from the car. One was stockily built with thinning hair, the other a tall spare man wearing well-worn tweeds. As they approached, Lorimer saw them exchange glances. They'd have seen his car in the driveway and put two and two together.

"Detective Chief Inspector Lorimer, I take it?" the tall man took the front steps two at a time and Lorimer found his hand grasped firmly. "I'm John Evans. And this is our guest, Sam Fulton," Evans turned to the man behind him who had bent down to fondle the collie by his side.

As Sam Fulton straightened up, Lorimer knew instinctively that the two men had discussed a strategy between them. He looked back at Evans for a moment, aware of the frank, hazel eyes regarding him with interest.

"Mr Fulton, hallo," Lorimer smiled and raised a hand in greeting. "I understand we've arrived at an awkward time. Mrs Evans here tells me your lunch is ready. Please don't let us keep you back." He turned and met the Welshman's eyes again. "We can talk while Mr Fulton is at lunch," he said. Evans nodded. His expression showed that he knew it wasn't so much a request but a demand from this Glasgow policeman.

"Aye, okay. I'll see youse later," Sam Fulton licked his lips nervously and slunk past them into the house, followed by Frances Evans who ushered him along the corridor like a recalcitrant child.

"This is my colleague Dr Brightman," Lorimer said, watching as Solly shook hands solemnly with the tall Welshman.

"Pleased to meet you, Dr Brightman," Evans had stooped slightly to meet the psychologist's eyes but was now looking over his shoulder. "I think we could talk in the lounge, but first, there's someone else you should meet."

Both men turned to follow his gaze. The figure that had been following the collie was heading up the path. Close to, Lorimer could see her raincoat flapping against a pair of stout legs clad in thick socks and heavy walking boots. The headscarf knotted under her chin made the woman's face appear like a pale, round moon. In one hand she carried a staff and each step she took was defined by a thump as she lumbered forwards.

"Sister Angelica?" Solomon looked enquiringly at John Evans.

"Yes."

"Wretched dog. Never comes back when I tell him to. You have to train your animals better than that, John." The woman puffed to a halt before them. "This the policemen, then?" she asked, indicating Lorimer and Solly with her stick.

"DCI Lorimer and Dr Brightman," Evans stated, standing aside for the woman to shake the out-stretched hands.

"I'm Sister Angelica. How are you? Don't answer that. I don't really want to know. Had enough of hearing how everybody is back in the Grange," she cackled.

"Frances is doing lunch then these gentlemen will want to speak to you," John Evans told her. Lorimer saw her hesitate for a moment. The psychiatric nurse had a firm manner that brooked no nonsense yet there was a reassuring gentleness in that Welsh accent.

"Suits me. Sam in already?" Without waiting for a reply the woman strode into the house, the collie wagging its tail at her heels.

"Please go into the lounge. I'll ask Frances to do some tea for us," Evans said and disappeared in the wake of Sister Angelica.

"What d'you make of them?" Lorimer sat down and whispered to Solly.

"Sister Angelica seems pretty well adjusted, don't you think? No sign of weakness in her personality at first sight. She's getting on with things, I'd say. Out with the dog in the fresh air. And she had no problem about facing us, did she?"

"What about the man? Fulton?"

"Didn't want to make eye-contact, did he?"

"You noticed that too?"

"And..." Solly broke off as John Evans pushed open the lounge door with a tray. He set it down on the table between the two men and began offering sugar for the steaming mugs.

"We found it rather strange that two patients who were in the Grange during a murder should be allowed to disappear up here the very next day," Lorimer began. "Mrs Baillie said the reasons were financial," he added, raising his eyebrows to show John Evans just how sceptical he was of this excuse.

"Did she?" Evans looked surprised. "I would have thought she might have explained about Sam and Angelica."

"What about them?"

"Well. Both patients had completed their course of treatment. They really needed the respite care we offer at Failte. You have to understand, Chief Inspector. They'd been through a very difficult time and for them to become embroiled in a police investigation might have seriously set either of them back."

"What about now? Will we damage their recovery?" Lorimer asked, sarcastically.

"Maybe. But they've had a while to rest and take stock of all their therapy. I think you can safely interview each of them without too much upset."

Evans crossed his legs as he spoke and leaned back into the armchair. He regarded Lorimer thoughtfully over the rim of his mug.

"Neither of your patients were in the Grange in January when the first murder took place," Solly pointed out. "Chief Inspector Lorimer will have to know their whereabouts for that particular date."

"You're not seriously suggesting that Sam or Angelica might be suspects?" Evans sat up suddenly. Neither man replied, letting the silence answer his question.

"But why? Just because they've been ill doesn't mean they'd be capable of carrying out something like that!"

"The perpetrator of those killings appears to be someone who may very well be ill," Solly answered slowly. "In building up a profile I have to consider the extent to which any risk of discovery was considered. Whoever did these killings was either very cunning or totally disregarded the thought that they might be caught. Someone whose behaviour was prompted by an uncontrollable urge might even have wanted to be discovered."

"And how do you come to that conclusion, Dr Brightman?"

Solly shook his head. "I'm sorry. I'm not at liberty to divulge that kind of information."

John Evans looked at each of them in turn, his mouth a thin line of disapproval.

"Well," he said at last, "I suppose we must be as co-operative as we can. Still, I do hope you can see our side of things. Mrs Baillie would not have seen her actions as obstructing the course of a murder inquiry. She would simply have put her patients as a higher priority."

Lorimer listened to the man's measured tones. There was no sense of outrage nor was there any attempt to thwart this stage of the investigation. Evans was a man of some sense.

"Were you always a psychiatric nurse?" he asked, curious suddenly about the Welshman's background.

Evans smiled and shook his head. "No. I retrained some years ago."

"I'd have hazarded a guess that you were an

academic of some sort," Solly stroked his beard thoughtfully.

"Well done, Doctor. Spot on," Evans replied, putting his empty mug back onto the tray. "I was at Cambridge for many years. Lectured in philosophy." He smiled again, looking straight at Lorimer. "You can check it all up if you like."

"So why did you change careers?" Lorimer wanted to know.

"Perhaps I saw that nursing had a greater value than teaching philosophy," Evans replied, his eyes suddenly grave. "You will take care not to put Sam under too much stress, won't you?" he added.

Lorimer and Solly waited in the lounge while Evans brought his patient to them. Sam Fulton shambled into the room ahead of the nurse, who placed an encouraging hand on his shoulder before stepping out and closing the door behind him.

"Mr Fulton, please come and sit down," Lorimer stood and indicated the chair recently vacated by John Evans.

Eying them suspiciously, Sam Fulton sat on the edge of the armchair, clasping his hands together as if to warm them.

"You know we are investigating the murder of Kirsty MacLeod, a nurse from the Grange?"

Fulton nodded.

"She was killed during the night before you left to come up here."

"Aye. Ah know. Me an' Angelica thought it wis mad comin' here when a' that wis goin' on."

"You didn't think it was wise to leave, then?"

"Wise? You kiddin'? It wis pure mental. That Baillie

woman's aff her trolley. We should've bin ther wi' a' they others, shouldn't we?"

Lorimer nodded. "We think so. Still, now that we have the chance to talk to you, Mr Fulton, perhaps you can help us."

"Aye," Fulton replied then screwed his face up. "How?"

"Can you describe what took place on the night of Nurse MacLeod's death? Just talk us through everything you did and can remember."

"Aye. Well," Fulton scratched his head and hefted his bottom more comfortably into the chair. "Ah did ma packin' fur comin' up here. Not that ah've goat much. Then went tae bed. Ah'm oan medication so ah went straight oot like a light. Didnae hear a thing until the screechin' began."

"What time was that?"

"Whit time? Jesus! Ah don't know. Ah wis that bleary wi' sleep. Ah came oot intae the corridor and Peter telt me there had bin an accident."

"Peter? That was one of the other nurses?"

"Aye. He telt us tae get back tae wur beds."

"Who else was out in the corridor with you?"

Fulton gave a sigh, "Ah cannae remember. There wis that much goin' on. Ah jist went back tae ma bed."

"When did you find out about Kirsty MacLeod's murder?" Solomon asked.

Sam Fulton turned as if he had forgotten the psychologist's presence. "The next morning. Mrs Baillie telt us on our way to Glasgow Airport."

"So you knew nothing about it before then?"

"Naw." Fulton's chin came up defiantly as he looked Solly in the eye.

"Where were you on the night of January 12 this year?" Lorimer asked suddenly.

Fulton frowned. "How the hell should ah know that? Ah've no been well. Ah cannae remember dates an' things," he added with a hint of a smirk across his face.

"Is there anybody who could help you remember?" Lorimer asked. "A friend or family member who could verify your whereabouts?"

Fulton licked his lips nervously. "Here. Whit is a' this? You sayin' ah done something? Is that it?" he leaned forward on the seat once more, his shoulders bunching around his ears.

"We have to eliminate as many people as possible from our inquiries, Mr Fulton. We are looking into the possibility that Nurse MacLeod was killed by the same person who carried out the murder in Queen Street station in January."

"Aw," Fulton's face showed some relief. "That one. Aye. Ah read aboot that in the papers. Naw. Ah wisnae there. Ah wis up the hoose maist o' that time," he turned to Solomon. "Wi' my *problem*," he said.

"According to our notes you became an in-patient at the Grange on January 25," Lorimer told him.

"Aye. Burns night. They had tae haud me doon," Fulton smirked again.

"Mr Fulton, forgive me, but wasn't it rather an expense for you to enter a private clinic for such a prolonged stay?"

"Oh, aye. It's a hell of an expense. But ah've goat kinda special terms, see?"

Lorimer nodded. He'd let that one pass. How a former shipyard worker who had been unemployed for as long as Fulton could have obtained private medical insurance, if that's what he meant by *special terms*, was something of a mystery, though. There were things about this man that didn't add up.

"So could you find anybody who would verify that you were housebound on the night of January 12?" Lorimer insisted.

"Aye. Nae bother. Ah'll speak tae wan o' the boys."

"Boys?"

"Aye. Ma lads. Gerry and Stephen. They'll tell ye ah wis hame a' the time."

"Thank you."

"When do you expect to return to Glasgow?" Solomon asked.

Fulton shrugged. "Don't know. Sometime. It's an open ticket we've goat. Maybe in a week or so. How?"

"We need to know your whereabouts, Mr Fulton. It's routine, that's all," Lorimer answered for him. "Anyway, thank you for your time. If Sister Angelica is ready, we'd like to speak to her now."

"That it?" Fulton asked, rising to his feet. "Right. Okay, well. I'll see if she's there," he raised his hand in a short salute of farewell and headed for the door. As he left, he turned and glowered at the two men sitting by the window. Solly, seeing his expression merely smiled and nodded in return.

The woman came into the room immediately. She was, they saw, dressed for the outdoors, her wax coat already buttoned up.

"Not a day for sitting inside. You can talk to me all you want but don't expect me to sit in here."

She paused for a moment, regarding Solomon and Lorimer who had risen to their feet. "Got any warm jackets? That's a north easterly wind, you know." Looking them up and down, she went back into the hallway calling, "Sula! Here, lass!" There was the sound of claws scrabbling along the polished wooden floor then a dog whining excitedly. "Come on, then," Sister Angelica flung over her shoulder, "What are you waiting for?"

Lorimer handed over the car keys to Solly. "Jackets?"

"If she says so," Solly raised his eyebrows.

The road from the house flowed over a rise and down towards the sea. Sister Angelica strode ahead, the collie barking at her heels. Overhead a gull squawked. Catching her up, Lorimer signalled the woman to slow down. Behind him, Solly walked, just within earshot.

"Right-oh. What d'you want to ask a mad old nun, then?" she grinned, turning to meet Lorimer's eye.

Lorimer smiled back. "Not so old and not so mad, I think."

Sister Angelica flung back her head and gave a hoot of laughter. "Well, maybe not so mad any more. Whatever they hoped to achieve seems to have worked. I'll grant them that. Still, you can't turn the clock back and I'm not going to see the right side of fifty again. There's no known cure for the ageing process."

"We need to ask you about Kirsty MacLeod."

The nun slowed her stride but kept on walking. "She's dead. Someone killed her and it happened in the Grange while I was there." She looked at Lorimer, a thoughtful expression on her face. "That's all there is to know. She was a thoroughly nice young woman and nobody had any right to take her life away."

Lorimer nodded. "That's how I feel. That's why we're here. To try to find out as much as we can about the people who were there in the Grange that night."

"Chief Inspector. I really don't see how I can help you. Some intruder obviously broke in and killed the girl. The back door of the basement was open, after all."

"How do you know that? You left early the next morning."

"Mrs Baillie told us. She said someone had broken in and attacked Kirsty. She said we'd be questioned by the police eventually. Sam thought it was a bit daft to go, just like that."

"So why did you leave?"

Sister Angelica gazed at the ground as if the wind-blown grasses could supply her answer then she looked up at Lorimer.

"Cowardice, I suppose. We just wanted to be away from the place. Even though I knew it was our duty to talk to the police we let Mrs Baillie persuade us. I'm ashamed to say we didn't take much persuading."

"Can you remember the events of that night?"

"Oh, yes. I remember them all right. I was sitting up in bed when Mrs Duncan began screaming at the top of her voice. We all began to drift into the corridor to see what had happened."

"What did you think had happened?"

"I thought someone had topped themselves. Peter said there had been an accident and we should all go back to bed but I stayed."

"Why?"

The woman shrugged. "Force of habit, if you'll

excuse the pun. I'm used to being around crises."

Lorimer let this go. It was probably true. "So, what happened then?"

"Mrs Baillie tried to calm her down and Peter let me come into the staff room to make some tea. They didn't seem to mind me being there," she added, as if this had only just occurred to her. "Mrs Duncan was shaking and sobbing by this time and I heard Mrs Baillie tell Peter she was going to telephone the police. That was when she told me to go back to my room."

"And did you?"

"Yes," she hesitated as if there was something more she wanted to say but couldn't form the words.

"Did you see anything strange that night, Sister?" Lorimer looked intently at the nun.

"Not strange, not really. Just," she gave her head a shake as if to clear her brain. "Just unusual."

"What was that?"

"When I got back to my room one of the other patients was kneeling by my bed. Praying."

Lorimer stopped and caught her arm. "I would say that was very unusual."

Sister Angelica gave a sigh. "More's the pity, I say. But, you're wrong as it happens. They all knew I was a nun and some of them would come into my room to talk about spiritual matters. I encouraged them. I even held a time of prayer each week. Well, they needed guidance if they were in a clinic for neural disorders, didn't they?" she said briskly.

"Who was in your room, Sister?"

The woman sighed again, her large white face turned up to Lorimer's. "It was Leigh," she said. "And he was crying."

Chapter Twenty

"Well, what do you think? Does Leigh Quinn fit your profile?" Lorimer asked, taking his eyes off the road for a moment and turning to Solly with a scarcely contained excitement.

Solly said nothing. This was the moment he'd been dreading. He'd been waiting for just such a question from the DCI and had absolutely no answer. No answer and certainly no criminal profile. His mouth shifted into a little bitter twist. Not so long ago Lorimer had thrown scorn upon the veracity of such techniques as profiling and here he was now, all eager to have a response as if Solly were some conjurer pulling a rabbit out of his hat. The truth was that he didn't have a clue. This case had puzzled him from the time he had visited the Grange. Nothing seemed to add up about the two killings. The different locations were odd for a start. The murder of a prostitute and a respectable nurse were at variance, too. Nor was there any matching DNA material. Yet the things that should have been significant remained: that flower and those praying hands. It had to be one and the same killer.

Not a soul outside the murder investigation knew about these details; even the Press had depicted a corpse with praying hands like an effigy, palms towards heaven, not like their victims at all. So he'd ruled out any possibility of a copycat killing. Now Lorimer wanted answers and he had none to give.

"You don't think it's Quinn? Is that it?" Lorimer's voice held just a hint of querulousness as Solly remained silent.

Solly heaved a sigh. "To tell you the truth, I'm not sure at all. It would be better to re-interview the man, of course, but from his notes he seems a pretty withdrawn sort. Not the type to have easily consorted with a prostitute."

"I would have thought those kind of loners were exactly the sort who'd need a woman like that!"

"But he's practically non-verbal. He'd have needed some conversational skills to persuade the woman to go into the station with him," Solly protested.

It was Lorimer's turn to fall silent. His sudden euphoria at the nun's revelation had evaporated. Solly's words made sense. And yet? Perhaps Leigh Quinn had been a different person back in January? Maybe his illness manifested itself in different ways? They'd have to re-examine the case notes thoroughly, that was for sure.

The sign for Callanish appeared and Lorimer turned off the road without consulting his companion. Right now he needed some fresh air and a chance to think without a nun and a dog at his heels.

As Lorimer switched off the engine and opened the door he glanced over to Solly, who was staring out of the windscreen as if he were miles away. Something was troubling the younger man. He got out, leaving Solly sitting where he was. If he wanted to follow him, fine. If not, he was happy with his own company. Aware that a rift had developed between them, Lorimer turned his back on the Visitors' Centre and walked purposefully towards the ancient ring of standing stones that stood out like giant fingers pointing skywards. There were no sounds of other vehicles on the road nor of aircraft overhead, only the thin cry of a bird that might have been a curlew. Lorimer squinted against the brightness of the sky and the water, shading his eyes to look for the bird.

Yes, there it was, almost hidden against the muddy browns of the lochan's shoreline: unmistakeable with that long, curving beak. Another note made him look up suddenly to follow the flight of a lark, soaring into the pale skies. Still gazing heavenward, he heard the tread behind him.

"Quite a place, isn't it?"

"Indeed," Lorimer replied, not looking down but still following the flight of the skylark as it became a dot against the clouds. When it had disappeared he turned to Solly and was gratified to see his face raised in similar rapture.

"The Lark Ascending," Solly nodded. "He captured it so perfectly. Vaughan Williams. Yet the real thing never fails to work its magic, does it?"

Lorimer raised his eyebrows. "Didn't know you were a bird lover too."

"Ever since I was a little lad being taken around Saint James's Park. It's all part of my scientific curiosity, I suppose. How about you?" Solomon looked quizzically at Lorimer through his horn-rimmed spectacles. There was a kindness to his tone as if he were speaking to one of the patients in the Grange. Trying to sound me out, Lorimer thought. Was there a tentative suggestion here for him to open up his private thoughts?

Or had Solomon already drawn some profiling conclusions of his own? Lorimer was tempted for a moment to reveal his desires to this young man in a way that he had once shared with Maggie. He wanted to tell how he sometimes longed for wild open spaces like these and fresh air to fill his lungs instead of living within the confines of the city's grid; how he wanted to turn his back on the paper trails that Mitchison left him to follow; how he felt that surge of freedom when gazing into the soul of a painting or following the song of a simple bird. These were desires of a kind that he kept strictly to himself.

But there was always that other desire, too, the desire to hunt out the truth. Sometimes it was like an itch that he automatically started to scratch without thinking, the kind of itch that made him demand answers to hard questions. Such as, who had killed a young nurse in Glasgow? Whoever it was had robbed her, forever, of the right to stand here as he stood now, simply glad to be alive.

Lorimer expressed none of these whirling thoughts to the man at his side, however much he might understand, but simply stood looking out over the landscape, his face as inscrutable as the mealiths themselves. The slanting grey stones thrust themselves out of the grass high above their heads. For a moment they stared at them silently. Lorimer felt the weight of years pressing down on the landscape. Did Solomon feel that too, he wondered?

"Yes. Tomorrow or the day after. That's right. The whole day, I'm afraid. The boats out of here aren't frequent. Sorry? Oh, just a small hotel near the harbour. Nothing fancy." Lorimer put a hand onto his stomach. That meal downstairs had been plain home cooking but the portions were obviously meant for appetites larger than his own.

"Yes, Solly's fine. Okay. See you sometime tomorrow night or else I'll phone you. 'Bye." Lorimer replaced the telephone on its cradle before realising he hadn't asked Maggie how she was or what had been happening at home. Cursing himself, he lifted the handset again to redial but just at that moment a knock on the bedroom door made him drop the phone back with a clatter.

"Thought you might fancy a drink. The bar downstairs looks friendly enough. What d'you think?" Solly grinned from the doorway, his eyebrows raised in anticipation of his reply.

"I'll just grab my jacket." He slipped his wallet into the inside pocket, picked up the room key and closed the door behind them, all thoughts of another phone call forgotten.

Maggie put down the phone thoughtfully. It was the same as usual. No information about what was going on with the case nor any inquiry as to how *her* day had been. Okay, so she was used to being told the minimum information or else none at all. That was standard procedure. So why did she suddenly feel so sidelined by her husband?

Maggie shivered despite the heat wafting from the radiator. She was sitting on the carpet by the phone, her back against the hall table. The wooden spar dug into her spine but she hardly noticed it. For a few minutes she closed her eyes, trying to imagine what he was doing up there in the Island of Lewis. It was a place they'd talked about visiting but never had. Like so many of the things they'd intended to do. Opening her eyes, Maggie's gaze fell upon the envelope. It looked like any other plain buff A4 envelope, nothing that should give rise to any excitement, but Maggie experienced a sudden lifting of her spirits just by seeing it there. It could be her passport to a different way of life. A life she'd be able to control for the first time in years. Why hadn't she done something like this ages ago? When they'd finally given up trying to have a family, for instance? She'd let things drift just as much as he had. That was the plain truth of the matter. And it had taken that American woman to make her see things in a different light. Divine Lipinski had made an impact on her, that was for sure. Maggie cast her mind back to the night of the nurse's murder when they'd been left so abruptly. She and Divine had talked for hours. About being a policeman's wife. About all the dreams she'd shelved because of his job. And about how she yearned to travel. Divine had provided such colour and warmth that night. She'd made Maggie laugh about her life in Florida. She even made her involvement with crime in that part of the US sound amusing. Then she'd spoken about the Everglades, the sunsets over the Keys, the lazy flight of the brown pelicans; listening to her, Maggie was spellbound.

"Come over, why don't you?" Divine had said. She'd brushed away all the excuses about Lorimer's job. Maggie remembered the gentleness of her voice and the way she'd looked into her eyes. "I'm talking about *you*, Maggie, just you. Don't you want to spread your wings just a little?"

Maggie stretched out her hand for the envelope and drew it towards her. The pages of the white form were stapled together at one corner. She flicked through the contents speculatively. There was a closing date for this application. It was ages away but still she felt an urgency to do something now. She should discuss it with him first, surely? Almost as soon as the thought had come into her mind she dismissed it. No. This was for her to decide alone. It was her future. Her career.

There was no knowing whether they'd take her anyway, another little voice reasoned. Besides, hadn't there been an element of fate in seeing that leaflet on the staff room noticeboard?

It hadn't taken her long to collect the necessary references, either. Things had fallen swiftly into place as if it was meant to be. But she still hadn't told a soul outside the school. Well, except for Divine.

Maggie pulled herself to her feet and strode through to the kitchen in search of a pen. She cleared a space and spread the form out on the table. A few minutes later it was completed. All she had to do to finish this application for a teacher exchange was to sign her name at the bottom. Then the wheels would be put into motion and she might just find herself flying out to the US for an academic year while another teacher came to take her place. Would he miss her? Would she feel differently about things when she came back? Questions reeled through her mind as the pen hovered over the last page of the document. Where was he now? a voice demanded. Away. As usual. Maggie bit her lip. Then suddenly she knew what she had to do.

The pen flew over the dotted line with a flourish and Maggie sat back in satisfaction, smiling at the two words: Margaret Lorimer. It was like looking at the name of a new and exciting stranger.

Chapter Twenty-One

Solly and Lorimer strode towards the narrow staircase that led to the hotel foyer and thence to the bar. The hum of talk was as thick as the cigarette smoke that hung like a hill mist in the airless room. In one corner a large individual in jeans and grubby t-shirt battled against aliens in the shape of a games machine. From his curses it sounded as if the aliens were winning.

"What'll you have?"

"Oh, why not a local malt, eh?"

Lorimer grinned. There was something about being with Solly tonight that made him feel as though he were on holiday. It wasn't a feeling he was very used to, he thought as he pushed his way between the rounded shoulders of two burly seamen. Lorimer caught the barman's eye and gave his order then, turning to see where Solly had gone, he watched as the man weaved his way to a vacant table by the window. His beard nodded up and down as he responded to some friendly remark from a total stranger. There was a touch of the exotic about Solomon Brightman that drew eyes to him, thought Lorimer. On his own patch, Lorimer knew he was pretty easy to identify as Plain Clothes. But that didn't seem to apply up here. He studied the faces around him, noting the weather-beaten complexions of the fishermen and trawler men who slouched against the bar.

There was a knot of older fellows dressed in shabby jackets and tweed bunnets. Lorimer pigeon-holed them as local worthies. Maybe they'd be good for information after a dram or two, he mused, the police-man's train of thought taking over. Behind them

Lorimer's eyes made out the paler faces of a group of skinny boys lounging in a dingy corner. They were likely drinking up the week's giros, if he read them aright. He'd no illusions about the unemployment difficulties in these parts but as he watched them his thoughts turned to those other youths who had left the islands to find work.

Inevitably his mind turned to Kirsty.

As Lorimer carried back the drinks to where Solly was sitting he glanced this way and that, watching for a stare or a wondering eye to catch but nobody seemed the least interested in him. He was just another tourist passing through. So it was with some surprise that he felt a tug at his sleeve.

"Mind if I join you?" Lorimer turned to see Rowena Evans, an insouciant grin on her face. Lorimer hesitated. Was the girl underage or not? Her manner suggested that she was quite used to coming into the hotel for a drink but that meant nothing. He followed the girl's eyes towards their table where Solly sat reading the Gazette. So that was her little game, was it? Well, Solly was more than a match for a warm-blooded teenager.

"Why not. We're just over here." Lorimer stepped aside to let Rowena slither through the gap between the tables.

"Oh, hallo," as soon as he caught sight of the girl, Solly rose to his feet, the newspaper slipping on to the floor.

"Here. A local malt, you said?" Lorimer put down the drinks as Rowena slipped into the chair opposite Solly. "What about you, Rowena?"

"Oh, just a diet coke, thanks. I'm driving," she

replied, a twinkle in her eye as if she had already guessed Lorimer's thoughts. As he left the pair at the table Lorimer wondered if Rowena Evans had deliberately chosen to come to the hotel knowing that Solly and he were staying over. Or was it just a coincidence?

"You're a criminal profiler, Dad says," she began. "Does that mean you have to interview lots of really nasty folk?"

Solomon laughed. "I don't really interview people much at all during an investigation. That's up to the investigating officer and his team. In this case, Detective Chief Inspector Lorimer."

Rowena turned to glance at Lorimer who was patiently waiting his turn at the bar once more. She shrugged. "So what do you do, then? Weren't you up here to question Sam and Angelica?"

Solly's smile died on his lips. The girl's eagerness to find out about his professional techniques seemed feigned suddenly. Had John Evans put his daughter up to this, perhaps?

"Rowena, this is a murder investigation. A young woman from Harris died in pretty horrible circumstances and we are all trying to find out everything we can about the world she came from and the people who knew her. Anybody from the clinic who had met her might be of help," he told her, his voice deliberately grave.

"So you don't think it was Sam or Sister Angelica?"

Solly stared at the girl, not answering, until she dropped her gaze and flushed.

"Sorry. I'm being a nuisance, aren't I?"

"You haven't known these two patients very long, Rowena. Why all this solicitude for them?"

"What?"

"Solicitude." Solly stopped. The girl wasn't one of his students; perhaps this was a term she might not understand. "Do you care about them a lot?"

"Are you kidding?" Rowena gasped with laughter. "I just want to know if I'm sleeping across the landing from a murderer!"

"And do you have any reason to think you might be?" Lorimer broke in, placing a bottle of Coke on the table.

"Gosh, you gave me a fright. I didn't hear you coming!"

"Nervous type, are you?" Lorimer joked, trying to make light of the girl's reaction.

"No, not usually."

"But you're worried about the present house guests?"

"Well, sort of. Not Angelica, really. She's all right. Sam's a bit creepy, though. Dad says he's been through hell and back. I suppose I should feel sorry for them all. They've been so ill and all they want up here is a bit of peace and quiet. Well, they get that okay, I can tell you. This place is *dead*. Okay, so I'm going with my pal to a disco tonight but that doesn't happen very often."

"Sam Fulton. Is there any reason to feel a threat from him other than your own imaginings?" Solly asked.

"What do you mean?"

"Has he actually done or said anything that gave you cause for concern?"

Rowena took a sip of her drink, considering Solly's words. "No. It's just that Dad seems to be with him all the time as if he's worried to let Sam out of his sight. Like he'll take him into town or they'll both go up the hill with Sula. They even watch T.V. together. I mean, Dad never watches T.V. He'd rather sit with his nose in a book."

"Me, too," Solly said and smiled as Rowena made a face at him.

Lorimer regarded the girl. She was restless on this island, a city girl who had been brought up here because of her parents' work. "How long have you been living at Failte?"

"Three years next August. I started at the Nicholson just after we came up."

"And have you any plans of your own for the future?"

"Depends on my exam results, doesn't it? Dad wants me to go to university but I'd rather get a job."

"In Glasgow?"

"No way. I'm off to London first chance I get," she scoffed. "As far away from Lewis as I can manage."

"You're not happy here, then?" Solly inquired.

"Oh, I'm happy enough. Mum and Dad are fine, you know. But I miss my friends from down South. Wish I could cadge a lift with you two or get a flight with Angelica tomorrow."

Lorimer raised his eyebrows. "She's leaving? Sister Angelica's leaving the island tomorrow?"

"Uh-huh. She told Dad she was going back to Glasgow just after you had left. Why?" the girl looked from one man to the other sensing the impact of her revelation.

"No reason," fibbed Lorimer though his mind was racing with all sorts of possibilities.

"Oh, here's my pal Heather," Rowena stood up suddenly, waving to a dark haired girl who was standing looking around the bar. "Thanks for the drink. Be seeing you." She gave the two men a quick smile as she left, her mind already on her friend and the evening ahead.

"So," Lorimer said, cradling the malt whisky in his hands. "Sister Angelica has had enough of the quiet life already."

"I wonder," returned Solly. "Is she regretting telling us about Leigh Quinn?"

"Or is there some other reason that's taking her back to Glasgow?" Lorimer frowned. The sooner they were on that boat back to the mainland, the better. This trip to Lewis and Harris had left him with more questions than answers.

Chapter Twenty-Two

It was the tune on the radio that brought everything back. Just a simple thing like that, Tom marvelled, and he was once more sitting by Nan's bed, her face turned to his, tired as always, slightly puzzled as if she still hadn't worked out why this disease had chosen her body for its host. Even when its final strains died away and the presenter began announcing something entirely different, the memories lingered like the scent of a woman's perfume, subtle yet all-pervasive.

Tom had battled with all his psychologist's expertise against the demons that had threatened to submerge him until he'd finally taken his own advice and sought professional help. But sometimes there would be a trigger, like that song, and he'd be swept into a series of pictures in his mind that refused to be dislodged.

Yet today it was not scenes of utter desolation and sickness that came to mind but the better days when he'd taken Nan for drives down the coast. She'd been light enough to carry out to the car, her wasted limbs slack beneath the rug, her arms not twined about his neck but hanging useless as he placed her gently in the passenger seat. He'd always played the car radio on those journeys rather than trying to make one-sided conversations. Nan's voice had reached that piping stage when it was impossible to make her out over the car engine.

Once they'd sung along to the radio, he remembered, when they'd been first married. Journeys into work had been happy, he suddenly realised, despite the daily gridlock. Wasn't it always thus? To find a memory of pleasure that had seemed so mundane at the time? That's what everyone had told him at the funeral. Hang on to the good memories. And he'd tried. God knows how he'd tried.

Another picture: Nan on her exercise bike, her feet strapped into the pedals in an attempt to strengthen her ankles. She'd not been able to walk but Kirsty had insisted that it was of benefit anyway. The routine had been well established by then. Mornings when he'd washed and dressed his wife, leaving for work only when the Community nurse and her assistant arrived. The full time carer came after that and was gone by the time he'd returned, his morning note embellished with words of her own. Often his classes were over in time for Tom to be there when Kirsty arrived for her third visit of the day. He'd watched her tend to his wife, her lilting voice utterly normal, never condescending like some of them. Nan had hated the ones who had treated her like some imbecile child. Thankfully they'd usually had Kirsty up until the end.

"You'll be wanting *Countdown* then?" she'd ask Nan. "I'll leave you to it. Never could do anagrams myself," she'd say with a self-deprecating laugh. She'd known somehow that Nan's mind was still quick even if her fingers couldn't hold a pencil any more. That was what he'd admired about the young nurse, her ability to see beneath the illness to the whole person inside. Not many people had realised what an asset the girl had been to them. And how many people would miss her now?

The radio presenter's voice brought Tom back to the present as he handed over the programme to the newscaster. Another bomb had exploded in the Middle East.

He listened as the facts presented themselves to his brain, Nan's face still floating before him, still smiling up at Kirsty as she made to turn on the television. Now last night's FA Cup results were being analysed. Her face became hazy, indistinct. A different voice told Tom that a band of rain would be sweeping across the country. He tried to hold onto the image dissolving in front of him, to keep the smile at least, but all he could see was that empty pillow.

Lorimer switched off the car radio. The weather forecast told him only some of what he needed to know. If only there could be a crime forecast, he thought wryly. *A band of robberies will sweep across England and Wales today, followed by a combined forces occluded front. A high of serial killings will be present over Scotland leaving floods of victims in its wake. Outlook: grim.* His mind toyed with more comparisons, their flippancy a relief from the thought that had been haunting him all morning. Mhairi MacLeod was all alone now, the last of her family now that Kirsty was gone. Just what thoughts she had hidden away under that wise exterior, he couldn't say. Did she ever wonder about the possible link between a Glasgow prostitute and her own darling girl? Nobody in the investigation had even begun to tar the nurse with the same brush as poor Deirdre McCann. Even the Press had shown some sympathy. Their take on things was that the killer was some nutter and Kirsty his random victim. But was she?

Victims were not restricted to the dead women in the mortuary, either. The old lady herself was a victim just like the McCann family. And the ripples spread outwards to all whose lives had been touched. The Grange had its own victims, too. How many poor souls were still shaken by their loss?

Lorimer glanced across at Solly who seemed absorbed in the landscape, miles away from thoughts of death and its consequences. Behind him on the back seat his mobile began its insistent ringing, making him look ahead for the nearest place to stop. Despite these fairytale mountains sweeping above, Glasgow could still reach out with its persistent demands.

Phyllis didn't really care if the new nursing assistant was an improvement or not.

"What d'you think of her, then, dearie?" Brenda had asked for her opinion and was watching Phyllis's face closely for a sign. The woman in the bed gave none, simply stared back into space as if she hadn't heard a thing. Muttering to herself, Brenda swept her hand over the creaseless counterpane and waddled from the room. Behind her a pair of bright eyes followed her progress and a small sigh escaped into the air. Phyllis fixed her eyes on the door that was always kept ajar. Beyond it there was another world. But here, for a time, was her territory. She let her gaze focus on a fly that was crawling steadily up the grey paintwork. Its erratic progress might let it reach the top of the door. Would it take flight then? The question for Phyllis was far more absorbing than anything big Brenda could offer.

Brenda Duncan knew fine that Phyllis had heard her. "Just can't be bothered, I expect." She told herself, adding a whispered, "Poor soul."

Time and again she'd tried to make a connection with the sick woman. Even a flicker of the eyelids would have been something. But, no.

Kirsty had had the knack, of course, Brenda thought. That one had been able to charm the birds off the trees and no mistake. They'd all been daft about young Kirsty. And she had even seen Phyllis nodding in response to the nurse's questions. Nothing great, mind. Just that slight movement. But it was a dash sight more than she ever got. These thoughts were going through Brenda's mind as she pulled her shopping bag out of her locker and dragged on her raincoat. Those other thoughts were suppressed now. She'd had counselling from that woman her GP had recommended. Hadn't wanted it, but she'd had no choice in the end. It was that or trail about forever like a zombie, doped up to the eyeballs.

"That you off, then, Brenda?" Sister Pearson was looking pointedly at the clock at the end of the corridor. It was still four minutes to the hour but Brenda had to clip the minutes off if she were to catch her bus. Pearson knew that fine well, she thought crossly to herself. Mrs Baillie didn't mind, so why should she?

"Aye," she responded shortly and heaved open the front door, activating the bleeper as she did so. The glass door swung shut, stopping the alarm abruptly. Brenda quickened her stride. She didn't want to be hanging about in this drizzle. There was no shelter at her stop and this was the kind of rain that soaked through everything. She visualised her umbrella, hanging from the coat hook in the hall. Fat lot of good it was doing there. So much for this morning's forecast, she told herself, clenching her teeth against an easterly wind.

It was supposed to be nearly summer, for God's sake. What bloody awful weather! Her glasses were streaming now and she had to keep her head down to avoid the worst onslaughts of the gusts. Her rubber-soled shoes made wet imprints on the pavements under the watery light from the street lamps. The dark sky had activated their photo-sensitive cells on an evening that was more like autumn than spring. Brenda's stout legs quivered with the effort of increasing her pace. She had turned the bottom of the hill and now it was that climb up to Langside Monument. Determined not to miss her bus, the woman plunged on, bag over one arm, clutching at her collar to stop the raindrops seeping in. She felt a sharp pain in her chest as the incline steepened. Too much weight, her GP had scolded her when she'd complained about her aches and pains. Brenda was conscious of her glasses slipping down her nose now, but she tried to ignore them, fearful of loosening her grip on the coat collar.

Just as she made her way to the brow of the hill she saw the bus pulling away from her stop.

"Damn!" she uttered aloud. "Damn and blast!" Her shoulders sagged and the shopping bag slipped from her grasp as she watched the bus sail past her, tyres swishing on the wet road. It was at least fifteen minutes until the next one, unless this was an earlier one running late. Brenda knew all about the erratic timetables. Bitter experience had taught her that it was no use taking a chance to go off to the café for a hot cuppa. You had to wait, just in case there was another bus coming.

She took her place at the head of the queue, tucking wet hands into the sleeves of her coat. She was oblivious to the other passengers forming a line behind her. The rain that was now coursing in runnels down the back of her neck had sapped all her energy and she stared moodily towards the direction from which her bus would come. She didn't notice a figure half-obscured beneath a golf umbrella in the queue behind her. Nor was she aware, when the bus did eventually arrive with a harsh squeal of brakes, of the same figure leaving the queue and heading instead towards the taxi rank by the Victoria Infirmary.

Brenda slumped into the nearest seat and stared out past the streaming windows at absolutely nothing at all. Her mind was jumping ahead to the meal she'd cook for herself at home; her body was simply grateful to be seated at last. Behind her two women chattered. If Brenda had cared to listen in to their patter she might have heard all about that-one-in-the-next-close and her fancy men. But the women's voices were simply part of the overall noise of bus engine and the presence of humans around her, a comforting sound that made her eyelids droop. She paid only the briefest of attention to the outside world; a flicker of a glance outwards to make sure she didn't pass her stop.

Here it was. She rose slowly from the seat with a creak of leather and shuffled forwards towards the platform. Her hands grasped the cold metal rail as the bus veered around a corner then shuddered to a halt.

Now she was walking, walking, forcing her legs to carry her up the familiar street. The red sandstone tenements looked warm and welcoming through the misty drizzle. Not far now.

The close mouth yawned open, the security door latched back on its metal hook. The stone corridor with its glazed wall tiles that led from the front steps to the backcourt was exposed for all to see. Yet it was only residents who were supposed to have keys for either entrance. She peered in, uncertain for an instant as to why this door was lying open. Then the smell reminded her. Of course. This was the day the painters were to be in. Brenda tiptoed past the Wet Paint sign chalked on the stone floor of the close.

Mustn't get any of that on my raincoat, she thought, pulling its folds tighter around her rotund frame. It was a fair step to the second landing.

Puffing, she stopped from time to time, admiring the newly painted walls. The lower half was a bright sky blue, defined by a neat black stripe from the cream upper walls and ceiling.

Brenda gave a sigh of relief as she reached the top step then rummaged in her raincoat pocket for the keys. The sigh became a yawn and she took off her glasses to rub tiredly at her eyes, fitting the Yale in the lock with her free hand.

Just as the solid wooden door swung away from her, she felt a tap on her shoulder. Brenda turned around with a start, surprised and instantly puzzled that she'd heard nobody coming up behind her. Her face, which had been tensed in alarm, relaxed immediately.

"Oh," she said, "it's you." Then, cocking her head to one side, she added, "What on earth are you doing here?"

Brenda's eyes widened in disbelief as the figure lunged towards her, hands suddenly grasping her throat. Her mouth opened in protest, then there was a gargling sound as she struggled against her attacker.

As Brenda jerked backwards onto the hall carpet, her glasses flew upwards into the air. They curved in a perfect arc then broke with a tinkle against the rows of brass hooks screwed into the wall. For a moment the landing held its breath. Then several small sounds interrupted the silence. Wood clunked on wood as the golf umbrella was propped carefully against the door-frame. Feet in wet shoes brushed back and forth, back and forth on the doormat; the sound of coming home; familiar, nothing to alert the neighbours.

The front door banged shut against the newly painted close, echoes spiralling down the stairwell. These were the sounds that everybody listened to at the time, but afterwards nobody remembered that they'd heard them.

Within the house, behind the solid door, Brenda Duncan lay sprawled where she had fallen, ungainly even in death.

Chapter Twenty-Three

The Cross café wasn't the nicest place to have tea and a chat, but it was a safe haven from the deluge outside. The rain had not stopped all day and runnels of water were swirling down the slopes of the pavement outside. Angelica sipped the hot brew, sighing with a mixture of pleasure and relief. It would be okay, now, she told herself. It was all over. Trying to make Leigh see things that way might be tricky but she had hopes.

As if on cue, the Irishman staggered into the café, his hair plastered black against his head. He gazed around him, lost for a moment in the sea of tables and chairs until he spotted her at the window. She'd sat there deliberately so he could see her but the window had steamed up, foiling her strategy.

"Angelica." Leigh's eyes softened as he sat down opposite her. "I thought...for a minute...you'd not come."

"I said I'd be here, didn't I?"

"Aye, that's so."

"I haven't let you down yet, my boy, and I'm not about to start now. Got that?"

Leigh nodded.

"What d'you want? Tea? Coffee?" Angelica asked as the waitress approached.

He shrugged as if it wasn't important so Angelica gave the waitress an order for another pot of tea.

"Now, down to business. The police were up at the respite centre in Lewis. That Chief Inspector wanted to know what you'd been doing the night of Kirsty's death."

Catching sight of Leigh's sudden frown, she hastily

added, "I told them that you were with me, of course. We'd been praying together. But somehow he seemed to think that was suspicious."

"Why?"

"It's the praying hands, Leigh. That's what they can't see past. You know and I know the significance for us both but they don't look at things quite in the way that we do. D'you understand?"

The man nodded then flinched as the waitress set down a pot of tea on the table. Angelica poured it for him, knowing he was still too shaken for even a simple task like this. The man's nerves were shot to pieces, she told herself. How he was going to stand up to that Lorimer when he came back from Lewis, only God knew.

"You still keeping an eye on Phyllis?"

"Aye."

Angelica nodded her approval. That was something at least. She leaned forward and patted his hand. "Now you're not to worry, but the police will be coming back. They want to talk to you again."

Leigh looked puzzled but said nothing.

"Here's what to do. Now listen. When they ask where you were the night Kirsty died, tell them you were with me. I'll back you up."

Leigh Quinn shifted in his seat, squirming around as he looked around the cafe. Suddenly every person there seemed to pose a threat. Angelica watched him intently, sensing his moods as she always did. She could almost smell the fear rising from him.

"Look, Leigh, it's going to be all right. You just have to trust me." Angelica fixed her eyes earnestly on the man's white face until he looked at her.

Then he gave a grudging nod.

"Good. Now drink up your tea. We have plans to make, you and I."

Chapter Twenty-Four

Lorimer's eyes were gritty from peering into the swishing windscreen wipers hour after hour. He'd been reasonably circumspect on the journey through the Highlands, given the rain sweeping across the winding roads, but after that call on his mobile the car had hurtled down from Loch Lomond, breaking every speed regulation in the book. Now they were entering the city boundaries at last. Solly had slept a lot of the way from Ullapool, folded into his black raincoat like one of those cormorants he'd seen around the Harris coastline. Lorimer was glad of the silence between them. It had given him time to think, time to digest that phone call from HQ telling him to get himself over to the south side double quick, there'd been another death.

He'd called Rosie at the University to see if she'd be at the scene of crime. Yes, she'd said shortly, and not with Mitchison if Lorimer could get his arse into gear. Her tone expressed distaste for Lorimer's boss that had made him chuckle. But his mirth was short-lived. There was nothing remotely funny about this.

"Brenda Duncan," Lorimer spoke softly to himself. "Who on earth would want to do you in?" It didn't make sense. First a prostitute in Queen Street station, then a nurse working the night shift. Now another member of the clinic's staff murdered in her own home. Had she seen something the night of Kirsty's death? Had she been keeping something back from Strathclyde CID? Or had something happened that she'd failed to register as significant? Either way it took him back to the same place: the Grange. One thing was certain, though; neither Sam Fulton nor Sister Angelica could have committed this latest murder.

Lorimer braked sharply as the lights turned to red.

"Here already?" Solly turned to look out at the familiar urban landscape. "How long till we reach Govanhill?"

"Another fifteen minutes, if we're lucky." He stared ahead at the build up of rush hour traffic. It would take them at least that to cross town, he reckoned. Maybe he should have crossed the Erskine Bridge. Hunger was gnawing at his guts. He should have made more time for a lunch stop. Maggie would be home by now. Maybe even cooking something decent for him, he thought wistfully. God, he'd missed her these last few days.

The journey across town via the Clyde Tunnel was a nightmare. Lorimer fretted and fumed aloud, cursing each and every driver that slowed him down. To cap it all, the tunnel was down to one lane. Solly, sitting beside him, kept a tactful silence. The psychologist looked out onto the darkening skies. He'd already worked one thing out for himself. Whoever had killed Brenda Duncan had known exactly where she lived and when she'd be off duty. Someone she knew, possibly. A colleague? A patient? Again, Solly felt a frisson as he thought of the killer and the risks he'd taken. There was both recklessness and a sense of calculation about the man that seemed at odds with one another. More than ever Solly was disquieted by the three murders; it was as if they had been carried out by a different hand each time. Still, there was a new crime scene ahead and that might throw light upon the puzzle.

Solly shivered. The sight of a corpse was not something he relished.

It was well after six o'clock when Lorimer turned the car into the street in Govanhill. Rosie Fergusson's BMW was parked outside the close mouth, a squad car just beyond.

"Coming up?" Lorimer asked, unbuckling his seat belt.

Solly just looked at him and nodded. He had to see it for himself. There was no other option.

Brenda Duncan's flat was on the second landing. Lorimer acknowledged the scene of crime officer with a nod as he reached the open doorway. He could see a uniformed officer at the far end of the passage where the glare of the arc lights washed over the scene. Rosie was examining the body as they entered the hallway. It was a surprisingly large area, reminding Lorimer of the old-fashioned room and kitchen belonging to an aged relative, long since deceased. The Glasgow tenements had fairly teemed with family life a century ago. But he was here to deal with death, he reminded himself, his eyes returning to the body beyond Rosie's white-coated figure.

The pathologist looked up at the sound of their footsteps. "Hi. Oh, Solly. You're here too. Good!" She waggled a glove-clad hand in their direction before continuing her examination.

Brenda Duncan's body lay close to the wall. Above her a huge gilt mirror reflected the grim tableau of Rosie and Lorimer now crouching over the body. Solly held onto the wall for support, his stomach suddenly queasy. Yet he could not look away from the mirror. It was there, all right. Clasped between her podgy fingers was a single red carnation.

His signature, thought Solly, his calling card. Sliding along the wall, he took in the whole length of the woman's corpse, the raincoat riding up above the fleshy thighs, legs falling apart. The hands were pressed together and pointing downwards. It was just like the others.

"You okay?" Rosie looked up suddenly, concern on her face.

"Not really," he replied. "Think I'll go outside for a minute."

Lorimer and Rosie exchanged glances as Solly made his way out of the flat.

"Who found her?" Lorimer asked.

"The neighbour across the landing. She has a spare key. Got worried when nobody answered the door all day."

"Didn't she think the woman was out at work?"

Rosie shook her head. "She knew it was Brenda's day off. Said she'd arranged to call in and have coffee with her." The pathologist crooked her finger at him and Lorimer drew closer. "See this?" Rosie turned the head gently to one side and pointed to the bruising. "He used both hands and you can see where his fingers pressed into the larynx."

"Any sign of a struggle?"

"Nope. She was dead by the time she'd hit the floor, I reckon."

"Then he had his little ceremony."

"The flower? Yes. We saw that right away."

"Was she in this position when that neighbour called?"

"Yes, the body hasn't been shifted much at all."

"So whoever killed her just locked the door and walked away?"

"I see what you're getting at," Rosie replied. "But there was no need to use a key to lock up. The door locks simply by pulling it to."

"Time of death?"

"She's been dead since last night. I should think around mid-evening. I can't be more accurate than that, yet."

"What about sexual activity?" Lorimer pointed at the exposed thighs.

"None. I'm not sure why he pulled her skirt up like that. There's a question for Solly, perhaps."

"Any chance of fingerprints on the throat?"

"I shouldn't think so. He wore gloves. Again. But there may be some traces under Brenda's fingernails. That's something we'll have to investigate."

"Evidence. We need some evidence," Lorimer muttered. He stood up and turned towards the door. "Solly and I had better head over to the clinic. I'll be in touch."

Lorimer looked down as a flashlight from the SOCO's camera illuminated the corpse. He blinked then nodded briefly towards the body. The dead woman was in safe hands with Rosie Fergusson.

"Chief Inspector," Mrs Baillie's hand was outstretched as soon as they entered the reception area. "This is unexpected," she said, ushering Lorimer and Solly into the Grange.

"I'm afraid we have some rather distressing news. Is there somewhere private we could talk?" Lorimer said.

"In my quarters. We won't be disturbed there," she added, tucking a bulky file under her arm.

Mrs Baillie's rooms were situated on the top floor of the building. She unlocked a door in the corridor that gave way to a tiny square hall. A set of golf clubs lay propped against a shelf that contained a few dusty looking books.

"In here, please," she motioned them through to the sitting room. The windows overlooking the front of the grounds gave a view of the road all the way down to Queen's Park. Lorimer looked around him. Whatever he had expected from the woman's living quarters, it certainly wasn't this. The room was practically bare. An open door gave him a glimpse of a tiny kitchenette; another door, firmly closed, probably led to her bedroom. It, too, would give that view over the front. The walls were painted in the same pale wash that he'd seen throughout the rest of the Grange and were totally unadorned; no prints, no photographs, nothing but a blank expanse. Or was it?

Moving closer to the wall opposite the windows, Lorimer noticed faint rectangular shapes where pictures of some sort had once been hanged. Was she preparing to have the decorators in, maybe? Would that explain the empty mantelpiece and bare walls? Sweeping a practiced eye over the rest of the sitting room, he saw only a plain teak coffee table placed between a basic two-seater sofa and one upright chair. A grey metal filing cabinet stood to one side of the chair as if Mrs Baillie was accustomed to doing her paperwork in the privacy of her own rooms. It reminded him suddenly of Kirsty's bedsit with its second-hand furnishings, except that Kirsty had tried to project some of her personality into her room. This place had been stripped of any personal touches.

It looked as if someone had packed up all the usual bits and pieces that transform a living space into a real home; the little clues his detective's eye instinctively sought. Curious, he thought. Was the woman preparing to move out? Did that explain why it all looked so spartan? Catching Solly's eye, he raised an inquiring eyebrow. Solly's glimmer of a smile told him that the same thoughts had occurred to the psychologist.

Behind the door there was a cheap telephone mounted on the wall. His eye fell on the box fixed to the skirting board. At least she seemed to have her own private line.

"Please take a seat," Mrs Baillie said, immediately opting for the upright chair so that Lorimer and Solly had to share the sofa. "I was just about to begin checking the time sheets," she said, patting the folder on her lap.

Lorimer was aware of Solly's eyes still roving over the room as he began. "I'm sorry to have to disrupt your evening, Ma'am, but there's been another murder."

Mrs Baillie's face remained impassive, her eyes waiting for the information Lorimer was about to give.

"Brenda Duncan's body was found this evening by a neighbour." Lorimer watched the woman's face turn pale. Her hands clutched briefly at the folder but then she stayed stock still as though frozen by the news.

"It appears that she was killed last night, shortly after she had returned from her shift here," Lorimer went on. "You have my commiserations," he told her, wondering just what emotions were circulating under that bloodless face.

"I can't quite take this in, Chief Inspector," Mrs Baillie began slowly. "*Brenda*? She was such a harmless big woman. Who on earth would want to kill her?" she said, echoing Lorimer's earlier thoughts. "Where did it happen?"

"In her own home."

Mrs Baillie frowned. "So, do you think it was the same person…?" she tailed off, her eyes flitting from one man to the other.

Lorimer took a deep breath. "We aren't at liberty to divulge details right now," he began, then took a swift look at Solly.

"If it was the same person, then there is an obvious link between the clinic and the killer," Solly said.

"We could station a uniformed officer here if you wished," Lorimer told her.

"No. No. That won't be necessary. There's been enough disruption already. This business has set back a good number of our patients. Imagine how they will feel if they think they're being watched. Some of them suffer from paranoia, you know."

"There will have to be a police presence here at some time, though. We still have to question your staff about Mrs Duncan."

"But why? If she was killed in her own home? Why bother us here?" The woman clenched her fists, her expression defiant.

"Brenda Duncan," Lorimer began, smoothly. "I understand she left here yesterday evening. What time would that have been?"

Mrs Baillie opened the folder that lay across her knees. She turned the pages of the file with great deliberation, unaware of the eyes firmly fixed on her, intent on every emotion flickering across her face, watching for every sign revealed by her body language.

"According to Sister Pearson's sheet, she left at four minutes to eight yesterday evening, Chief Inspector. Today was her day off."

The papers had stopped being rustled and Lorimer had the impression that Mrs Baillie could have given that information without the need to sift through the time sheets. The woman's white hands were folded in front of her on the documents. She looked from Lorimer to Solly with an apparent coolness that was betrayed by two pink spots highlighting her cheekbones.

"The shift doesn't finish until eight on the dot but we are fairly flexible with our staff." There was a pause as she eyed them both. "She had a bus to catch over the hill. Anyway," she tapped her fingers in irritation, "Brenda was a good time keeper. Never had a problem with her."

The woman's words jarred. She'd said much the same about Kirsty.

"Even after Kirsty MacLeod's murder?" Lorimer swiftly interjected. Mrs Baillie's shoulders tensed. Lorimer could feel the anger being controlled. It was a cruel question but he wasn't in this job to ask easy ones.

"She went for counselling at my request. Through her own GP, of course."

"So she was off work?"

"Not for very long. Five days in all. She seemed fine once she was back into the routine." Mrs Baillie leaned forward slightly to press home her point.

"That's what the Doctor recommended, a return to the normal working day. And it worked," she added defiantly. Lorimer didn't doubt it.

"But I thought she worked nights?" Solly asked innocently.

"It wasn't thought suitable for her to return to night-shift work. A later shift beginning at noon and finishing at eight was deemed more appropriate," Mrs Baillie fixed Solly with a stare that brooked no nonsense then turned to Lorimer.

"Actually," the matron gave him a lopsided smile, "Brenda had spoken to me privately about handing in her notice."

The smile stayed glued to her mouth but failed to reach the eyes that continued to betray their hostility towards the two men. Her hands were clasped firmly in front of her. Lorimer was instantly reminded of his guidance teacher way back in secondary school when he and his mates had been caught drinking Carlsberg Specials in the boys' toilets. He stared her out too, if he remembered rightly.

"And did she?" he asked.

"I persuaded her otherwise," she said. "She didn't enjoy being grilled by the police. None of us did. You seemed to ask the same questions over and over as if you didn't believe what we were telling you. Brenda was most upset."

And now she's dead, Lorimer wanted to say. The woman didn't appear to have taken that news in properly, yet. There was a hostility here that he couldn't comprehend, something that threatened to create a chasm between the Director and himself. Fear could cause that, he knew. Had she something to hide, he wondered?

"This is quite normal procedure, Mrs Baillie," he began, keeping his tone neutral, almost bored. "You may expect to answer the same questions several times. Memory's a funny thing. Suddenly there are aspects people remember days later. Even when they were certain they'd recalled everything there was to recall."

Mrs Baillie inclined her head in a token of deference.

She doesn't buy that one, thought Lorimer. Let's try a different tack.

"We visited Failte in Lewis and spoke to Sam Fulton and Sister Angelica."

"Well, I'm sure they enjoyed that little change to their routine," she remarked, the sarcasm scarcely concealed.

"Sister Angelica told us that Leigh Quinn had been very upset the night of Kirsty MacLeod's murder. He'd actually been in her room shortly after the body was discovered. Praying."

"Really?"

"Where was Leigh Quinn last night, Mrs Baillie?"

For the first time the woman looked flustered. She unclasped her hands and wiped them down either side of her skirt.

"Here, I suppose. They're not prisoners, you know, Chief Inspector. Only those patients who might be a danger to themselves are kept under close scrutiny."

"And Leigh Quinn doesn't come into that category?" Solly asked mildly.

"No. Leigh has severe problems but he may come and go as he pleases."

"And does he?" Lorimer asked.

The woman hesitated before answering. "Sometimes he'll go out for a walk. He doesn't sleep well, you see. Other times," she broke off, biting her lips as if she had already said too much.

"Yes?" Lorimer prompted.

"Other times he sits with Phyllis in her room." She looked from one man to the other. "Phyllis doesn't mind," she insisted. "We'd know if she didn't want him to visit her room."

Lorimer nodded. Could anything be gleaned from that crippled patient downstairs to confirm Quinn's whereabouts last night?

"Brenda Duncan," Lorimer switched tack again. "Have you any record to show when she and Kirsty worked together and with whom? Nursing staff as well as patients."

Mrs Baillie clasped then unclasped her fingers and Lorimer saw the knuckles white and bloodless under her tight grasp. He suddenly had the impression of a physically strong woman beneath the navy suit.

"That's not a problem, Chief Inspector. We have duty rosters made up and signed after every shift. I can let you have a photocopy of the more recent ones." She paused and gave a small frown as if they were two tiresome small boys taking up her valuable time. Lorimer thought back to Kirsty's diary. It had yielded very little after all. No personal information had been recorded other than birthdays; her work rotas had simply been marked *early* or *late* depending on the shifts.

"And I believe you were not here yesterday evening, Mrs Baillie," Lorimer added.

"That's right. I..." The woman stopped in mid-sentence, staring at him as the full import of his words hit home.

"You're not suggesting that I had anything to do with Brenda's death? Dear God!" she exclaimed, her hand clutching the pearls at her throat.

"I'm not suggesting anything, ma'am. But it would be helpful to know where you were last night." Lorimer sat up abruptly, his shadow now cast over the coffee table between them. Mrs Baillie stared at him blankly then twisted round to search for something in the handbag that was looped over the arm of the chair, head lowered to cover her confusion.

When she looked up her face was flushed.

"I can't find it," she began. "My cinema ticket. I thought I'd kept it but I must have thrown it away." Then she straightened up and smoothed her hands along the front of her skirt. "But I don't suppose you're really looking for an alibi for me, are you?" She smiled again, her confidence returning.

"No, no. Not at all," Solly reassured her before Lorimer could speak. "What a pity you hadn't been here, though. Isn't it?" Solly smiled and shrugged.

"Anyway," she stood up and turned towards the filing cabinet, "I can give you the duty rosters for the last month." Lorimer watched as she walked her fingers through the files. At last she stopped and pulled out a green folder. Her back was to them as she leafed through its contents but even so, Lorimer and Solly could see the raised shoulders stiff with tension.

"Here," she pushed the file across the table to Lorimer. "All the rosters for April and May. You should find what you're looking for in there."

"Really?" It was Lorimer's turn for sarcasm now. "We're looking for a murderer."

Their eyes met in a frozen stare then, to Lorimer's satisfaction, Mrs Baillie dropped her glance.

"Thank you," he said as if nothing untoward had happened between them. "I'll see this is returned to you as soon as possible," he added, tapping the green file and easing himself out of the sofa. Solly followed his lead, springing to his feet. Mrs Baillie simply stood there for a moment, her tall figure ramrod stiff.

"I'd better show you both out," her voice was dry.

Nothing was said as the three made their way downstairs to the main entrance. The woman's hand flicked over the security buttons then pulled the door wide open.

She made no attempt to return Lorimer's "goodnight" as he strode towards the drive, Solomon in his wake.

Once in the driveway Solly tugged his sleeve.

"What was all that about? You were practically rude to her. Don't you want her co-operation, Lorimer?" Solly raised his arms then let them fall in a moment of bewilderment.

"Oh, she'll co-operate all right," he smiled. "She'll be only too pleased to co-operate once we've gone through the other files."

"What other files?"

Lorimer looked down at his quizzical expression and smiled. "Before we left Stornoway I got a rather interesting fax."

"Go on."

"I didn't mention it at the time but it seems that this clinic has been experiencing financial difficulties

after all. Despite the accountant's previous assurances."

"So?"

"So. A number of things. On their own they could be nothing to worry about but put together they make me uneasy. For a start the last accounts show a big loss. That could be okay on its own but the most recent accounts haven't been lodged and they've recently changed their bankers. That's always a bad sign." Lorimer paused. "But there's something else that's got me worried."

"What?"

"The building contractors who were doing renovations have slapped an inhibition order on the whole business."

"You don't think any of the contractors could have kept a key to the basement door, do you?"

Lorimer shrugged. "Who knows? They've been questioned just like everybody else who has something to do with this place. No. What's concerning me is money. The builders haven't been paid and they've obviously run out of patience so what they can do to get their money is to take steps to stop any of the properties being sold until the directors cough up."

"But I thought Phyllis Logan owned them. Surely the directors can't market the properties without her permission."

"I don't know. There's something odd going on and it's not just to do with her saving money on airline tickets to Lewis. Did you see that place of hers? Didn't you think it looked like she was in the throes of moving out? There was hardly a decent stick of furniture in the entire flat."

"I still don't see what it's got to do with the murder of three women," Solly replied.

"Nor do I," Lorimer frowned suddenly. "But my policeman's nose tells me something's rotten in that place. Maybe something Kirsty and Brenda knew about, too. I want to sniff around a bit and find out what it is." He unlocked the car and leaned on the door. "And another thing. I've rarely seen anybody display so little grief. Shock, maybe, but not a word of sorrow. Explain that to me, eh?"

Solly pulled open the passenger door and slid into the leather seat. "Can't fault her there. Some people hide their emotions very well. She may well be crying her eyes out right now for all we know."

"Hm," Lorimer sounded sceptical.

"Anyway, aren't you forgetting Deirdre McCann? She's got nothing to do with the Grange," Solomon bit his lip suddenly. This was what he had wanted to discuss with Lorimer but each time he came close to it something stopped him. He'd been trying to see and feel his way into a killer's mind and all he could think was how disparate it all was, especially since Brenda Duncan's murder. He gnawed at the edges of his moustache. How could he tell Lorimer how he felt? It was as if there were two shadows following them, just out of sight, each intent on strangling some poor woman.

As the car roared into the night, Solly looked out into the streets and all he could see was a red flower crushed between dead fingers.

"It's me," the familiar, husky voice breathed through the intercom.

"Come on up."

Solly grinned. Rosie was just what he needed right now, he realised, his tiredness vanishing. It was late. She would stay the night, surely? Or was she merely bringing him up to speed with this latest murder? Solly caught sight of his boyish expression in the hall mirror and laughed softly. She'd have phoned if it was just about work.

Leaning over the banister, he looked down at the fair head bobbing below him as she climbed the stairs. His hands gripped the metal rail. Brenda Duncan might have stopped at such a place watching out for her assailant. But had she? Or was the freshly painted close with its yawning mouth an open invitation for a stranger to walk right in? Solly shook his head. No way. Brenda might not have expected a visitor but she would have known who he was.

Thoughts of the woman's corpse disappeared as Rosie smiled up at him.

"Hallo, you."

She raised herself up on tip-toe to kiss him full on the mouth. Solly's arms were around her in a welcoming embrace, drawing her to him.

"Mm. That's better," she murmured. "Can I come in, now?"

Solly gave a laugh, pulled the door wider and then closed it firmly behind her.

"Oh, what a day!" Rosie flopped into the nearest comfy armchair, dropping her handbag and jacket onto the floor.

"Drink?"

"Any of that gin I brought you?"

"I even bought in some tonics, specially for you."

"Ah! That's my man!"

Moving into the kitchen to fetch her drink, Solly warmed to her words. *Her man.* Not her waiter, her butler, but her *man. Her* man.

He sat at her feet, his head resting companionably against the chair as they drank in silence. It was comfortable, secure, so he could tell her what he'd been thinking, couldn't he?

"I've had some thoughts about the profile."

"Because of tonight, you mean?"

"Not really, but this death does rather consolidate my ideas."

"Go on."

Solly remained silent for a few minutes. Rosie let it linger. She was familiar enough with those silences of his by now so she waited, sipping the gin slowly.

"It's the flower that bothers me most."

"His signature?"

"Hm. Signatures can be forged, don't you know."

"Solly. What're you trying to say?" Rosie leaned forward, her eyes on his dark profile.

"Not all of it makes sense. A murderer who kills a prostitute in a station then two nurses, one at her work and the other in her own home. What kind of man is that?"

"Reckless? A risk-taker?"

Solly shook his head. "Not just that. There aren't any proper links. Just that flower and the praying hands."

Rosie laid her glass down suddenly. "Hey! Are you saying we've got more than one guy doing these killings? Or is there some sort of religious fundamentalist gang targeting women victims?"

Solly heaved a sigh. "Not a gang. Nor do I think the two killings show a pattern."

"Three. Three killings," Rosie corrected him.

Solly turned and faced her, his expression suddenly grave. "Yes, but there are only two killers and I doubt very much if they have ever met."

"But the flowers?"

"Yes, that's what I keep coming back to. In profiling you must look at the location first to see what opportunity the killer might have had and if he lives anywhere near the choice of locus. With the station that was difficult at first."

"He could've come by train?"

"Not in the middle of the night. He has to have something to do with Queen Street station. He knows the layout well, gets away without anybody noticing him or being caught on a security camera. Now, if the second murder had been in the vicinity of the city, even a mile or so away, I wouldn't have bothered so much. But the Grange is away over on the south side."

"So?"

"So, there's no pattern. You see, serial killers tend to work in ever increasing circles away from a base, which is usually where they live. With each killing they become bolder and travel a bit further afield. Okay. It's not a rigid model. There are cases like the long distance lorry driver who murdered those children. But even then there was a pattern defined by his delivery schedules. Here I can't find any evidence to show me a killer who progresses from a prostitute in a station to a nurse at work."

"Unless he's a nutter inside the Grange already."

Solly didn't answer her. For a moment he stared

into space, unblinking.

"With Brenda Duncan's death I feel justified in proposing that we have two killers. Whoever killed Deirdre McCann is a person in serious need of help. He's a danger to himself as well as to society."

"And Brenda? Kirsty?"

"Ah. I'm not entirely happy with the disturbed personality theory everyone is so eager to believe. There's a reason for those deaths. Someone badly wanted these two women out of the way. The flowers are a blind."

"You mean someone is trying to make you think there's a serial killer on the loose?"

"Exactly. There are two profiles here and my job right now is to untangle them."

"What does Lorimer think about this?" Rosie took one look at Solly's face and laughed. "You mean you haven't told him yet?"

"No. But I will. I'll have to, won't I?"

Solly pulled himself up and perched on the arm of the chair. "What about you? What's next on your agenda?"

"Oh, back to the lab. *Early*," she added with a grimace.

"Well," he hesitated and then smiled as if a happy thought had just occurred to him.

"Hadn't we better go to bed now, then?"

Chapter Twenty-Five

It was still daylight when Lorimer reached his street. The longest day was barely a month away and there was a pearly glow from the sky that comes after a rain shower in late Spring. It could have been any hour of the day.

Lorimer pulled into the driveway, carefully avoiding the stone gateposts, and parked outside his door. The front drive was ancient tarmac with the weeds poking through. It did fine for a parking space, if Lorimer had ever thought about it (which he didn't). It was Maggie who mowed what little lawn their property possessed and fitfully tended their ragged flowerbeds. Lorimer turned the key in the car door, reminding himself yet again to buy new batteries for the key fob. He looked up automatically at the lounge window. There was a light flickering against the glass. The television was on. Surely it wasn't *Newsnight* already?

The slam of the door behind him sounded hollow, as if all the carpets had been lifted. The house had an abandoned feel to it but Lorimer knew Maggie was in there somewhere.

"Hi. Anybody home?" he called up the unlit hallway. There was no response but he could hear the sound of voices from the television beyond the lounge door.

Lorimer rapped twice on the door before pushing it open. "It's only me," he joked, then stopped as Maggie leaped up to switch off the television, a look of alarm on her face. The alarm changed to something else. Relief? Lorimer couldn't decide. Then she was in his arms, clinging round his waist as if she'd never let him go. Lorimer felt her tension. Maybe she'd been watching a scary movie. He stroked her hair and kissed the top of her head. Suddenly his tummy rumbled below Maggie's clinging grasp and they broke apart, laughing together.

"No dinner again?" she shook her dark curls reprovingly.

"Sorry, Miss," Lorimer pulled a contrite face. "Didn't have time."

"How about poor Solly?"

"Oh, he never seems to remember such mundane things as meals. Time we found him a good woman."

"Like Rosie."

"Indeed." Lorimer slumped into a sagging armchair. "Oh, it's good to be home. Just the two of us."

Maggie nodded. It seemed ages since they'd been at home together.

"Anything to eat, kind lady?" Lorimer put on his most disarming face.

"Typical," she rejoined. "Doesn't see me for days and what does he miss? My home cooking!" And with a great pretence at being offended she set off for the kitchen.

Lorimer stretched his long legs out and, giving a huge yawn, muttered, "Too right." Then he closed his eyes.

When Maggie returned five minutes later with a tray full of soup and sandwiches she found her husband fast asleep.

Quietly she set the tray down on the coffee table then lifted the remote control. The videotape ejected noiselessly. Holding her breath she retrieved the tape, fitted it back into its sleeve then slid it deep down into her open briefcase. For an instant the echoes of those American voices reverberated in her brain telling her all about the opportunities teacher exchange could bring. Opportunities Maggie wasn't ready to share with her husband. Not yet. She looked down at the man sleeping below her gaze. His mouth was open slightly and she could see two days' stubble round the slack jaw. The lines round those bad blue eyes seemed deeper than usual. We're getting older, thought Maggie wistfully, both of us. But she wasn't past it yet. Oh, no. Not by a long way.

"Hey," she whispered at last, "soup's getting cold."

Lorimer came to, blinking as if he'd slept for hours rather than minutes.

"'S'nice of you to bother," he mumbled, sitting up and taking the tray onto his lap. Maggie watched as her husband spooned up the soup and munched on the ham sandwiches, never pausing for breath.

A lock of dark hair tumbled over his brow and she had to stop herself from putting out her hand to smooth it aside. Finally he put down the spoon and laboriously cleared the sandwich crumbs from his plate. Maggie observed the sagging shoulders and outstretched limbs. She'd seen the signs often enough to know that he'd sleep where he lay if she let him.

"Come on," she said softly, "let's get you to bed."

Lorimer reached out and slammed the top of the alarm clock, killing its insistent, drilling ring. He could feel Maggie's warmth curling around his legs, her hair soft against his naked back. He wanted to stay in this bed forever, slumbering against his wife's closeness. The sigh he exhaled told him a million things. How he'd be better off in a nine-to-five job, how he really missed the comforts of a proper home life. Lorimer straightened out under the duvet as sleepiness evaporated and he began taking stock, recalling Mrs Baillie's responses to his questions. What was going on over there? Was the clinic in such dire straits that it faced closure? The woman's flat looked as if she was planning to move out. But what would happen to the patients? And who would care for that poor woman lying paralysed down in the back room?

Maggie, sensing the shift in her husband's preoccupation, was up and out of bed before he'd had time to notice.

He watched her for a few minutes as she went through the morning routine of opening the bedroom curtains then pulling a hairbrush through her unruly dark hair. His eyes followed her as she unhooked her negligee from the back of the bedroom door then she was gone. Lorimer listened to the sounds of the bathroom door closing then the shower shushing its spray onto the tiled walls. He heard Maggie slamming shut the cabinet door. Closing his eyes, he imagined her body reaching up to the jets of water, her skin turning to wet silk under the spray.

There was a dull thud as the newspaper hit the hall carpet and he flung off the covers, grabbed his dressing gown and padded barefoot downstairs.

The headlines were predictable. Yesterday's news had been full of Brenda Duncan's murder. Now today's paper had inevitably linked it with Deirdre and Kirsty. There were some quotes from the residential patients to make it look as if there was a general panic amongst them. Mrs Baillie wouldn't like that. There was a quote, too, from Mitchison.

Investigations by senior officers have been taking place both in Glasgow and the Island of Lewis. It is too early yet to make a definite link in respect of the deaths of three women in Glasgow but forensic evidence may prove to be crucial in that respect. I would urge the families of patients at the Grange to remain calm and support the excellent staff who are doing their utmost to keep the clinic running as normally as possible.

Lorimer grimaced. Here was one senior officer who wouldn't mind a quick report from forensics. He'd give Rosie a ring just before he left, just on the off-chance that she'd come up with something. Then there were the computer checks on all the patients and staff at the Grange. And at Failte, he reminded himself.

Lorimer waved briefly as Maggie clattered out the front door, her jacket slipping off her shoulder as she struggled to close the bulging briefcase. It wouldn't fasten so she hoisted it up under her arm, feeling with her free hand for the car keys somewhere deep within her shoulder bag. He watched her from the open door, biting his lip as he waited for Rosie to come to the phone. The car started up then his wife was gone.

"C'mon, Rosie, where are you woman?" he whispered under his breath, listening into the airwaves that were blessedly free from any taped music-while-you-wait. At last Rosie's "Hi, Lorimer," came down the line. She sounded weary.

"Okay, Doc, whatcha got for me?" Lorimer put on his jokey Columbo voice, but his face became serious as he listened. Rosie Fergusson took her time as she filled him in on what she'd found since last night.

"We've run tests on the fibres from all three and there are definite matches between Kirsty's and Brenda's, so far. There were traces that may have come from surgical gloves. There's static showing up in several sets of fibres, particularly around their throats."

"That makes sense," Lorimer said, visualising only too clearly how the women had been strangled.

"No matches with Deirdre McCann, then?" he frowned.

"Nope, but there are still loads of things to work on. There is something else, though."

"Go on."

"There were traces on the hall carpet that show a dirty footprint. Remember it had been raining really heavily that day."

"Any indication of foot size?"

"A size eight shoe as far as we can determine."

"So. You're saying it's a man's print?"

"Come, on. You know me better than that. When did I ever jump to those kinds of conclusions? No. I'm simply saying someone had on a pair of wet shoes in a particular size. Not necessarily a man." Lorimer grinned at the indignation in her voice. "Anyway, the imprint suggests a size eight shoe. The heel mark was quite distinctive. And the traces from the carpet fibres showed all sorts of stuff. Mostly to be found in the Glasgow streets," she added wearily.

"So. A very big lady or a small man?"

"Even a man of average height might have a smaller shoe size. You know that, Lorimer," Rosie protested. "My cousin Ruth's only about five foot three and she takes a size seven."

"What about the post mortem?"

"This morning sometime. Coming down?"

"Will I make it by ten? The Super wants to see me first thing."

"Okay. Have fun," Rosie's voice was loaded with sarcasm. Mitchison obviously wasn't her flavour of the month either.

Lorimer gazed into space, thinking about what Rosie had just told him. Surgical gloves. A man's footprint. Were they dealing with a member of staff from the Grange, then? That's what had been running through his mind since last night. The sooner they had these computer checks available the better. Then he could focus on the picture more clearly. For now it was blurred round the edges, just like that grainy Press photo lying on the floor.

Mitchison was on the warpath. The latest broadside from the Press had obviously got under his skin. And now there was another victim to add to the tally of unsolved murders.

"How do you account for the time spent? One interview with a relative and a brief visit to Failte! You've been away three days, Lorimer!"

Lorimer ground his teeth. Whose case was this anyway? He was the investigating officer, for God's sake! But he kept the thought to himself, refusing to give Mitchison the satisfaction of his outrage.

"Another thing. I don't see anything in writing from the second victim's relative," Mitchison went on, flicking through a file that was indeed painfully thin. Lorimer knew he'd not be happy until there was a

Bible-sized report on his desk.

He ached to take the man by the collar and give him a good shaking. Victim. Relative. They were statistics to this man, not the flesh and blood figures that peopled Lorimer's every waking thought.

"There hasn't been time yet to write up a report. With the discovery of Brenda Duncan's body I decided to go straight over to the Grange last night. Besides," he continued, "Dr Fergusson's report should be included."

"Anything new there, yet?"

"Dr Fergusson's team have found traces of latex on Kirsty and Brenda's bodies. It may suggest the involvement of a member of the medical staff." Lorimer stopped short of divulging any other information. He wasn't prepared to go into the whys and wherefores of the Grange's finances just yet. He'd follow that up as and when he could. But he certainly didn't need this kind of earache.

Mitchison pressed his fingertips together and frowned. "I don't want the Press involved with members of staff until we know more. Tell Mrs Baillie."

Bit late for that now, thought Lorimer, remembering the morning's headlines. Let the Police Press Office sort that out. He had enough on his plate right now.

The Superintendent sat up as if he were about to dismiss Lorimer then changed his mind, leaned forward and added, "A Press conference with members of the Duncan family might be helpful after the PM. Get the TV boys in to video it. See how the family members react."

Lorimer shrugged. Was Mitchison hedging his bets

or did he simply want to control the Press boys as well? He'd be lucky, thought Lorimer; there was no way he was going to go down that path. The less the public knew right now, the better.

"You missed the course with Miss Lipinski," Mitchison told him. "Pity, that. You might have learned something."

The Superintendent's change of tack didn't fool Lorimer for a minute. It was his way of reminding his DCI who was Boss. Reminding him who sat in the Super's chair. Reminding him yet again that he hadn't got George's old job.

The City Mortuary was situated in one of the oldest parts of Glasgow, rubbing shoulders with the modern High Court building next door. Lorimer had often conjectured that the killers up before a judge and jury could be mere yards away from their victims held in cold storage in the mortuary.

Brenda Duncan's body was already in Rosie's "In-tray" as one of the mortuary assistants had jokingly coined it. Rosie was in her bright yellow wellies and green plastic apron, her assistant, Don, by her side as she performed the post mortem examination. Lorimer stood at the window that looked into the PM room. He had no problem with this aspect of detective work. Some policemen and women simply couldn't take it even after years of seeing dead bodies revealing their innermost secrets on the pathologist's slab. There was an intercom between him and the PM room. Not only could he hear Rosie's instructions to Don while they worked, but it enabled her to keep a running commentary of her examination for Lorimer's benefit.

Lorimer looked at the body of Brenda Duncan. She'd been a large, heavily built woman in life, he remembered. But now death had shrunk her body as she lay, the vital organs openly displayed to curious eyes. Her killer had taken everything from her, even her last dignity.

"Yes. There we are. Larynx compressed against the cervical spine. Injury to the hyoid bone. The cricoid cartilage has been damaged also. Someone pretty strong who knew exactly what they were doing, Lorimer. The element of surprise, too, of course. But she was a big woman and you might have expected her to fight back. He had used both hands so she'd have had her hands free."

"So, why didn't she?"

"Fright. Coupled with the fact that she was breathless from climbing the stairs. She had a weak chest. Being overweight was really to her disadvantage. And she was of an age that made fractures to the laryngeal cartilages more likely. A younger, fitter person would have fought back."

"Any resemblance to the injuries Kirsty MacLeod sustained?"

"He came at Kirsty from in front, too. But Kirsty's death was inflicted by one hand while he held an arm across her chest."

"And Deirdre McCann was strangled with her own scarf," Lorimer mused.

"No carbon copies of murder for you, I'm afraid. Just the killer's signature for Solly to deal with," she sighed.

"But I can tell you we are probably looking for a strong, fit person of at least average height, someone who works out, maybe. It takes a lot of strength to strangle a person who's standing upright."

Lorimer tried to picture the man in his mind. A shadowy figure that leapt at the women's throats, someone of significant strength to force them to the ground. He bit the end of his fingernail. There was something not right. He thought about the latex gloves and the security door.

Everything seemed to indicate that this was a murder where the victim had known her assailant. And had Kirsty known her attacker also? Was he in fact one of the patients at the clinic? And had he been responsible for Deirdre McCann's murder several months ago?

He felt a pulse in his temple throb against his hands as the image of Mrs Baillie came to mind. She was tall and probably strong. But was she strong enough to strangle two of her employees? Wonder what shoe size she takes, Lorimer mused, gnawing at his lip as he dismissed the idea. It had to be a man. Deirdre McCann's killer proved that. And the red carnation, as Rosie had reminded him, linked all three women. That part of the signature was known to the general public, all right, but the actual position of the praying hands was information that only the investigating team knew. Solly, Cameron, Alistair Wilson, Rosie...the list went on to include those who had discovered the bodies, he realised. And Brenda had discovered Kirsty's body.

Perhaps he should talk again to that chap from British Rail. Push a little harder. But, try as he might, he couldn't rid himself of the feeling that an answer to these murders was to be found in the Grange.

Chapter Twenty-Six

These spring mornings gave Phyllis new heart. It happened every year. Even with this disease wasting away her body, she experienced a surge of optimism each bright morning. In her waking hours Phyllis could close her eyes against the tedium of the room and see once again the avenue of trees unfurling their green leaves. By now the beech hedges would be a mass of bright green and the chestnuts would have uncurled their sticky buds. The azaleas would be a swathe of colour, the scent of the yellow blooms sweet and damp. In her mind Phyllis walked once more through the estate. She'd had dogs then, silly spaniels that raced through the woods after rabbits, real or imaginary. She smiled to hear them barking as she lay inert below the spotless sheets. Outside her window she could hear the sound of a pair of collared doves as they croo-crooed. In her mind they rose above the treetops heading towards the house. She could feel the tread of her feet on the earthen track. She could smell the wild garlic that wafted up from the banks of the stream.

Phyllis had been born at this time of year. Deep down she suspected that was why it was special to her. Other folk felt it too, she realised, opening her eyes as she heard someone singing in the corridor. It was little wonder. May was such a relief of light and colour after the long yawning stretch of grey winter months. Phyllis treasured these spring days. Would they be her last? There was no thudding of the heart as she anticipated death. Her illness was so far advanced now, realistically there couldn't be much time left. There was little more to be done. Her affairs were tidy. She was a financial burden to no one. Very few would mark her passing. Her solicitor, maybe. One or two of the staff here, perhaps. She really didn't care. Tying the house up as a clinic had been quite selfish, really, giving her a safe haven without the need to part with her own home.

In the long hours before daylight, Phyllis thought about death and what it would bring. An end to everything? Or a release into a new dimension? It was frightening to contemplate a new life free from the prison of this useless body. Not that she didn't want to believe in a life after death, an existence where her spirit swept untrammelled by flesh and bones. No. It was frightening because she wanted to believe in it so much. She had been let down by too much wanting already.

It was better to concentrate on outside. On the birds frantically feeding their young or the light that pierced the blinds and fell in shafts of dust towards the floor.

She hadn't been disturbed again by that voice or by those searching eyes. Maybe it was all over now. Maybe she'd never have to think about them again. Yet even as she tried to recapture the vision of her old garden in all its spring glory there came to mind the cries in the night and the threat that had followed.

Ellie Pearson's hands shook as she replaced the handset. That was another one calling in sick. She doubted if they'd come back at all. Not that she blamed them, really. Who'd want to work in a clinic for neural disorders where one of the patients might be a mad strangler? Stevie had been hinting only last night that she should find another post. The NHS was crying out for staff, he'd told her. Ellie had just shaken her head and tried to concentrate on *University Challenge*. She didn't want to leave. A stubborn loyalty for the Grange subdued any fears she might have. Anyway, Stevie picked her up at night now, like so many of the husbands. And the night staff all came in by taxi, Mrs Baillie had seen to that. She smiled wryly. After Ellie's own breakdown the Director of the Grange had been surprisingly sympathetic. Losing the baby had been the worst thing ever to happen to Stevie and her. The doctors had been terrific, though, really helping her to focus on positive things and to take time to mourn the baby properly. It was as if they'd all been through exactly the same kind of grief.

Ellie's eyes fell on the dust cover shrouding the computer on the reception desk. Cathy had been the first to leave and so far there was nobody to take her place. Glancing at her watch, she realised that the next shift was due in soon. She'd commandeer one of the girls to take the receptionist's place until they could find an agency temp.

A shadow on the frosted glass door made her look up a split second before the bell rang out. It would be the police. Again. They were practically on first name terms with some of them now, but not the man in charge, Chief Inspector Lorimer. There was an authority about him that made people keep their distance, Ellie thought.

"Good morning, come in," Ellie held open the door and looked up. She kept forgetting how tall the Chief Inspector was. Professional interest made her scrutinise his face.

The tired eyes were heavy with creases as if he hadn't slept much and the downturned mouth merely straightened into a polite line as he took her hand. That dark brown hair flopping over his forehead was badly needing a cut, she thought absently. Still, it was a good head of hair, not like Stevie's premature baldness. DCI Lorimer was good-looking, too, in a rugged sort of way. Ellie wondered absently if he was married. There was no sign of a wedding ring.

"Mrs Baillie's away today," Ellie told him. "So you'll have to make do with me."

Lorimer raised his eyebrows in surprise as Sister Pearson took them through the hall to the reception foyer. Now the sun filtered in through the vertical blinds casting slanted shadows across the room.

"We'd like to speak to Leigh Quinn," he began. Alistair Wilson hovered deferentially at his elbow as Lorimer waited for the Sister to reply.

"He's due to be with his psychiatrist in half an hour, will that be enough time for you?" Ellie Pearson looked at Lorimer doubtfully. The police had spent so much time interviewing staff and patients alike in the days following Kirsty's murder that she'd thought they must know about everyone by now.

"I think under the circumstances we might just take priority, Sister," Lorimer told her quietly.

Ellie felt her face begin to burn. She felt suddenly like a small child in a grown-up world that was beyond her. "Yes, yes, of course. If you'd like to wait here I'll find out where he is."

"Think you'll get anything out of him this time?" Wilson asked.

"Who knows? He was practically non-verbal last time we interviewed him. *Lost in a world of his own.* Wasn't that what his case notes said? *Post traumatic stress disorder resulting in non-communication.*" Lorimer remembered.

"What sort of treatment has he had?"

"They seem to have tried all sorts. One-to-one counselling. What did they call it? Brief therapy, or something like that. And group sessions."

"I bet they were a pure waste of time. I can't see Quinn participating in anything."

Lorimer shrugged. Solly had filled him in on some of the methods the clinic employed. His colleague, Tom Coutts, had been really helpful in that direction. Coutts was due to go to Failte, too, he thought. Perhaps he could see what the Psychology lecturer made of that experience. The patients' case notes had been made available to the team. Some of them made heavy reading; several depressed souls had tried to end it all. Those for whom life had become intolerable seemed to have reached a black hole, yet the patience and dedication of the staff here had helped not a few of them out of these pits of despair. Coutts had been lavish in his praise of the Grange. But then, it had worked for him, hadn't it? Whether Leigh Quinn, the Irishman, would succeed in throwing off his demons remained to be seen.

Lorimer had spent plenty of time reading the man's file. Born in Dublin, the son of a Union leader, there had been a background of involvement in grassroots politics, especially in the years he'd spent at university. After graduation he'd been in local government for a few years but had lost that job as a result of his heavy drinking.

That hadn't been all he'd lost, though, the case notes told Lorimer. Quinn had been married with a baby son. Both wife and child had perished in a house fire. Quinn had escaped, physically unhurt but with unseen scars that refused to heal. The file had recorded how he'd left Dublin to look for work in Glasgow. For six months he'd held down a job as a hotel porter before slipping into spells of depression that led him onto the streets. Rescued by the Simon Community, it had appeared that Quinn had tried to pull himself together but the depression had worsened until he'd been admitted to the Grange.

Lorimer had tried to make enquiries about his admission, but had drawn a blank so far. How could a down-and-out like Quinn afford the private fees demanded by a place like this? He recalled Sam Fulton. Something was going on here that didn't make any sense. How could men like that pay for such specialist attention?

His thoughts were interrupted by Sister Pearson's return.

"I've asked him to talk to you in his own room, Chief Inspector, if that's all right?"

"Fine. Thank you," Lorimer replied. The woman turned to lead them back along the corridor but Lorimer stopped her.

"Nobody on reception today?" he asked.

"Oh." The woman bit her lip. "Actually, our receptionist left us suddenly. We haven't had time to find a replacement yet."

"Did she give a reason for leaving?" Wilson asked.

Sister Pearson's shoulders slumped suddenly. "You

can't blame her really. Two nurses dead like that. We've had other resignations as well." She looked up at Lorimer, meeting his gaze defiantly. "It's hard for the patients, too. Until you catch this man they feel they're under suspicion," she said.

"Well, Sister, that's just what we're trying to do," Lorimer said quietly.

Ellie dropped her eyes. The man sounded so tired. God knows what sort of job he had to do. Of course the police would be doing their best. She looked up again. "Leigh's in here," she motioned towards an open door off the main corridor.

She rapped on the door. "Leigh. Visitors for you." Ellie pushed open the door and stood back to let Lorimer and Wilson into the room then, catching the Chief Inspector's eye, she retreated.

Behind her, Lorimer pushed the door shut. The Irishman was sitting by the bay window with his back to them. Instinctively Lorimer looked out at the trees framing the sky. Leigh Quinn's accommodation certainly didn't lack for a good view. Again the question of how he came to be there in the first place niggled at the edges of his mind. A quick look around the room showed a bed and a couple of easy chairs clad in matching turquoise fabric. The walls were painted in pale green emulsion broken up by prints of Monet's garden. A pair of slippers lay neatly by the bed and several books were piled up on the bedside table. Apart from that there were no signs of personal possessions. The man could have been a hotel guest on an overnight stay rather than a long-term patient.

"Mr Quinn," Lorimer said, expecting the man to turn at the sound of his voice but the Irishman stayed motionless as if glued to whatever he was seeing. Lorimer shifted his position so that his reflection was directly in the man's line of vision, noting a slight movement of the dark head. Even seated, he could see that Quinn was a tall man, though his frame was so gaunt that Lorimer supposed that his depression had affected his appetite.

With a nod, he motioned to Alistair Wilson and his sergeant placed himself on one side of the patient while Lorimer took a chair from the side of the bed and sat down on the other.

"Mr Quinn," he began again. "We would like to ask you some questions." The man continued to stare out of the window but Lorimer had the distinct impression that he was taking in every word.

"I went to visit Sister Angelica. She told me you had been very upset on the night Kirsty MacLeod was murdered. Can you confirm that, please?" Lorimer's voice was quiet but firm, devoid of any supplication.

Leigh Quinn turned his head and stared at Lorimer. The man was breathing in short spurts as if he'd been running hard. Was he about to suffer a panic attack? He fervently hoped not.

Then a long sigh escaped the Irishman and he shook his head wearily. "She should not have been killed," he said at last, looking away from Lorimer and gazing into his cupped hands. "She was a wee flower."

Over his head, Lorimer caught Wilson's eye.

"You were fond of Kirsty?"

The dark, shaggy head nodded again and Quinn put his hands over his eyes as if to blot out a memory.

"Sister Angelica told us she found you praying in her room. Is that right?"

The hands were still covering his eyes as the man nodded again.

Outside a blackbird called in liquid notes from the treetops, heightening the silence within the room. Lorimer waited for a moment before speaking.

"Brenda Duncan has also been killed, Leigh. Did you know that?" Lorimer's voice dropped to a conspiratorial whisper. He saw the man's head nod into his hands.

"Who told you?"

Quinn took his hands away from his eyes, clasping them together on his knees. "A nurse."

"Have you been out of the clinic in the last two days, Leigh? For a long walk maybe?" Alistair Wilson asked, diverting the man's attention from Lorimer.

Quinn's head turned towards the sergeant, a puzzled frown on his pallid face.

"Do you know where Brenda lives, maybe?"

Quinn's face froze in sudden understanding.

"No. I've been for...walks, sure," he began slowly, stumbling over his words. "Not out of the grounds." He shook his head and turned to Lorimer as if this was something he should know.

"Can anybody confirm this?" Wilson persisted. Quinn shook his head, his eyes still fixed on Lorimer's. The man's gaze was shrewd, Lorimer thought. He knows fine what we're asking him.

"Do you remember the night before last, Leigh? It was pouring with rain," Lorimer asked.

Leigh Quinn pushed back the chair and stood up, putting his hands out against the glass of the window. Lorimer watched as the man's breath clouded up in little circles against the cold pane. Wilson started as if he was going to pull him back down but Lorimer raised a hand and shook his head, seeing Quinn push his face right up against the glass.

What was the gesture meant to signify, he wondered, suddenly wishing that he had Solly Brightman there in the room. Was the Irishman trying to escape from them or was he simply trying to make the two policemen disappear?

"You're not thinking of leaving the Grange, are you, Leigh?" Lorimer asked suddenly.

He heard a sniff from the man and a muffled "No" then watched as the man rested his head on his forearms and began to sob.

Lorimer stayed still. Were those tears of remorse? Or was Leigh Quinn still grieving for a young Island girl who'd befriended so many of the patients here? He waited until the sobs quietened. Quinn pulled out a pocket-handkerchief and blew his nose then slumped back down on the chair.

"I didn't kill anyone," he sighed. "That's what you're thinking, though." He looked across at Lorimer, defeat in his eyes.

"We need to check the whereabouts of everybody who was here two nights ago," Lorimer told him. "If you can find somebody who would vouch for your presence here from eight-thirty onwards, that would be a help."

Quinn nodded then stared back into space.

"Can you?"

There was no reply as the Irishman failed to react. He'd said all he was going to say, for now, Lorimer realised, watching the dark eyes glaze over. Even so, having him talk at all was a major breakthrough. He signalled to Wilson and they got up to leave. Turning before he left the room, Lorimer saw the face of Leigh Quinn reflected in the glass like a faded print, the luminous eyes unblinking.

"Chief Inspector." Lorimer turned to see Ellie Pearson hovering in the corridor.

She beckoned them with a finger as if afraid to disturb the silence in the room. "Dr Richards would like a word with you." Lorimer and Wilson followed her down the corridor to a room simply marked "Staff."

Sister Pearson knocked and opened the door. "Dr Richards. Chief Inspector Lorimer and Sergeant Wilson."

Lorimer smiled. Solly had told him about this psychiatrist. A miracle worker, Tom Coutts had called him. Perhaps Leigh Quinn's ability to verbalise had more to do with the doctor's expertise than a sudden need to defend himself.

A man of medium build, with thinning hair and a pair of half-moon glasses perched on his nose rose from behind his desk to greet them. "Maxwell Richards," he said, hand grasping Lorimer's firmly. "Chief Inspector, thank you for giving me a little of your time. Gentlemen, please sit down. Ellie, is there any chance of some tea or coffee?" He beamed at the Sister before turning his attention to the two men before him. Lorimer took in the dark pin-striped suit and pink polka-dot bow-tie. On Maxwell Richards the ensemble was sartorial rather than effete, he realised. He looked like a psychiatrist and somehow that immediately dispelled any mystique. Lorimer found himself warming towards the man who continued to smile at him.

"You came in to see Leigh, I believe?"

"That's correct, sir."

"Perhaps I can fill you in on my patient, gentlemen. He won't have spoken much to you?"

Richards' eyebrows rose questioningly above the glasses. "No, I thought not," he continued as Lorimer hesitated. "Let me see. Where should I begin?" he mused, steepling his fingers and twirling his thumbs around as he considered.

"Perhaps you might tell us how Quinn came to be here in the first place," Lorimer broke in.

"Ah, I wondered if somebody might ask me that. Hm. Confidential, really, but in the circumstances…" Dr Richards took off his spectacles and rubbed the side of his nose before replacing them. "The Logan Trust," he began. "It was set up by the owner of the Grange some time ago. When she was still in charge of all her faculties, you understand."

"Phyllis Logan? The Multiple Sclerosis patient?"

"Indeed. Phyllis established her Trust to enable the clinic to treat people with neural disorders. There are funds set aside for several patients who could not otherwise afford our fees. Leigh Quinn is one such," Dr Richards explained.

Lorimer nodded. Sam Fulton, no doubt, would be another.

"Why should she do something like that?" Wilson wanted to know. "I'd have thought she'd have given preference to MS patients like herself."

Dr Richards smiled. "Yes. One would think so but there are aspects of her life that make such provisions understandable," he hesitated to look closely from Wilson to Lorimer. "This is in the strictest confidence, of course, gentlemen," he added. "Phyllis Logan's husband committed suicide after suffering depression for many years. Giving help to other people has been a sort of catharsis for her."

Lorimer nodded. That explained a lot.

"Doesn't she have any family?" Wilson asked.

Dr Richards shook his head. "No, nor many friends. Since her illness she has become something of a recluse. The clinic was set up to give her a permanent home with the best of care. She is very well looked after here."

Lorimer picked something almost defensive in the man's tone. Had there been any comments made to the contrary?

"What happens when, well," Wilson hesitated, "when she goes?"

"Ownership of the Trust reverts to the Grange and its Directors."

"I see."

"Leigh Quinn," Lorimer put in. "What can you tell us about him?"

Dr Richards sat back in his chair. "Well, now. What can I say that you haven't read in his case notes? He's basically a very kind man. He cares about other people far more than he cares about himself. You'll have noticed that already, though. His personal grooming is quite neglected. Not a materialistic sort of man at all, though he does value his books," Dr Richards smiled. "He actually has a soft spot for Phyllis," he went on. "Goes into her room to sit with her. As far as we know he doesn't say anything, just sits or rearranges her flowers."

Lorimer stiffened. The image of Brenda Duncan's

cold hands clasping that solitary red carnation came unbidden into his mind.

Richards continued as if he hadn't noticed the policeman's discomfiture. "He is usually very withdrawn. Didn't communicate at all when I first met him. But he does keep a diary."

"Oh, yes?" Lorimer was suddenly interested.

"Yes. But he scores everything out and begins again each day. Not a healthy sign, I'm afraid. The denial of his day-by-day experiences, I mean. Perhaps one day he'll allow himself to acknowledge that he has a life. Meantime he seems to find solace in the world of nature. He takes long walks by himself. My colleague in the Simon Community tells me that he used to spend hours simply staring into the river."

Dr Richards clasped his hands on the desk in front of him and fixed Lorimer with a penetrating stare. "What you really want me to tell you, of course, is if I consider Leigh Quinn capable of murder."

"And is he?"

"In my opinion, no. There's a gentleness about the man that I think precludes any ability to hurt another person. Besides, he's been diagnosed as suffering from manic depression. He's not psychotic."

"And would you be prepared to stand up in court and say this?"

"Of course. But I don't really believe you're going to charge Leigh with murder, Chief Inspector."

Lorimer clenched his teeth. There certainly wasn't enough evidence for that but there were coincidences that bore further scrutiny, like the flowers in Phyllis Logan's room and the image of the man on his knees after Kirsty's death.

Psychiatrists had been wrong before, in his experience. No matter how highly this one was rated, he might not be correct in his assessment of the Irishman.

Chapter Twenty-Seven

The embankment was covered in brambles and elder saplings pushing up through the litter that seemed to grow like some perennial weed. No matter how often he picked it up and bagged it, the cans, papers and other foul stuff simply returned. His legs were beginning to ache from walking along the steep slope for so long. Trying to keep balanced while holding the sack in one hand and the grabbers in the other made unreasonable demands on his calves and thigh muscles. Still, there was a sense of duty in it all. He was performing a cleansing task. The green would re-emerge once he'd cleared the rubbish away and someone travelling along might see God's gift of beauty in the wee flowers that were struggling to appear. All along the track itself were pink weeds that threw out their suckers year after year. How they survived the trains sweeping over them, he couldn't imagine. But they were brave, these little flowers, and persistent, like himself.

He felt a glow of pleasure as he thought of his work. To clean up the embankments was not his only occupation, oh, no. Sighing with pride, he recalled the voice that had appointed him to rid the stations of other foul weeds.

Then, as if to spoil his morning, a sudden memory of the woman and her temptations shamed him.

She'd lured him towards his sin. But this time he wouldn't weaken. All through the cold months of winter he'd waited for a sign and then had acted upon it. Now he felt the restlessness that had preceded that first sign. Was it time to commit another act of cleansing?

Chapter Twenty-Eight

It was time to come clean. All day Maggie had felt a restlessness that had more to do with guilt than with the anticipation of Lorimer's reaction. More than once she'd found a pair of eyes staring at her from the rows of desks, waiting for a reply to a question she'd never even heard. It was totally unlike her not to be on the ball. Not within the sheltered haven of her own classroom, anyhow. She'd fought for months to have her own room, a place where she could keep papers and books, where she could work undisturbed. There was a poster opposite her desk, just above eye level. It was a souvenir from last year's trip to Stratford. They'd taken the Fifth and Sixth Years in the slot after exam leave and before they all scooted off for the summer. It had been an idyllic interlude for the kids, and for Maggie. She'd felt a hundred years younger walking through the cobbled streets with those kids. The weather last June had been hot and breezy. If she thought about it hard enough she could still conjure up the feeling of her long linen skirt wrapping itself around her legs and her hair blowing free as they'd walked along the banks of the Avon. But the memory that stuck longest was the sense of disappointment at having to come home to an empty house.

As ever, her husband had been out on some police matter or other.

Maggie had wept that night in sheer frustration at having no one, no one at all to communicate her days of pleasure and nights of magic, transported by the spell of The Bard. It wasn't the same to phone her old mum, even if she'd been awake at that hour. She'd wanted someone to talk to; a soulmate who would hold her in his arms and look at her in understanding of all she had to tell. She'd wanted Lorimer.

The clock on the wall told her it was high time she took herself out of there. The rush hour traffic would be its usual slow, gas-guzzling mass with motorists caught between rolling back the sunroofs or cooling themselves with recycled air. Maggie made a sour face. It was all right for Lorimer with his Lexus. Ancient it might be, but the comfort and air-conditioning were there okay. Still she sat on, torn between a desire to have it all over and done with and a fear at what he would say. What would he say? She'd gone over and over this question for days, steeling herself to come to this moment of truth.

Maggie stretched herself and pushed back the metal chair. Okay. She'd do it. Now. Tonight. She was sure he'd be home tonight. After how tired he'd been he would try to come home at a reasonable hour. Surely. Maggie straightened her back and gave her dark curls a shake. She was going to America for a year and her husband would just have to accept it.

Jo Grant's brow creased in a frown as she scrolled up the list of figures. Lorimer had been right. There was something out of order in the clinic's accounts. At first she'd assumed that the Logan Trust had been responsible for the gaps, but they were way too frequent and didn't tally properly. She could see that now. Jo gave a smile.

I.T. had a way of showing up things that could save hours of old-fashioned detective work. She pressed the print button. Lorimer would like this. There were several large sums of money missing from the Grange's accounts. The patients' fees simply weren't covering the expenditure. Someone had been on the fiddle, she guessed. Her years in the fraud squad had given Jo a nose for that sort of thing.

"We need to see the clinic's own paperwork," Lorimer told her. "Mrs Baillie keeps the records. See what you can worm out of her."

He watched as Jo left the room. She was good, that one; sharp as a needle. He'd felt there was something wrong about the finances and now she'd proved him right. But was there any link to the murders? Lorimer leaned back in his chair, swivelling it back and forth as he pondered. Mrs Baillie had been so tight with information. She'd also shown little real remorse after the deaths of her two nurses. He'd like to be a fly on the wall when DI Grant started to ask more questions. The Procurator Fiscal had issued a new warrant to search locked premises so Mrs Baillie couldn't refuse access to any of the clinic's files. Lorimer smiled to himself. Something was beginning to unfold.

Maggie had prepared a pot of chicken broth. It was totally unseasonable but she had felt the need for comfort food and the soothing feeling that came from cutting up the vegetables as she'd listened to Classic FM. Now the soup was congealing in the pressure cooker as she waited for the sound of his car.

She'd rehearsed over and over in her mind what she would say to him, but she still jumped nervously as the Lexus braked in the drive below. She could hear him take the stairs two at a time as if eager to be back home.

"Hey, something smells good. That wouldn't be one of your brilliant soups by any chance?"

Suddenly he was there and Maggie shrank back into a corner of the kitchen as if seeking refuge by the cooker.

She turned to face him, tried to smile and failed miserably.

"Mags?" Lorimer reached out for her, immediately sensing her distress.

One moment she was in his arms and the next she was struggling to be free of him, angrily pushing him away. Lorimer took a step backwards, trying to see his wife's expression but Maggie had turned away. He stood, hands helplessly by his side.

"What the hell's going on?"

"I'm sorry." Maggie looked at him, seeing the puzzled, hurt look in his eyes then, she took a deep breath. "I think we'd better talk." She motioned through to the sitting room.

Lorimer sat on the edge of the sofa but Maggie chose the armchair opposite as if touching him would somehow weaken her resolve. He watched her chest heave in a sigh that made him want to fold her up into his arms.

Her eyes were cast down towards the carpet as she spoke. "I've applied for a new post. A temporary post. It's just for a year. An exchange, actually." Maggie's voice rose in a squeak that betrayed her nervousness. She looked up to see her husband frowning at her, trying to figure out what she meant.

There was a tentative smile hovering around Maggie's mouth as she told him.

"I'm going to America."

"What?" Lorimer stared at his wife in disbelief. He wanted to replay that last moment, let her words sink in. America? She hadn't just said that, had she?

There was a silence between them that seemed to go on and on. In the silence Lorimer's worst fears about his marriage were brought to the surface like scum on a pot of bubbling stock. What was she saying? He listened numbly as Maggie suddenly rattled on about teaching opportunities and career advancement. He wasn't hearing this properly at all. All he could think of was that he felt like she'd swung a wet dishrag across his face.

"Hang on. Let me get this right. You want to spend a year abroad. On your own?" He heard his voice rise in protest. When he spoke again the words came out in a mere whisper. "Why? Why do you have to do this, Mags?"

"For me. I've wanted to do something like this all my life. Can't you understand? I'm tired. So tired. All the time I wait for you to come home. I feel as if I've spent, no let's be truthful about this, I've *wasted* so much of my own life. You're never here. I want to talk to you. I want to spend my evenings with you. Oh, I know all about the pressure of police work. Believe me I've tried so hard to put up and shut up."

Lorimer flinched at the bitterness in her voice.

"I need to do something for myself. Before I end up simply an appendage of DCI Lorimer."

"Maggie, this is beginning to sound all very mid-life crisis to me," Lorimer began.

"Don't you dare start to tell me I'm becoming menopausal or whatever. Just don't dare!" Maggie's eyes were so fierce with passion that Lorimer sank back against the sofa cushions wondering what on earth to say next.

"What have I got that's my own? Eh? Tell *me* that? A job. A house. Okay we couldn't have kids. No one's fault. I'm not trying to lay any blame. All I want is a year to myself doing something I might enjoy." Her eyes were pleading with him now. "Don't you understand? I want to be me. Do something on my own."

What about us? Lorimer wanted to say, but something he couldn't define stopped him from uttering the words. Instead, in a voice stiff with emotion, he asked, "And at the end of the year?"

Maggie shrugged her shoulders. Her eyes were focused on the pattern of the carpet again. "We'll see."

Lorimer took a deep breath. He spent a lot of his working life trying hard to put himself into the shoes of other people; victims of crime, hoods, murderers, witnesses too scared to speak. But it seemed he'd failed to empathise where it mattered most, in his own home. He gazed sideways out of the window at the still clear blue sky. America. Suddenly a thought struck him.

"Why America? This wouldn't have anything to do with that woman, Lipinski, would it?"

Seeing Maggie's expression gave him his answer. "I might have known! She's been encouraging you to make a break for freedom. Is that it?"

"Don't you think I've got a mind of my own? Okay so Divine told me a bit about Florida and, yes, that's where I'm going on an exchange. But you're entirely wrong in imagining that she put me up to it," Maggie snapped back at him. Then her face softened as she added, "I wouldn't be doing this if I didn't want to."

Lorimer nodded. He wouldn't let this escalate into a row. Looking at his wife's face he realised how important this moment was. If he made too much fuss then he could alienate her all together. All his expertise as a police officer had taught him that he must play this quietly. The best thing now was to reassure her, not to let her see how she'd hurt him.

"Right. Come over here and tell me about it all over again," he patted the sofa cushion beside him.

Maggie hesitated for a fraction of a second then got up to join him. Lorimer resisted the urge to hold her tight and simply took her hand, giving it a friendly squeeze.

He tried to make out that he was listening carefully as she told him all over again; about the job in Sarasota, about the high school system, about the accommodation being made available to her, and about the holidays.

"I could see you at Christmas," she whispered, a little sadly.

"I should hope so," Lorimer replied, his tone light, belying the heaviness he really felt inside.

Chapter Twenty-Nine

It was a perfect night. The moon had slid behind the blue-black clouds leaving just the glow from city streetlamps shining on the parked cars. He leaned against the wall and waited. There was no hurry and certainly no fear of being seen. Apart from the fact that the CCTV cameras didn't work in the staff car park, he was simply part of the natural background of the station, a railway worker going about his lawful business.

He shivered, anticipating the real business of the night. It was more lawful than anyone could guess, commanded by the highest authority. The woman had been hanging around for three nights in succession, eyeing up the stragglers from the last Edinburgh train, flashing her bare legs around the taxi rank. She'd disappeared with a man every night and somehow he knew she would keep coming back. A quick glance at his watch told him it was nearly time.

He heard her high heels click-clacking over the pavement before he saw her walking briskly towards the automatic doors, her short red skirt riding up against those white thighs.

"Hey!" he called out softly and grinned as he saw her pause mid-stride and peer into the darkness.

Moving out of the shadow he waved his hand, gave a flick of the head indicating that she should come over.

As she smoothed down her skirt and sashayed over he could see that she was younger than he'd thought. A momentary qualm was quickly replaced by disgust at how much she'd sullied her youthfulness. The grin on his face was a rictus. It would never do to reveal how he really felt towards her. The woman stopped in front of him, flicking back her white-blonde hair, a black shoulder bag clutched tightly with one hand. He could see beyond the caved-in cheekbones and the dull eyes to the girl she might have been before she'd chosen this way of life. With one crooked finger he beckoned her further into the shadows.

"Ye wantae do the bis'ness?" She was chewing gum, her jaw moving in wide circular movements. The sound of saliva slapping against her tongue was like a dog wolfing its meat. Something turned in his stomach.

He swallowed hard, nodded and took the woman's arm. "Over here," he said, leading her into the shadows of a small building tacked on to the back of the station. It was where all the green rubbish bins were corralled together behind a mesh fence. A padlock swung loose on its hasp.

"Ah'm no gonnae go in therr," she protested, tugging against his grip.

"Aw, c'mon," he coaxed. "Give's a kiss." With one hand he swung open the gate and pushed her inside the compound, his body already hard against hers. There was no struggle as his mouth enclosed her thin lips, more an acquiescence. He could feel her body relent as he pulled her hands around his waist, walking her slowly over to the nearest bin.

It was when she fumbled for his zip that he uncoiled the scarf from his neck and slipped it around her throat.

The "Noooooooo!" was cut off abruptly as the ligature tightened. He felt her body struggle against his in a passion that had nothing to do with sex any more. Her leg came up in a vain attempt to lash out at his crotch but he side-stepped, hanging on to the scarf, yanking against it with all his strength. Suddenly a gurgling noise issued from her throat and she buckled under his grasp. He let go and she fell to the ground with a soft thump.

He took a step back, looking at her for a moment then knelt beside her. The grin that hadn't left his face was like a mask now, something he couldn't remove. Not yet. There was still the ceremony to perform.

He clasped her fingers straight within his own, glad of the leather that separated their flesh. How small they were, the warmth seeping through the gloves. He was aware of these things even as he uttered the prayer. The words that he spoke were of forgiveness for sins. She would not commit any more acts of depravity. Sitting back on his heels, he turned to look for the package that he'd left here earlier that evening. It was still there, hidden under the concrete edge of the shed. He slid it out and unwrapped the carnation from its cellophane wrapper. There were tears in his eyes as he forced the stem between her dead palms. It was such a lovely flower, so fresh and sweet. But it was a mark that she was saved now. They would find her and know she'd been redeemed.

He rubbed his gloved hands against his trousers as he stood up. Finished. He was done. The gate made virtually no sound as he fastened the padlock onto its hasp.

It was only a short walk back to the car and there was nobody about to see him slip into the driver's seat. He peeled off the heavy gloves, letting them fall to the floor. There would be new ones issued tomorrow, unsullied by her kind of filth.

Two black cabs turning into the area made him stop for a moment. Then he released the brake and drove slowly out of the station, up the hill towards Cathedral Street and away, his night's work complete.

Chapter Thirty

They'd arranged to meet late afternoon. Solly would be free by four o'clock, he'd said, but Lorimer knew from past experience that he was rarely on time. He'd taken the clockwork orange (which was the locals' name for the Glasgow Underground) as far as Hillhead station, deciding to stroll along Byres road to clear his head.

The woman's body had been identified as Geraldine Lynch. She was a known prostitute in that area, the railway staff had said. Already there were punters coming forward with information about her. Lorimer's mouth hardened. She'd been dead for hours before they'd found her, dumped beside the huge industrial rubbish bins at the back of Queen Street station. One of the Transport officers had made the discovery. That, at least, had had the advantage of keeping the area sealed properly for forensics.

There had been an angry scene outside the Gazette's offices, girls and women who had known Geraldine Lynch and Deirdre McCann making their presence felt. Jimmy Greer's piece about Glasgow prostitutes had enraged them. None of them ever denied what they did, but to have the city's newspaper deriding them the way Greer had done was particularly insensitive. It was the usual ploy, Lorimer guessed, to generate letters to the editor.

The Police liaison team had invited the women into Pitt Street to discuss their security. It was doubtful that many would turn up, though. These Glasgow girls liked to think themselves tough, and some of them were, but others were just wee lassies finding themselves at the bottom of the drugs spiral.

Lorimer tried to rid his mind of the murdered girl's face as he walked along the road, taking note of the shops and buildings. Much of the area had changed dramatically since his own student days, but there were still landmark pubs like the Rubaiyat further down where he was to meet Solly, and of course the Curlers next to the Underground. They'd been revamped over the years but they continued to provide that ethos of camaraderie and heavy drinking a student clientele had come to expect.

Outside the station Lorimer side-stepped the flower vendor with his basket of brightly coloured blooms. He paused for a second. He'd never been in the habit of buying flowers for Maggie except on the rare occasions when they'd been supermarket shopping together. The vendor, a slim boy with lank, dark hair, caught his eye even as Lorimer hesitated.

"Nice roses. Two bunches for a fiver?" the boy held up several bunches of the long-stemmed blooms for Lorimer to see.

"No thanks," he shook his head briefly, eyeing the single carnations stuck into a green bucket. Inquiries had been made all over the city. This boy had probably been questioned more than once. Should he stop and buy some flowers for Maggie? He had walked away from the stall even as the thought crossed his mind. No, they'd only wither by the time he reached home, he argued with himself. Anyway, she'd maybe think he was trying to apologise for something.

As Lorimer waited for the lights to change on the corner of University Avenue his attention wandered to the shops on the other side of the road. On day-glo orange stickers, Going Places travel agency was proclaiming cut-price fares to Florida. He could always see what flights were available in October, say?

The lights changed to the wee green man and Lorimer strode across, his mind drifting away from fares and flights to Geraldine Lynch. The only place she would be going was into Rosie Fergusson's postmortem room.

As he crossed over, his eye was caught by three older men deep in conversation. Two had greying beards compensating for what they lacked on top and the third was a tall, angular fellow whose mane of white hair made him an imposing figure.

Three academics, Lorimer smiled to himself as they swept past. They still seemed to favour baggy linen jackets and distressed leather briefcases, just like his old Prof. He'd felt at home here once, Lorimer realised. What would life have been like if he'd pursued his original studies to their conclusion? Would he have ferreted into all the intricacies of Art History instead of investigating contemporary crimes? Would Maggie have been happier married to an academic?

Walking in the direction of Partick, he caught sight of another familiar landmark. The newsagent was still there. Lorimer saw with a pang that several youngsters were busy taking down details of flats to let from the cards in the window. This unofficial letting agency had been there for as long as he could remember. He had a sudden memory of standing in the pouring rain in his ancient duffel coat scanning the cards for a room to let where he and Maggie could set up home. They'd talked such a lot about moving in together but it had never happened.

Instead Lorimer had left university for his police training while Maggie had finished her degree. They'd done the conventional thing after all, working and saving to buy the house before they'd finally married. His young man's dream of a love nest had been set aside when he'd left the university world behind for the new experiences of the police force.

The pub on the corner seemed caught in a time warp, Lorimer thought as he pushed open the door. The Rubaiyat might have a name that conjured up a literary world but it wasn't so far from the traditional spit and sawdust. The same scuffed brass foot rail had been there in his day and although the banquettes were newer, their vivid patterns continued the attempt at evoking the idea of ancient Persia. Lorimer ordered a pint and settled into the curved seat opposite the door.

"Lorimer. Hallo," Solly's face displayed his usual boyish grin as he caught sight of him. Seemingly oblivious to the warmer weather, he was wearing a long gabardine raincoat over his leather jacket; he unravelled himself from these layers of clothing, discarding them in a heap over his bulging briefcase.

Lorimer smiled. Solly would never change.

"What are you having?"

"Ah. Something nice and cold. I don't mind," he answered vaguely.

"White wine? Beer? Orange juice?"

"Yes, lovely," he replied.

Lorimer raised his eyes to heaven and ordered another pint for himself and a glass of squash for Solly.

"So," Solly suddenly put the drink down, giving Lorimer a considered look. "We have another young woman who's been strangled."

Lorimer sighed. "I can't believe four women have been killed and we've no trace of their killer."

"No," Solly replied. "It's a difficult one." There was a pause as he seemed to examine his glass carefully, then he placed it on the table and shifted close towards Lorimer. "More difficult than I think you realise."

"Oh? How's that?" Lorimer looked at Solly. There was something familiar in the sad smile, something that told him Solly was about to be the bearer of bad news, as if he hadn't enough to contend with.

"We don't have one killer. We have two."

Lorimer nodded slowly. It was something that he'd fleetingly considered himself. "That would be a lovely idea, pal, but how do you account for the modus operandi? Besides, the guy places flowers into her praying hands each time. Same signature."

"But a different locus. And a different type of victim," Solly tapped the edge of the table to underline his point.

"Granted. But how can you explain the hands? Even the Press didn't get hold of a picture of any of the bodies. Their mock-up shows a different position altogether. It has to be one and the same person who's carrying out these killings."

"I don't agree," Solly told him quietly. He heaved a sigh. "The whole picture didn't make sense from the time of Kirsty MacLeod's death. I simply couldn't build a profile. Now I think I know why. There are two people to profile, not one."

Solly watched as the policeman's mouth set in a

grim line. The murder case sat heavily on his shoulders. Until they could solve it there would be a feeling of inadequacy heightened by something he couldn't yet put his finger on, an extra weight that he was bearing. His energies were directed at finishing off this job if he could. That was good for the case and good for Strathclyde CID, but was it good for William Lorimer?

Just then a crowd of students piled into the pub, their voices loud with post-exam relief. Soon it would be standing room only in the Rubaiyat.

Lorimer bent forwards, suddenly aware of any ears that might be tuning into their conversation. "Look, why not finish off here and we'll go for a walk? Fancy the Botanics? It's a nice night."

Solly nodded and raised his glass. The two men sat back opposite one another, drinking in a silence that was full of questions.

"We'd have to check all the members of the team, too," Lorimer told him. "If your theory's correct, and I'm not saying you're wrong, then someone inside the investigation has let slip details of the signature." Lorimer didn't dare voice any other thoughts than that. Carelessness, that was the only crime any of his team could be guilty of, wasn't it?

"It could have been the railwayman who discovered the first victim," Solly reminded him.

Lorimer gnawed a raggle on his fingernail. Nobody had noticed the flower until he'd arrived at the scene. Still, it was worth checking out. "If the nurses have been killed by a copycat killer then we're still left with a helluva lot of questions. Like, why?"

Solly didn't reply. He was walking slowly along the

path, face towards the ground as if he was looking for a lost penny. Lorimer glanced sideways at him.

What was going on in that brain? He'd given the psychologist the benefit of the doubt and, in an uneasy way, he felt he was on to something.

"What about the prostitutes, then?"

Solly looked up and stopped, smiling sadly. "Oh, that's easy, I'm afraid. The killer is suffering from some kind of delusions. Religious delusions. Fairly common, I have to say. He's probably hearing voices telling him to take away the bad women of the night."

"A religious nut, then? What we thought all along?"

"Yes. And I think this latest crime shows he's definitely got a link with Queen Street station."

"The staff car park's close circuit camera is out of order," Lorimer told him gloomily.

"There. Have a closer look at who has access to that area at night. Or even during the day."

"Anything else?"

"If forensics haven't found any DNA matches between railway personnel then maybe you could dig a little deeper into each member of staff's background."

"What are you looking for?"

"White, single male. Thirty to forty. There's possibly a history of being in an institution. I suppose he must have a car, too," Solly mused, stroking his beard absently as if he were seeing a shadowy figure in the recesses of his mind.

"And the other murders?"

"Ah. Now that's more difficult. We're dealing with somebody very clever indeed."

"Someone inside the Grange?"

Solly frowned before answering. "I'm not sure. It's possible, but then again…" he trailed off.

"Look, why don't we go for a curry? See if we can get into the Ashoka?" Perhaps with some food inside him Solly would become more expansive, he thought. Besides, Lorimer wasn't in the mood to go home just yet.

It was dark by the time the taxi drew up outside the house. Maggie stumbled a little in her high heels as she tried to tip-toe to the door. She failed to see the swish of curtains from upstairs as her key turned in the lock.

Her husband appeared to be asleep when she crept into the bedroom.

Maggie slipped easily out of her skirt and top, letting them fall onto the carpet. She was unfastening her suspenders when Lorimer spoke suddenly, making her jump.

"Been out on the town?"

"Good God! You gave me a fright. I thought you were asleep."

Lorimer half sat up, regarding his wife in the darkness. She saw him shake his head.

There was a silence as she finished drawing off the stockings and underwear, a silence that was charged with embarrassment as if he had no right to be watching her. She fished out a nightdress from under the pillow and slipped it hastily over her head. His eyes were still on her as she climbed into bed beside him. There was a continued silence that was full of unspoken questions about where she'd been, who she'd been with.

Heaving a sigh, Maggie gave in.

"I was out at the Rogano having a drink with Sheilagh. Okay?"

There was no reply. She turned her head towards him and in the darkness she could make out the smell of onions on his breath.

"Been out for a curry?"

Lorimer gave a laugh. "Want to join my team, Sherlock? Or is it that obvious?"

Maggie giggled, the tension suddenly evaporating. "You stink! You always eat far too many spiced onions," she complained.

"I was seeing Solly," Lorimer said, as if that was an explanation for the state of his breath.

"And?"

"He's got this idea that we're dealing with two separate killers."

Maggie twisted towards him, interested in spite of herself. "And is he right?"

Lorimer lay back on the pillows, one hand behind his head. "I don't know. If he is, though, I may have to start looking a lot closer to home."

"You mean someone in the force?"

Maggie could hear her husband sigh in the darkness. It was a sigh that went all the way through him. She snuggled up closer, her cold skin touching Lorimer's warm body. He didn't answer her question but wrapped an arm round her shoulders, pulling the duvet in tighter to keep her cosy.

There was nothing sexual in his action, it was a gesture of pure affection, the kind of thing she'd been missing for so long. After only a few minutes Lorimer's breathing became heavier and Maggie knew he was asleep. Still he held her close, folded into his arm. So why did she feel that overwhelming sense of loneliness?

As Maggie laid her head against his chest she felt the tears hot against her lashes.

Chapter Thirty-One

It was already daylight and he'd only slept for about three hours but Lorimer felt wide awake as he lay on his back staring at the bright gap in the curtains. He'd been dreaming about the St Mungo's case. In his dream he was being chased by a figure in the park that had somehow turned into to Maggie. He'd woken with a start, relieved to see her sleeping soundly by his side. But it had got him thinking.

He remembered the moment in that other case when he'd suddenly realised he'd been looking at things all the wrong way round. Maybe he was doing it again. Lateral thinking, he told himself. Open up your mind.

The image of the rusted railing leading to the basement of the Grange came back to him. If the killer had come in that way then how had he crept up on Kirsty? Lorimer traced the whole route in his mind from the stairs leading into the corridor and through the double doors leading to the main building. No. Wait a minute. There was something missing. The room where Phyllis Logan lay, her body full of tubes. Lorimer recalled those bright eyes. She couldn't talk, he'd been told. But nobody had said she couldn't hear, had they?

For a moment he lay quite still. They'd interviewed the other residents, but not her. Was it worth a try? If the woman had heard something maybe there could be a way of finding out what it was?

Phyllis felt the sun warming her hands. She observed them on the white cuff of the sheet, drained of colour in the brightness, thin membranes stretched over knobs of bone. Her nails grew hard and gnarled, pale ochre, the colour of an animal's hoof. It was an irony (one of many she'd noted with a bitter smile) that she'd suffered split and brittle nails in her younger days when such small vanities had mattered, and now her fingernails grew strong and hard when nothing like that was of any importance. It was simply a result of the drugs she had to take. That's what young Kirsty had told her.

Phyllis remembered her lilting voice and the way she'd made conversation as if Phyllis could actually answer her back. She'd felt easy and comfortable with that young girl. She'd longed to be able to talk to her, to share some of her own past, the way Kirsty had shared hers. She knew all about the drowned father, the loss of her mum, the growing up years she'd spent on the croft with her old auntie. They'd been kindred spirits in some ways, though she'd never been able to tell Kirsty that of course. Phyllis, too, had been a solitary child. No brothers or sisters. She wondered what life would have been like having siblings. Would they have cared for her at home? Or would she have ended up staying here, no matter what? The ideas she pushed around her head were totally objective. Phyllis was long past the stage of self-pity. Yet it was pity she felt for Kirsty. Pity and grief that her young life had been so cruelly cut short.

A spasm passed through her hand, making it flicker with a sudden illusion of life. It was a nervous shudder, no more. The sun must have passed behind a cloud for the warmth had gone out of the room and now her hands were like two dead fish, pale and untwitching.

Phyllis turned her eyes at the noise of swing doors

opening and shutting a small distance away. She could hear voices. There were people coming along her corridor, a man and Maureen Baillie. She couldn't mistake her voice. She was in and out of Phyllis's room quite often these days, making sure everything was in order.

Mrs Baillie didn't knock.

She watched the woman stride into the room, hands bunched into fists at her side. There was a determined set to her jaw as she spoke.

"This is Chief Inspector Lorimer, Phyllis. He's investigating the events that happened here. He'd like to talk to you. Is that all right?"

Phyllis's eyes travelled over the man as he came into view. She saw a tall figure whose dark hair straggled over his collar. She focused on the face. There was a certain weariness etched into the lines around his mouth but the eyes that regarded her were a bright, unforgettable blue. It was him. The one who'd come before. That night. So he was a policeman, was he? That pleased her. She liked to know who was on her side.

Lorimer had noticed that the Director had failed to knock but simply swept into the room and now stood with her back to the window. He looked from her face, which was in shadow, to the immobile figure in the bed. The eyes looked back at him, unflickering. Lorimer saw a keen intelligence there.

Mrs Baillie folded her arms, looking as if she were waiting for Lorimer to begin. Just then there was a light tap on the door. PC Annie Irvine stepped into the room, a large square bag slung over her shoulder. The policewoman smiled then gave a nod to the Director. Lorimer stood aside to let her move into a position where Phyllis could see her.

"You can go now, Mrs Baillie. My officer will let you know if there's anything we need. Thank you." Lorimer held the door open as if to emphasise the point. She wasn't wanted. Police interviews were conducted in private, no matter what the circumstances.

Mrs Baillie looked as if she might argue the toss but a glance at Lorimer's face showed she'd decided against it. They heard the sound of her feet quietly padding down the corridor as Lorimer closed the door.

"Here's a couple of chairs, sir," Annie had spotted the grey stacking chairs and was lifting them over the side of Phyllis's bed. "Is it okay, ma'am?" she added, looking directly at Phyllis.

The woman in the bed gave a tiny nod and Lorimer saw a faint smile play about her lips. Maybe this wouldn't be so impossible after all. He positioned his chair close to the bed so that the woman and he were facing one another.

"Hallo again," he began. "You do remember me, don't you?" His tone was gentle but firm. He didn't intend to insult her by being condescending. There was nothing worse for disabled folk than being talked down to like children. She gave that slight nod again and her smile deepened.

"The last time I was here it was to investigate the death of a nurse, Kirsty MacLeod," he continued, still gazing at her face, her penetrating eyes.

She closed them and opened them again. Was she trying to blot out the memory of that night? He hoped she wouldn't, for his sake and for Kirsty's.

"May I ask you about that night?"

Phyllis frowned at him as if he'd said something out of place so he added quickly, "Look, I know you can't talk to me, but I'd like to think we can communicate all the same. Give a nod if you mean "yes". Close your eyes if it's a "no". Can you do that?"

There was a tiny movement of the woman's head that Lorimer took to be a nod. Lorimer turned to Annie, who was busy unpacking the video camera she'd brought.

"We'd like to make a recording of this interview. It's a little unorthodox, perhaps, but then your situation is, let's say, a bit different."

The woman had her gaze trained on his, he noticed. She could hear him, no bother, then. But just what was going on behind that steady expression?

"PC Annie Irvine recording in the Grange clinic for neural disorders. DCI Lorimer interviewing Mrs Phyllis Logan. Date and time pre-set," Annie's voice broke into his thoughts. Okay, this was it.

He took a deep breath before asking, "We need to know exactly what took place in the clinic on the night that Kirsty died. And I'd like to know if you heard anything."

The nod she gave was quite definite now and her eyes were staring at him, huge and fearful. She'd heard something all right. Lorimer edged his chair closer to the bed. He spoke slowly and deliberately, watching Phyllis's every reaction. Her eyes flickered once in Annie's direction then passed back to him as if she was indifferent to the presence of the camera.

"Right, now. Did you hear anything unusual outside your door on the night of..."

Lorimer broke off. The woman in the bed was

making high-pitched mewing sounds, as if she was trying to tell him something. Tears threatened to spill over from those huge eyes.

Lorimer leaned closer. "You heard something?"

Phyllis gave a nod. Her eyes were round and staring.

"Was it a sound like something being dragged past your door?"

Again that tiny jerk of the head meant yes.

"Did you hear any noises coming from the far end of the corridor?"

The woman's brow furrowed for a moment.

"A noise like something heavy falling down a flight of stairs?"

She gave another frown then shut her eyes quite deliberately before nodding again.

Was she telling him "Yes and no"? How the hell could he draw out all the details? For a second Lorimer clenched his teeth in frustration. Then he looked at the woman in bed. Dear Christ! If this was how he felt what on earth must it be like for her? He breathed in and out, deliberately relaxing himself before continuing.

"Did you hear a door banging shut? A heavy door?"

The nod confirmed her answer this time.

Lorimer paused, still holding her eyes in his, trying to see what she had seen.

"Phyllis, did you hear footsteps coming *back* along in this direction?"

Lorimer watched as her mouth worked noiselessly, trying to form words that nobody could hear. A plaintive sound came from within her, repeated over and over again as her head tilted up and down in agitation.

Then suddenly her eyes flitted past him and stared wildly at the door, making Lorimer turn to see who had come into the room.

There was no one there. What was she trying to tell him?

He could feel a growing excitement inside as he asked her, "Phyllis. I want you to think very carefully before you nod again. Did you see anybody in here just after you'd heard the noise of the door banging?"

Her eyes switched back to his. He could see the sigh unfold in her chest as if she'd been waiting for this question that he'd finally asked. She gave a nod.

"That's "yes", Phyllis. You're telling me that you saw someone in here that night?"

The nod came again but Lorimer could see the strain on her face. The effort of making even these small movements was exhausting the sick woman.

"Was it anyone you knew?"

Her eyelids fluttered. Was that a "no" or was she simply unable to keep her eyes open?

"Did Leigh Quinn come into your room that night?"

The movement of the woman's head was imperceptible. Not a nod at all, more of a gesture of inquiry as if she was puzzled by the question.

"Phyllis. Did a man come into your room?"

She nodded but the movement was clearly an effort as her head hung forward, its weight drawing Phyllis's face towards the sheets.

"Was this man a stranger to you, then?"

Had she nodded? He couldn't be sure.

Lorimer gazed at her wasted body. Could he really put his faith in this invalid? A niggle of doubt began to bother him. Was she a reliable witness? Should he even be questioning her like this?

Lorimer's eyes travelled back to her face. The body might be wasted but here was no doubting the intelligence locked inside that impaired nervous system. As Phyllis's eyes met his, he realised that he had no need to doubt her. That steady expression told him that she was willing him to see whatever she had seen.

"Did he speak to you?"

Lorimer saw the muscles in her face twitch as a spasm passed through them. Her eyes widened in fear but her head nodded forwards.

"And threaten you?"

Her eyes bored into his as she gave a nod.

Lorimer glanced up at Annie Irvine. They were on the brink of something momentous.

"Phyllis. Do you believe that you saw the person who killed Kirsty MacLeod?"

There came a small weeping from the woman in the bed, tiny stifled cries as the tears flowed down into the pillow. Slithers of mucus dropped from her open mouth. For an instant Lorimer stared at her, absorbing her grief. Then he felt in his pocket for a clean handkerchief. Folding it around his index finger, he wiped away the tears. Carefully he gathered up the wet trails hanging from Phyllis's mouth and dried her chin.

Her breath shuddered suddenly. Lorimer's simple actions seemed to have calmed the woman. Her head was drooping low and she looked awkward, propped up on a bank of pillows that no longer gave her any support. Lorimer didn't hesitate. He knew he was probably breaking all sorts of rules, nevertheless he thrust an arm around the exhausted woman's shoulders then pulled her further down into the sheets until her head was resting against the pillows once more. Well, he'd broken rules before and, hell, all those leading questions might be thrown out in a court of law anyway.

This video could turn out to be a total waste of time. Lorimer sat back looking at the patient. Her body was rigid with pain. It was not only pointless but cruel forcing any more out of her now. Besides, she'd given him plenty to work on already.

"DCI Lorimer terminating the interview," he said. He heard the buzz from the video camera as Annie retracted the zoom and ended the recording. He was pretty sure that there were several leads he could follow from what Phyllis had given him. Part of him wanted to be up and off to study the footage they'd just recorded but there was something he had to do first. Right now he had a duty to protect this vulnerable witness.

"Ask Mrs Baillie to come back in here, would you, Annie?"

As the policewoman left the room there was a low moan from the woman in the bed. Lorimer returned to his place beside her and took her hand. It felt cold and bloodless.

Phyllis turned her head away from him and then moved it back to look into his eyes, making sure he was watching her. Then she turned once more, staring at the large vase of flowers set on top of her locker.

"Is it the flowers, Phyllis?" Lorimer felt the cold hand in his, motionless. She continued to stare at him, then, imperceptibly, she nodded.

Suddenly Lorimer realised what it was she had been

trying to tell him. The flowers!

"Did the man take a carnation from your vase, Phyllis? A red carnation?"

The woman gave Lorimer a long hard stare then, quite deliberately, nodded her head, once, in definite affirmation.

Her shoulders relaxed in the sigh that followed. Now she really had expended all her energy. Her eyes closed and Lorimer heard her breathing steadily until he was sure that she had fallen asleep.

"You may also think you have a witness statement from the Logan woman but it might be quite inadmissible in a court of law, you know," Mitchison continued, the finger wagging just a fraction too close to Lorimer's face.

"If you would just take a look at the recording, sir?"

Mitchison gave a theatrical sigh, "Oh, very well, then. Let's have a look."

The Superintendent watched as Lorimer slotted the tape into the video machine. The two men listened as Annie Irvine's voice began the interview. Lorimer stared at the face on the screen. He had every detail of the tape off by heart now. There was no interruption from Mitchison as they listened to the recording. At last it was over and Lorimer looked questioningly at his superior.

Mitchison was frowning at the empty screen, an expression on his face that Lorimer couldn't quite fathom. It was almost human, he thought cynically.

Finally the Superintendent broke the silence between them. "She's a very sick woman," he began to say, slowly.

"Yes, she is," Lorimer replied. There was no point in denying it after what they'd both witnessed on the tape.

"I wonder if the courts would consider her a reliable witness?" Mitchison seemed to be asking the question of himself. Then he shook his head. "Oh, I don't know. We'd need all sorts of expert medical witness statements to back up the validity of this statement. If you can even call it that."

Lorimer clenched his fists out of sight, under the desk. Would Mitchison try to stop the tape being used as evidence after all her efforts? He mentally rewound the video, seeing the woman's anguished face. It took all his powers of restraint to keep the passion from his voice.

"Sir, although she has no power of speech, she's no dummy. Mrs Baillie can vouch for her mental health."

Mitchison's face twitched as if a spasm of annoyance had passed over it. For a moment he didn't speak but simply continued to stare at the blank screen. Lorimer wondered what was going on in the man's mind. At last Mitchison swung around in his chair, his usual expression of superiority back in place. "Oh, very well, let's get on with it. But I have to warn you, Chief Inspector, I'm really expecting some results now. There have been too many man hours frittered away on this case already."

Lorimer took a deep breath. "I'll be showing this to Dr Brightman, sir."

Mitchison looked askance at his DCI. "Our criminal profiler? Why not. He hasn't come up with anything yet, has he?" he asked, as if Solomon was yet another tiresome burden he had to bear.

"No, sir," Lorimer lied, his fingers crossed under the table. Let Solly's theory about two killers simmer for a bit, he decided.

Having Mitchison's blessing about Phyllis Logan meant more right now, especially with the idea that had taken root in his brain. If Solly was correct and a killer was closer to home than they thought, then Phyllis Logan might be in more danger than they imagined.

Solly recrossed his legs thoughtfully. They had watched the video footage twice together now and he'd not offered any comment. He could feel Lorimer's eyes burning into him, waiting for some word of encouragement.

"Well, what do you make of her?" Lorimer asked, obviously bursting for a response from the psychologist.

Solly shook his head slowly, tugging absently on the curls of his beard. Then he sighed. "What a terrible imprisonment for her. To be so confined. Just like poor Nan Coutts. Yet she must have developed an inner self." He spoke softly, almost to himself as he stared at the screen. "She's been terrorised all right, though, don't you think?" he added, turning to make eye-contact with Lorimer.

"Oh, I don't think there's any doubt about that. Only by whom? That's where our problem lies. Leigh Quinn was my first thought, but now I'm not so sure. It's certainly a man, so we can eliminate the female staff and patients from the scenario along with the cleaners and other women.

Including Mrs Baillie," he added.

Solly tried to hide a grin. The director of the Grange had ruffled DCI Lorimer's feathers considerably during the investigation. And there was still that question mark hanging over the finances of the clinic.

"Phyllis Logan's been there long enough to know the staff and long term patients by name, surely," his voice trailed off and Lorimer was left watching him as Solly's face took on the dreamy attitude with which he was becoming so familiar. There was something brewing in that brain of his.

"I took a long walk around the whole area," Solly began. "It struck me that somebody walked straight into the Grange and straight out again the night that Kirsty was murdered. I think we're pretty much agreed that this killer knows his way about. He knew Brenda's movements too. There's a coolness about his character. He has something to do with the clinic, that's clear enough to me. He can disappear into the background like so much wallpaper. Nobody sees him as out of place."

"Nobody seems to have seen him at all except Phyllis Logan!" Lorimer protested.

"I wonder," Solly mused. "Brenda Duncan and Kirsty MacLeod were doing their usual rounds, checking up on the patients. They had to go into everybody's room, isn't that so?"

Lorimer nodded, puzzled. They'd been over this again and again. What was Solly getting at now?

"Well, it's a pity we can't ask either of them, but I wonder…"

Lorimer bit his lip impatiently.

"The patients on suicide watch have a designated

nurse with them during the night, don't they?"

"Yes," Lorimer frowned. What was he trying to say?

"Well, suppose one of them left their post for a bit? Both they and their patient would be vulnerable, wouldn't they?"

"Vulnerable to what?"

"Suspicion, of course!" Solly exclaimed, surprised that Lorimer hadn't followed his line of thought. "And I don't see any of the nurses owning up to being away from a patient's bedside when that would provide a perfect alibi, do you?"

"But, hold on, let's look at this another way. Say you're right and there's one killer of prostitutes who likes to hang around Queen Street station then another who bumps off two nurses, what about motive? Are we looking for two nutters, d'you think?"

Solly shook his head. "Whoever murdered Kirsty and Brenda knew exactly what they were doing and why. The real problem is how they came to find out about the signature." Solly looked hard at the policeman. "Rape can escalate into murder. The women in Queen Street may well have been raped. Sexual activity was present in both cases."

"But they were prostitutes! Of course there were signs of sexual activity!"

"But neither Kirsty nor Brenda were assaulted like that. He simply walked up and strangled them. The element of shock was that they knew their attacker and trusted him."

"Would they have trusted a patient?"

"That depends. If they knew him well enough, yes.

Still considering Leigh Quinn?"

Lorimer's face twisted in a grimace. It fitted almost too neatly: a depressive who had some sort of flower fetish. But why would he have killed Kirsty? He'd liked her. And Brenda Duncan? What possible reason could he have had for stalking her home like that?" Lorimer shook his head. "Not really," he sighed. "He had no grudge against either woman as far as we know."

"Interesting you should use the word *grudge*. Something may have happened to poison a mind already holding a grudge. Something that triggered off this chain of events."

Lorimer reached forward to eject the tape. The MS patient had given them both plenty to think about.

Solly would try to develop his profiles while his own team would continue the painstaking work of cross-checking the background of every man connected to the Grange. And now that included every member of the team itself.

Chapter Thirty-Two

Father Ambrose let his spectacles fall on top of the evening paper. Four women had been strangled now and still he sat here worrying about them. Praying too, he admitted, but he would have done that anyway. The picture in the evening paper showed a young woman smiling into a camera. The headline had shouted out her crime, and his. Poor child, he thought, to have stooped so low. The journalist had painted a life of drugs and deprivation. Father Ambrose could imagine what that might have been like. One of his parishes had been in the inner city, long ago, before they'd torn down the sagging tenements and given people decent homes. He'd been party to some terrible confessions in those days, he remembered.

It was the flowers that had first bothered the priest. Red carnations slipped between the praying hands of a killer's victims. There had been a shiver of unease to begin with until memories came flooding back, memories of other hands that had selected the choicest blooms. A vivid picture of a body in a coffin came back to him, the flower like a gash of blood against the whiteness of the shroud. The hands that had placed those flowers had been clasped in prayer each day, right by his side. Until the scandal that had shocked them all.

Father Ambrose picked up the paper with shaking hands. He knew what he must do. All along he had known it, but he'd suppressed that event over the years until it had almost ceased to exist. Now he had to face the truth.

Chapter Thirty-Three

Lorimer could have gone home but tonight he just didn't feel like sitting staring at the television while Maggie was up to her eyes marking these interminable papers. So here he was, waiting to be served in the canteen. The fluorescent bulbs glared overhead, at odds with the spring light that poured into these upstairs windows. Mitchison could make a start by saving dosh here, thought Lorimer moodily. Like the waste of money Maggie was always going on about in her school where the heating was kept turned up all year round, even in the holidays. Maggie again. He must stop thinking about her.

Lorimer looked around the canteen. There weren't many folk in tonight but he recognised DC Cameron sitting alone, hunched over a plate of spaghetti. Lorimer noted with interest that he wasn't eating it. He was stirring the strands of pasta round and round his plate with a fork but was making no attempt to put any of it into his mouth. Lorimer's curiosity made him watch the young officer.

"Chief Inspector, what's it to be?" Sadie, a wee woman with a voice that could have scoured a burnt pot was standing, ladle in one hand, looking at him expectantly. Lorimer turned to give her his full attention. No one messed with Sadie.

"Just some soup, thanks. Oh, and one of your brilliant Danish pastries, Sadie," Lorimer gave her his best smile as usual but this was one woman who was oblivious to the Chief Inspector's famous blue eyes.

"Wan soup, Betty!" she shouted towards the kitchen. "Yer Danish is up therr, son," she added, jerking her head to the plastic-covered shelves that Lorimer had already passed. Lorimer nodded and turned to fetch his pastry, marvelling as he always did at Sadie Dunlop's ability to make them all feel like school kids. She was wasted here. She should've been Governor of Barlinnie at least.

"Mind if I join you?" Lorimer grasped the back of the metal chair next to Cameron's. The DC sat up with a start as Lorimer spoke.

"Not fancy Sadie's pasta special tonight, then?"

Cameron shook his head and attempted a smile.

"How about a drink? I was going to drop into the Iron Horse. Okay?"

Cameron's pale face flushed slightly as he answered, "I don't usually drink, sir. I'm TT, you know."

"Ah, the strict Hebridean upbringing," Lorimer teased. Then his face grew more sombre as the germ of an idea began to form in his head. An idea that might take root, depending on what Cameron could tell him.

"Come on down anyway. The ginger beer's on me," Lorimer's voice held a note of authority that he knew Cameron recognised. The DC looked up at his boss then pushed the congealing mess of spaghetti away from him.

They were practically out of the canteen when a familiar voice stopped them in their tracks.

"Haw, ye's've left yer dinners. Ah thought ye wanted that Danish? Right waste of good food that is, 'n'all!"

Lorimer glanced at Cameron who was dithering in the doorway. "Come on, before we get arrested for dinner neglect!" Lorimer grinned conspiratorially and gave the DC a friendly wink.

It was quiet in the pub. Seven o'clock was a watershed between the quick after-office pint and quiz night. Seeing the bar staff polishing glasses and catching up with the day's paperwork, Lorimer knew they wouldn't be disturbed.

He had chosen a booth at the rear of the bar. On the table sat a pint mug of orange squash and Lorimer's two preferred drinks, a pint of draught McEwan's and a half of Bunnahabhain. Lorimer stretched his long legs under the table, feeling the heels of his shoes dig against the ancient wooden floor. The Iron Horse had made few concessions to modernity, which, for Lorimer, was part of its charm. He sank against the burgundy-coloured padded seat, feeling something close to relaxed. Pity he'd have to spoil the moment.

"How are you settling in to the job, now? Glad to be out of uniform?"

Cameron shot Lorimer a wary look before giving a shrug.

"You could tell me to get lost, but I think it might do you good to have a wee talk if there's anything on your mind."

"There's nothing, really," Cameron began in a tone that told Lorimer just the opposite.

"Is it the case that's bothering you? Still feeling bad about Kirsty MacLeod?"

Lorimer looked intently at Cameron. The lad's mouth was tightly shut and he could see his jaw stiffen. If it had been anyone but Lorimer asking such questions he'd probably have been told to mind his own damned business. Except that Cameron didn't even swear. The young detective constable had been looking past him as if intent on the framed engraving of James Stewart on the wall above their booth, but then he turned suddenly, meeting his superior's gaze.

"Yes, I feel bad. I thought I could handle it, but maybe I was mistaken."

"You handled yourself well enough at the mortuary. Dr Fergusson even commented on that."

"Well, that was different. It wasn't so personal."

Lorimer took a mouthful of beer and licked his lips. Just what did the lad mean by personal, he wondered.

"Did you ever meet Kirsty down here in Glasgow?"

"No." The answer came just a shade too quickly.

"Sure about that?"

"Of course. Why would I lie?" the flush had crept back over Cameron's neck.

"You tell me."

"Look, Chief Inspector, Kirsty was a girl from home. She was a friend of my wee sister's. I hadn't seen her for years, okay?"

"Okay, calm down. How about that place Failte, then? Did you know anybody there?"

Cameron shook his head. "Before my time. It was a holiday place for as long as I can remember. There are plenty of houses empty most of the year just waiting for incomers. It's only been a respite centre, or whatever, for the last two years or so."

Lorimer nodded. That had been his information too. Phyllis Logan's family had kept the house as a summer residence then it had lain empty for years before becoming a part of the Grange.

"D'you remember that first murder back in January?"

"Of course. I'm not likely to forget it."

"The woman who was killed had a flower between her hands. Did you actually see it that night?"

Cameron stared at him, surprised by this sudden change of tack. He frowned as if trying to recall the images of that freezing January night.

"I remember seeing her lying there and DS Wilson calling her Ophelia. That was after we saw the flower, wasn't it?"

"Can you remember how her hands were held?"

"Well, I know how they were held, it's in all the reports, isn't it?"

"But do you *remember* it?"

"I think so. Why?"

"You didn't by any chance describe it anybody outside the case, did you? Anyone from home, for instance?"

Cameron looked at him curiously then shook his head. "I don't talk about my work to the folks," he said. "They don't even know I'm involved with Kirsty's murder."

Lorimer was looking at him keenly as if to weigh each of the DC's words carefully. Niall Cameron returned his gaze with apparent coolness. There was no longer any tell-tale flush warming that Celtic pallor.

He wanted to believe the younger man. Experience told him he was hearing the truth, but there was someone who had inside knowledge of the first case, someone who had used it to copy the killer's signature. And Niall Cameron had known the girl from Lewis. It had been his call, too, that had alerted Lorimer that night, he remembered. He picked up the whisky and drained the glass in one grateful swallow, suddenly needing the burning liquor to take away a taste he didn't like.

The vibration from his mobile made him put down the glass with a bang. "Lorimer?"

Cameron's eyes were on him as he listened to the voice on the other end. He was vaguely aware of the younger man picking up his jacket and giving him a wave. He nodded in return, watching the Lewisman walk out of the pub and into the Glasgow night.

"Who is this Father Ambrose?" Lorimer asked, listening as the duty sergeant told him of the priest's telephone call.

"And he's coming up to see us?" Lorimer bit his lip. This was news indeed. A priest from the Borders who had information about Deirdre McCann's murder, or so he claimed. As he pressed the cancel button, his thoughts drifted back to Lewis and to the house called Failte where he'd met the nun. Where was she, now? And had she anything to do with this sudden need for an elderly priest to speak to Strathclyde CID?

Chapter Thirty-Four

Father Ambrose was a small rotund gentleman dressed in clerical black. His thinning hair showed a well-scrubbed scalp that shone pinkly through wisps of white curls. A cherubic face smiled up at Lorimer's.

"Chief Inspector. I'm so glad to meet you," Father Ambrose said in a voice as gentle as a girl's. But the hand that grasped Lorimer's was firm and strong.

"Father Ambrose. You rang last night, I believe?"

The priest ducked his head as they walked towards the stairs. "Yes. Though I should have contacted you sooner."

Lorimer raised his eyebrows. Ideas of confessionals sprang to his mind. But weren't those secrets told during the confessional sacrosanct? As he pulled open his door and ushered the little man inside, his head was buzzing with speculation.

"Some tea, Father?"

"No thank you. I will be seeing an old friend later this morning. She will be filling me with pots of the stuff, I assure you," he smiled, a dimple appearing on his cheek.

"Well, what can we do for you, sir?"

"Ah. Now, it's what I can do for you, Chief Inspector. What I should have done for you months ago, when that poor young woman was killed."

"Deirdre McCann?"

The priest nodded sadly. "I read about it in the papers. It troubled me greatly at the time but it was not until this latest death that I made myself face some unpleasant facts."

"Oh?" Lorimer leaned back slightly, appraising the

man. Father Ambrose had folded his hands in front of him as if to begin a discourse. Lorimer waited to hear what he had to say.

"There was something that happened several years ago, something that I had wished to forget. It's no excuse, of course, for procrastinating. Indeed, had I acted sooner perhaps these other women might not have been murdered." Father Ambrose's voice dropped to a whisper. He gave a short, resigned sigh and continued. "I became a priest and was trained by the Jesuits. I have probably had one of the finest educations in the land, you know," he remarked. "Anyway, my work took me into teaching for a time and I was responsible for the young men in a novitiate in the Borders."

"A novitiate? Is that like a seminary?"

"No, Chief Inspector. A seminary exists to educate those who wish to become diocesan priests. Rather like students for the Ministry in other denominations."

"So what does a novitiate do, exactly?"

"Well, we have a year of discernment where men, usually young men, learn about the Order. The novices study but also do many tasks around the Parish House." Father Ambrose smiled wryly. "We like to give them quite menial jobs as a way of testing their resolve."

Lorimer nodded, encouraging the priest to continue.

"This is not something we take lightly, Chief Inspector. It is the highest of callings and any novitiate must be suitable as well as serious in their intentions. About fifteen years ago we had a young man who had come from a farming family in Lanarkshire. He was a huge chap, great shoulders on him, hands like hams. He had the physique of a farmer. But Malcolm wanted to join our Order and I was appointed to be his novice master. He was so eager and willing to help and I admit he was of great use around the Parish House when anything of a practical nature was required. That was how he came to help us with the funerals." He paused and stared at Lorimer.

"We were part of a large Parish at that time and our own church was shared with the local parishioners during massive renovation work. Malcolm began by doing the heavy work, lifting coffins, packing away hurdles, that sort of thing. But then he began to take an interest in the laying out of the deceased." Father Ambrose tightened his lips in a moue of disapproval. "Normally there would be vigil prayers the evening before a funeral and the coffin would be kept overnight in church. One evening, just before leaving, we caught sight of Malcolm placing a flower in the hands of a young woman who had passed away. It was a red carnation."

Lorimer sat up smartly.

"It was a nice idea, we thought, and the relatives rather liked it, so it became a habit of Malcolm's to select a flower for the coffin thereafter. Of course that stopped when he went away."

"He left the Order?"

Father Ambrose sighed once more. "Not exactly. He was asked to leave. There was an incident," he hesitated, his pearly skin flushing. "Malcolm was found interfering with a corpse, Chief Inspector."

"What exactly do you mean, Father? Interfering

in what way?"

"Normally the coffins were screwed down after vigil prayers and somehow that job always fell to Malcolm." The old man wiped a hand across his eyes as if trying to erase a memory. "One of the other novices had left something in church and went back for it. That's when he saw Malcolm."

"What was he doing?"

"He was trying to make love to the corpse." The priest's voice had sunk to a whisper again as if the memory of that shame was too much to bear. "We realised then what we had suspected for some time, that he was not quite right. Academically Malcolm was fairly poor and his progress towards the priesthood would always have been in question, but there was more to it than that. I think there may have been some problem. There was talk of behavioural difficulties when he was little. Perhaps I'm trying to find an excuse for what happened, I don't really know. Anyway, it was a terrible time. We managed to keep it out of the papers but it rocked the whole novitiate. Malcolm was sent home and I left shortly afterwards."

"But it wasn't your fault, surely?"

"I was responsible for the boys and their welfare, Chief Inspector. My integrity was in question. There was no way I could continue as a novice master," the priest replied firmly.

"So," Lorimer began, "you think this Malcolm may have had something to do with the murder of Deirdre McCann and the other women?"

"I do. Although," the man hesitated again, "I worried about the nurses. I couldn't see him murdering good people like that. Still, the mind does odd things,

isn't that so? No, it was the killing of the two prostitutes that concerned me."

"Why was that?"

"Malcolm was adopted, Chief Inspector. His parents were farming folk who had no children of their
own and they took him in and gave him a good home
and a loving upbringing. Perhaps that love was just too
giving, in the end. You see, they told Malcolm about
his real mother. She had been a prostitute in Glasgow
and had given up her baby for adoption. That was the
reason Malcolm gave for wanting to enter the priesthood. He had a vocation, he said, to rid the world of
that kind of sinfulness. Of course, we took that to
mean that he wanted to save their souls."

"And now you think he may have been on an
entirely different crusade?"

"Yes."

"Tell me a bit more about this man. Malcolm...?"

"Malcolm Docherty. There's not a lot I can tell
you. He must be in his late thirties by now. I can give
you the address he had in Dumfries," he said, handing
Lorimer a piece of paper. "But I don't know what
became of him after he left us."

"And there's nothing else?"

"No. Just my feeling, I suppose. Well, more a cer-
tainty, really." Father Ambrose looked Lorimer
straight in the eye. "I just know that Malcolm is the
man you're looking for."

It didn't take long after the priest had left for
Lorimer to run a computer check on their existing
data. The names and details of all who had been interviewed were listed in a file. Running his eye down the
names, Lorimer wondered if Malcolm Docherty,

disgraced novice priest, had even kept his own name.

He had. There, amongst the list of railway employees, was one Malcolm Docherty, aged thirty-nine. Lorimer sat back, stunned. They had him! After all his team's intensive investigating it had been the conscience of one elderly priest that had cracked it for them. Taking a deep breath, Lorimer lifted the phone.

"Alistair, get the team together. Now. There's been a development."

Malcolm was picking up an empty lager can when he saw them approach. His stick froze in his hand as he watched the figures draw closer. There were about five of them, all in uniform, and they were coming down the side of the railway line. His first instinct was to warn them off, they were too close to the rails. But these were no wee school kids shouting names at him as he chased them away from his line. These men walked towards him with a purpose. Malcolm dropped his plastic sack and turned to run. But just as he began the ascent of the embankment he saw two more uniformed figures sliding down the grassy slope towards him.

He raised his stick and charged, yelling at the top of his voice. Suddenly his legs were swept away from him and he felt a sickening thud as his mouth connected with the hard turf. As he stared at the ground and listened to the harsh voice telling him that he was under arrest, all Malcolm could see were the pale blue speedwells shivering on the grass. He put out his hands and grabbed the tiny flowers, squeezing them tightly in his huge fists, then felt them being wrenched away and cuffed tightly behind his back.

All eyes were on the man as he was led away through the station to the waiting police van. The platforms that had been cleared for this operation were now full of commuters alighting from their trains. Even a Press bulb flashed, prompting an officer to throw up an arm as if to protect his prisoner. But there would be plenty of stories told by the passengers held back by the police cordon. Once the news broke, they'd be able to tell how they'd actually witnessed the arrest of the man who'd become known as the Station Strangler.

Chapter Thirty-Five

Solly shook his head as he read the evening headlines, *Killer of Four Women Caught*. They were wrong of course, just as Superintendent Mark Mitchison was wrong. Malcolm Docherty had not murdered Kirsty MacLeod or Brenda Duncan. Solly's mouth twisted at the irony of it all. The signature that had identified the man was being used as evidence that he had murdered all four women. And so far Lorimer had not intervened. Mitchison had insisted that he be charged with all four killings. Was Lorimer really doing nothing to prevent this? Somehow he couldn't imagine the DCI condoning a miscarriage of justice, not to mention the fact that Solly was convinced that a killer was still at large. And Lorimer knew that.

He hadn't been invited to sit in on the interview. In fact, there had been no communication at all from Strathclyde Police. Perhaps he ought to make it his business to be there all the same, Solly thought, watching as a black cab rolled down Byres Road, its orange light glowing. Making a sudden decision, Solly raised a hand and watched as the vehicle drew in to the kerb.

There was an atmosphere of jubilation at headquarters when Malcolm Docherty arrived. Lorimer felt guilty that he was about to spoil it. The last months had been a slog for all of them and Docherty's arrest seemed to be the culmination of all that painstaking effort. He'd called the whole team together once Docherty had been safely conducted to the cells for a medical examination.

Lorimer looked from one smiling face to another. Jo Grant was looking positively smug, as well she might. Even the serious Lewisman had a grin on his pale face, though it wouldn't be there for long.

"I'm sorry to spoil the party," he began, "but there is a development that I want you to be aware of."

All eyes turned to him and he could see their smiles fading as they heard the gravity in his tone.

"As you know, Dr Brightman has been attempting to profile our killer. I'm pleased to tell you that Malcolm Docherty fits a profile that has been drawn up."

There were murmurs of approval but among them Lorimer detected Alistair Wilson, hand on his chin, giving his boss a speculative look. The detective sergeant knew Lorimer well enough to tell when something was wrong.

"However, this profile was developed with some difficulty. Dr Brightman did not find it possible to draw his profile until he came to a conclusion about the murders." Lorimer paused to see if he had their attention. There was a kind of hush as all eyes were turned his way.

"He believes we have not one, but two killers," Lorimer told them.

"But that's impossible!" someone exclaimed.

"What about the flowers?" another voice demanded.

"I know, I know. I've been asking myself exactly the same question. There's a chance, however, that the murders of Kirsty MacLeod and Brenda Duncan have been carried out by a copy-cat killer. Until we interview Docherty, we can't be certain of this, of course.

It may well be that he confesses to all four murders. If so, we can open a few bottles and go home. And no one would be happier than me, I can assure you," he added. "However," he raised his hand to quell the murmurs that had broken out, "If we have no real evidence to link Docherty with those other two deaths, we may have to consider something else." Lorimer took a deep breath before continuing. "If Dr Brightman is correct then we have a real problem on our hands. It would mean that information has been leaked from somebody on the team. Now, I don't have to tell you about security during an investigation. You all know how things operate. But the fact remains that the killer of those two nurses knew exactly how Deirdre McCann's hands were folded around that flower. The Press got that aspect wrong and we weren't about to correct them, I can tell you. So. Whoever killed Kirsty and Brenda had to have seen an incident report."

"Or been the same killer!" Jo Grant declared, a mutinous look on her face. Lorimer's heart sank. Jo had been one of Mitchison's sidekicks in the past. Would she make trouble for him now?

"That's right," he told her. "But we have to prove that, ladies and gentlemen. I wanted you to be aware of this before I have Docherty up for questioning. If any of you have been guilty of a breach of security then now's the time to tell me. Otherwise we may have to turn this place upside down."

"Superintendent Mitchison does not share Dr Brightman's theories, I might add," he said, looking deliberately at Jo. But the DI showed no triumph at his remark. In fact, she was frowning now and

Lorimer wondered just what she was thinking.

"I'll have a copy of Docherty's statement circulated to all of you as soon as it's available. Let's just hope he tells us what we want to hear."

Lorimer took his detective sergeant aside as the other officers departed. "I want you downstairs with me when Docherty's brought up," he told him. "We'll not have his DNA results for a bit and they may prove crucial. Meantime he's in for a grilling."

"You really believe Brightman's theory, don't you?" Wilson asked, a rueful smile on his lips.

Lorimer nodded. "Aye, more's the pity. It just makes so much sense, you know. The logic of it all hangs together apart from anything else."

"And has he come up with a profile for killer number two yet?"

"I think he's still working on that. But I'll let you know. *If* Mitchison lets him carry on, of course."

"Any chance that the Super will halt the investigation?"

"Don't even ask me that yet. Wait till we've heard what Docherty has to say."

It was a different figure from the man they'd seen escorted between two burly police officers. Malcolm Docherty's shoulders were slumped and his head hung down as if a weight drew it earthwards. The police doctor handed Lorimer a file, nodding towards the prisoner seated at the table.

"No problems, Chief Inspector. We'll let you know the results ASAP. Okay?"

"Thanks," Lorimer replied and walked around the

table to face Malcolm Docherty. The man did not look up as Lorimer stood at the table, nor did he flinch when the DCI scraped a metal chair across the floor, its grating squeal setting everyone's teeth on edge. At first Lorimer simply stood there appraising the prisoner. His mind flicked back to the January night when this case had begun. The swirling fog had cleared away now and he felt a weird sense of peace in the interview room. Euphoria had given way to calmness now that the man was finally here in front of him.

One glance at his feet made the line on Lorimer's mouth tighten. This man's shoes were size twelve, at the very least.

Alistair Wilson waited patiently out of Docherty's line of vision. His boss would begin whenever he was good and ready. At last Docherty looked up as if some magnetism stronger than his own will was forcing him to acknowledge Lorimer's presence. Lorimer sat down, Wilson beside him.

"Interview with Malcolm James Docherty beginning at 15.00 hours. June sixth. Detective Chief Inspector Lorimer and Detective Sergeant Wilson in attendance," Lorimer began in a voice that sounded utterly bored by what he had to do. It was a useful ploy. It made a suspect feel both inferior and at ease, often resulting in a sense of outrage. *How dare this cop treat me as if I were some unimportant part of his daily grind?*

Docherty's eyes gave a glitter that told the two policemen that the ruse had worked.

"You are Malcolm James Docherty of 19 Peninsula Crescent, Springburn?"

Docherty glared at Lorimer then shifted his eyes to

take in Wilson who nodded encouragingly. "Aye," he said at last.

"Where were you on the night of January 12th this year?"

Docherty licked his lips nervously, eyes shifting from Lorimer to Wilson and back again. His silence was not unusual. Many suspects were at a loss how to begin answering questions in an interview room, especially those who had no previous experience of the situation. Lorimer waited as if he had all day. If Docherty stalled too long, he'd simply pick up the Gazette and begin to read bits out to Alistair Wilson about last night's football results. That was another ploy that got under their skin, he knew.

But he hadn't long to wait. Docherty sat up a bit straighter and looked at Lorimer.

"It's my work," he began.

Lorimer nodded encouragingly, but not too eagerly. He'd make Docherty do the talking if he could.

"You see, I clean up the railways." He paused, uncertain of how to continue. "There's a lot of rubbish everywhere. Everywhere," he added, a dreamy look appearing in his eye.

Lorimer tried hard to sit still although his impulse was to lean forward to catch any nuance of speech.

"I was *asked* to do these other jobs," he told Lorimer, a note of querulousness creeping into his tone.

"What other jobs?" Lorimer asked.

Docherty looked surprised. "Clearing up the station. Those women can't come in and do things there," he protested, sitting up in his chair with an air of righteous indignation.

"What women?"

Docherty bent across the desk and glared at Lorimer as if he were stupid. "Prostitutes," he hissed, his teeth showing in a grimace of hatred.

"What method did you use to clear these women from your station, Malcolm?"

"I put them down."

"Could you describe exactly what you did, Malcolm?"

Docherty hesitated as if he were trying to find the correct answer then he moved his hands up and clasped them together as if they were round an invisible throat.

"Like this," he said.

"You strangled them?"

Docherty nodded.

Lorimer swallowed hard. His next question was crucial. Trying to sound as if this was a normal conversation he asked, "How many women have you strangled, Malcolm?"

The sound of Docherty's feet shuffling under the table could be heard as Lorimer waited for the answer.

"Just two," he said. "I'm sorry."

Lorimer took a deep breath, suddenly understanding what the man was apologising for. It was not contrition about taking lives. It was that he'd only taken two of them.

"Are you sure it was only two?"

Docherty nodded sadly. "Aye. Two prostitutes, they were."

"Tell me what you did after you'd strangled them, Malcolm?"

The man seemed to brighten up a little at the question. "Oh, I sent them on their way. I gave them a flower and let their hands do a prayer. I said a prayer too. They're quite safe now, you see. They'll not harm anything ever again."

Beside him Lorimer could feel Wilson shift uneasily in his seat. They had a right one here and no mistake.

"Did you give a flower to any other young women recently, Malcolm?"

"No. Just those two. It's not my fault," he told them, round-eyed. "I didn't get any other orders."

"You said earlier that you were told to do these clearing up jobs, as you put it. Who exactly was it who told you to kill these women, Malcolm?"

Docherty gave a smile. "God."

Lorimer nodded as if this was something he heard every day in the course of his investigations.

"And how did God make his instructions clear, Malcolm?"

"He talked to me. He showed me the flowers. *His* flowers. They're perfect, you know. All His creation is perfect. But *they* weren't perfect. They had to be cleared away. Like the rubbish."

A nutter, Lorimer thought. A twelve-carat nutter. Voices in the head from God. Sometimes they actually heard them from the television. That kind of mental illness wasn't really so uncommon. But had he had anything to do with the killing of the two nurses? Lorimer had to ask.

"Where were you on the nights of May 7th and May 14th?"

Docherty shook his head. "I don't know. What

days were they? I work during the day. But I don't go out much at night."

Lorimer told him.

"No, I'd be at home. I watch TV at night then go to my bed. Sometimes I go out for a fish supper. Can't remember, really." He shrugged as if the dates were of no importance to him.

"Two nurses were killed on those dates. They were strangled and somebody left a flower in their praying hands, Malcolm. Just like you did."

"What?" Docherty suddenly sat up, a horrified look on his face. "But that's terrible! Who'd do a thing like that?" The man's expression was almost comical, thought Lorimer, one serial strangler condemning another. But then his expression changed as the awfulness of the news sank in.

"You don't think...? No. Oh, just a minute, hold on now," Docherty rose from his seat, fists clenched, his face a mask of fear.

"Mr Docherty has got up from his seat," Wilson intoned into the listening tape.

His words seemed to calm the man for he sank back down, a look of horror still on his face.

"Do you deny strangling Kirsty MacLeod and Brenda Duncan?"

"Of course," he whispered. "I never killed them!"

Lorimer believed him. But would Mitchison expect him to grind the man down in order to elicit a confession from him? If so, he'd be sadly disappointed. That wasn't Lorimer's way. The DNA results might confirm what they were hearing and what Solly had suggested. For a moment Lorimer wished that he could have the psychologist here with them. He might know how to tune in to Malcolm Docherty in a way that would prove his innocence as well as his guilt.

A tap on the door made all three men and the uniformed officer turn round. DC Cameron's face appeared, signalling for Lorimer to join him outside.

"DCI Lorimer leaving the interview room."

Lorimer stopped in his tracks. Beside Cameron was the familiar figure of the psychologist. It was as if his wish had suddenly spirited Solly there. Was the man psychic as well as everything else?

"What are you doing here?"

"I wasn't asked to come in, if that's what you mean. I just wanted to be here," he explained with his usual little smile.

"Well. I'm not sorry you did," Lorimer told him. "We're in the middle of interviewing the suspect. He's already confessed to the two station murders but says he knows nothing about the other two."

"And you believe him," Solly said. It wasn't a question. He could see his answer in Lorimer's face.

"Will you come and sit in?"

"Thanks."

"Chief Inspector Lorimer re-entering the interview room accompanied by Dr Brightman," Alistair Wilson told the tape recorder.

"Malcolm, this is Dr Brightman from Glasgow University."

Docherty stood up and took Solly's outstretched hand in his large fist. "But I've seen the doctor already," he muttered, giving Solly a dubious look. "Why do I have to see another one?"

"Dr Brightman is here to keep us company, Malcolm," Lorimer reassured him. It was like talking to a wee boy, he thought, except that most wee boys of his acquaintance were a dash sight more streetwise than Malcolm Docherty appeared to be.

There was something otherworldly about this man that had nothing to do with his experience as a failed novitiate. Lorimer had seen so many criminals whose lives were lived in a world so different from his own, yet all worlds impinged on each other, he thought. There was never really a place to hide from the evils that existed. Not even in the Jesuit Order.

Solly had listened as Lorimer and Wilson took turns to ask the man questions. His behaviour intrigued the psychologist. It was as if he were a perfectly normal citizen in his own eyes, assisting the police with their enquiries. Any minute now, he thought, and he'll get up and ask if he can go home. There was no remorse, no worry at all about the crimes he had committed, nor any awareness of the boundaries that he had trespassed. That was the real difference between the criminally sane and those criminals who were mentally ill. Culpability was indeed a state of mind.

As he heard the questions and answers about Docherty's methods of strangling the two prostitutes, Solly's stomach turned. To dispatch these poor women as if they were so much dross! Lorimer and Wilson kept their feelings well under check, he noticed, though he knew well what they thought. *Any murder is an affront to humanity*, he remembered Lorimer insisting. And he agreed. But this man, this huge man who looked like a farmer with his weather-beaten skin and massive shoulders, he had no sense of humanity at all. Only a warped brain that took twisted messages from a false god.

Malcolm Docherty was well capable of murder. The man's physique was such that it was no longer difficult to imagine a swift strangulation at these hands. Rosie had worried about that, he knew. How could someone kill these women with no sound of a struggle?

The same applied to Kirsty MacLeod's death, though, a little voice reminded him. She'd been dealt with swiftly, too. But there was no way on earth that Solly could believe the man in front of Lorimer was responsible for that death. Nor for Brenda Duncan's. Solly was still a way from completing his profile but he knew the mind that he sought was altogether sharper and clearer than Docherty's. That was a calculating, reasoning person who was not quite in focus, yet. And it was not Malcolm Docherty.

Chapter Thirty-Six

Rowena sighed as the pick-up gathered speed. She could see the new man's hair curling sweetly around the curve of his ear and over the brown cord collar of his waxed jacket. Dad was wittering on about the flight and telling the man how much he was going to enjoy Failte. Give Dad his due, it sounded so sincere and welcoming, but Rowena had heard the same spiel each time a new one arrived at the airport.

She was glad that last one had gone. Sam Fulton had given her the creeps. Dad had kept a real good eye on him, though. Mum had insisted on that. After Sister Angelica's abrupt departure, the Glasgow man had sought out Rowena's company just a bit too often. She'd been pretty uncomfortable with him, not liking the way he joked about women as if they were all an inferior species. It was all a bit of fun, he'd told her. No harm meant. But Rowena had kept her distance from him all the same. Dad never told any of them what a patient's background was. She understood how it was important to maintain their privacy. She wouldn't like any of them to know all of her secrets either, Dad had once pointed out. Still, she had the feeling that Mum knew more about Sam Fulton than she was letting on. And this fact alone had increased her uneasiness. Still, he was gone now, back to Glasgow, supposedly over the worst of his depression.

Rowena smiled to herself. The new patient had shaken her hand as if she was a proper grown-up, not some silly wee schoolgirl. She recalled his grave eyes and that tired, kindly smile. She'd maybe ask him to come for a wee walk up the road with the dog after dinner, though Dad liked his guests, as he called them, to have complete rest after they arrived. Still, this one was only here for a long weekend.

Funny about the other man, though. They'd waited for him yesterday with a placard that said Failte in bold lettering, but nobody from the Glasgow flight had acknowledged them. Dad had phoned Mrs Baillie who had shrugged it off but there was always a worry that somehow a patient would simply slip past them and roam about the island, unsupervised. It hadn't happened yet, but there was always a first time, Mum had warned them. Still, they had another new one now.

Rowena settled back to enjoy her thoughts. She'd rehearse what to say before they went out. Then maybe she'd be able to slip in questions about that Dr Brightman. Had they met at the Grange? Was he married? Her fantasy continued down towards the house, the passing landscape a familiar blur of greens and blues.

Chapter Thirty-Seven

"You want *what*?" Superintendent Mitchison's voice rose in a squeak that might have been funny in other circumstances.

"Complete freedom to carry out a surveillance operation. I've spoken to the patient and she has agreed to my suggestions."

Mitchison sat silent for a while, his face showing the struggle within. Lorimer could almost hear the cogs turning. Would the cost of the operation, never mind its risks, be outweighed by the capture of the second killer? Mitchison had railed long and hard against Lorimer's decision not to charge Docherty with all four murders. But the DNA results were pretty conclusive. Whoever had killed Brenda and Kirsty, it was not now likely to be the prisoner currently undergoing psychiatric testing. Which left them with a huge problem. Lorimer had sat down with Solly to confess his innermost fears; someone on the team was involved. Mitchison had been reluctant at first to have them all DNA-tested but it made sense for the purposes of elimination as well as to restore some kind of peace in the ranks. This weekend all his men and women would be in for their tests, whether they liked it or not. Lorimer and Solly would be there too.

Undergoing the test would give the team a sense of solidarity as well as letting him observe their various reactions. Staff and patients at the Grange had already been tested by the police doctor, giving Rosie's lot plenty to keep them busy.

At last the Superintendent looked up. "I don't like your ways, Lorimer, but that's neither here nor there.

A surveillance operation like the one you are suggesting carries a high risk. Not just for the patient, but a risk of failure. And I don't need to tell you how much the Chief Constable abhors a waste of time and money."

"We really need to try, sir. It's almost certain that we have another killer on the loose and that he has something to do with the clinic." Lorimer paused. Should he reveal his disquiet about the Grange's financial affairs or would that muddy the waters at this stage? No. He'd beaver away at that problem on his own, for now.

"Give me a complete breakdown of all the personnel you would need and the timescale, then," Mitchison decided. "And," he paused and drew a hand across his brow, "take care of that poor woman, won't you?"

Lorimer was taken aback. Concern for Phyllis was not what he'd have expected from the Super. Maybe the man had a heart after all.

"Mind if I come into your room, missus?" The man in white overalls carrying a cantilevered toolbox stood uncertainly at Phyllis's door. Phyllis eyed him with curiosity. That new nurse said that someone would be arriving today. To fix the television set. A wave of the old frustration swept over her. She couldn't explain she didn't watch the thing. It was pointless to do anything to a set that hadn't been used in years. Why not dismantle the whole thing and take it away?

As she watched him there were other questions that digested themselves in her brain until Phyllis had produced a satisfactory answer; questions that were

explained by the repairman's unusual activities. She
didn't know the first thing about televisions but she
didn't think the set would function in its normal way
with all its innards removed and replaced by what
seemed to be a smallish camera.

They were watching her. Perhaps she should be
relieved that those secret eyes were looking after her
but all she could feel was a sense of intrusion into a
world that was already far too confined.

Lorimer swung round in his chair to face the window,
the solicitor's words still singing in his brain. There
had been a lengthy delay in responding to his query
about the woman's will. He glanced down at the figure
on his notepad as if to check that it was correct.
Phyllis Logan's estate was estimated to be in the
region of three and a half million pounds. What would
his team make of this? One thing was certain, they'd
have to be especially careful of the sick woman now.

Lorimer looked back at the solicitor's report. The
main beneficiary of the woman's estate was the clinic
itself, wrapped up in a trust fund. There were several
provisions made to help patients who could not otherwise afford the fees, that money coming from interest
in share capital. Lorimer frowned. With the collapse of
so much on the stock market in recent years, just what
were these shares worth? But it was the other beneficiary that caught his attention. To the director of the
Grange, Mrs Maureen Baillie, Phyllis Logan had left
£250,000. A sweet quarter of a million!

Recalling the woman's spartan living quarters and
the suspicion that all was not well with the clinic's
finances, Lorimer felt a niggle of worry. People had

been murdered before for a lot less than that. But why would Kirsty and Brenda have been killed over a financial scam? It didn't make sense, unless they knew something that made their continued existence a danger to somebody. You've got a dirty mind, Lorimer, he told himself. Still, he'd keep digging this particular seam until he hit gold.

Why would Kirsty have been killed that night? Phyllis had been so vulnerable to the killer's hands. It would have been so easy just to have dispatched her there and then. If that was the underlying motive. He gnawed his fingernail until he felt it split under his teeth. There was something there, but what?

A bird flying past his window made him glance up and catch sight of the clock on his wall. Time to go. They'd all be waiting for him.

They were all in the muster room. Lorimer walked in to face the semi circle of officers who sat on steel chairs. He noticed that Jo Grant had chosen to perch on the wide windowsill that overlooked the car park.

"Right. We've got the go-ahead. I want to introduce you to two of our undercover officers from D. Division, Patricia Crossan and Marion Warbrick." He turned towards two young women who were sitting at the edge of the circle. One, a blonde girl hugging a stone-coloured raincoat around herself, was slouched into her chair. She gave a perfunctory nod. The other girl raked back her seat and stood up. Her black leather jacket and short cropped hair showed drops of water from the recent rain shower.

"Hi there," she smiled at the other officers. "I'm Pat and this is Marion." There were murmurs of acknowledgement from the rest of the room. As she sat down again, all eyes turned towards Lorimer.

"Next time you see Pat she'll be on duty at the Grange. Marion has come in specially to meet you before she hits the sack." The blonde girl managed a watery grin as Lorimer continued. "Erica, the third of our undercover officers, is keeping an eye on Phyllis Logan right now and Pat will be doing the next shift later on. I don't need to tell you how important it is that you treat all of these officers as if they were perfect strangers. As far as you are concerned they are agency nurses who are helping out at the clinic, okay? The one thing we don't want to do is to arouse anyone's suspicions. And I'm talking about staff, patients, visitors, anybody who comes through their doors on a regular basis."

Lorimer let his gaze travel over every officer's face as he went on. "If their cover's blown the whole operation could be scuppered. As far as the people in the clinic are concerned they're simply three new pairs of hands. Luckily, each of them has bona fide nursing experience. Guess the glamour of police work lured you away from your last jobs, eh, girls?"

There were snorts of derisive laughter from several directions, including, he noticed, Jo Grant tucked into her windowsill.

"There's been no suspicion at all at the clinic, has there?" Lorimer addressed Pat.

"They've accepted us without question, sir. Frankly, they're all relieved to have some agency nurses," she replied.

"Yes. There's been a bit of an exodus amongst the staff since Kirsty and Brenda's deaths," Lorimer agreed.

"So, ladies and gentlemen, we now have a round-the-clock presence at the Grange." He measured each word carefully as he continued, letting his blue gaze fall on each officer in the room as he spoke. "Now, here's the risky bit. We've let it be known to the nursing staff that Phyllis Logan has information about the night of Kirsty's murder." He paused to let his words sink in.

"We've not said in so many words that she actually saw the killer but the implication is there all the same. Pat, Marion and Erica have been asking both staff and patients all about the murders like the rookies they're supposed to be," he told them. "One way or another we've made sure that word has spread. Not too difficult in a small community like that. The patients will no doubt pass on the gossip to their nearest and dearest. I just hope to God the Press don't get wind of it."

He tapped his thigh as if considering what to say. Sometimes stating the obvious helped to concentrate the mind.

"The murders of those two nurses took place exactly one week apart. Okay, the loci were entirely different but each of them took place on a Monday night. Now that may have absolutely no significance but it's never something that can be ruled out of an equation, as you all well know. So this coming Monday is our choice. We've got the weekend to let the rumour factory do its worst, then we move in."

Lorimer heard their sounds of approval with a sense of satisfaction. There had been some voices of dissent when Solly had dropped his bombshell but now it seemed that they had come round to respect his opinion.

"We set up surveillance over the weekend and then wait to see if Phyllis Logan has any unexpected visitors."

"What if nothing happens, sir?" Niall Cameron was red in the face but he seemed determined to risk the question nonetheless.

"I expect Superintendent Mitchison will send us to the salt mines for wasting public money, Cameron," Lorimer growled at him.

"We've laid our bait in the trap. With her full co-operation, remember. Now we have to watch and wait. You're all experienced enough to know that's the hardest bit in any operation. You'll be on duty from just after nine o'clock right through till I say when."

He turned to the board behind him. A large-scale plan of the Grange had been fixed to the board with pieces of masking tape at each corner. Lorimer pointed to each area as he spoke.

"We'll have officers in unmarked cars all along the road to the front. There's waste ground at the rear. Alistair, you and Davie will take up positions between the basement door and the shrubbery. The gardeners have been given a holiday that week," he grinned. "You'll cover that exit. The patients will all be receiving visits from Health Board "officials" in the shape of Eddie and Vince," he indicated two of his detective constables, "since neither of you have been out at the clinic. The story is that you're there for a routine check. We've done the homework on it and it's a normal procedure. There should be nothing to create suspicion. The camera's in place and it'll be monitored from our British Telecom van out in the street. That's where I'll be with Dr Brightman and DC Cameron.

We'll be out of sight but in constant contact with all units. Erica and Pat will alert us to anyone coming into or going out of Phyllis's room. She's a target but remember she's also our main witness. Right?"

He turned to the board again and drew aside a fresh sheet of paper. "And," he added, "there's this." Taking a marker pen, Lorimer wrote down the figures he'd obtained from Phyllis Logan's solicitor and a brief note of her will.

He heard an incredulous whistle as he faced them again. "So now we have even more reason to look after our witness. *And* keep an eye on certain members of staff. Okay?"

There were murmurs of assent as the team prepared to leave the muster room. Lorimer found that he was surprisingly calm. Cameron's question had been quite valid, even if unwelcome. What if nothing did happen? He was gambling with the hope that the killer would take action, believing Phyllis to be a real threat. But what if the information so carefully dropped simply made him take to the hills? Was there any reason to suppose that the killer was still around anyway? Solly firmly believed that he was, and right now that was enough for Lorimer.

Chapter Thirty-Eight

Niall Cameron was sweating. Lorimer had chosen to take him personally under his wing. What could that mean? Did the DCI have doubts about his ability? Did he feel that as the relative newcomer to the job he needed to be supervised? Or was there another reason?

As he walked along Bothwell Street, the young man kept looking out for the clocks that signified the Standard Life building. That was where he was to meet the guy. Lorimer had indicated that the Grange's accountant had been trawling through the clinic's books with a fine-tooth comb and that he wanted to discuss certain things with Strathclyde Police. Cameron had been dispatched for this particular duty, and right now he was feeling more like an office boy sent on a simple errand than an officer involved in a murder case.

There they were, great gilt clocks high up at either end of the building. Automatically he checked their time against his watch to see if the time was correct. It was. Cameron stepped into a vast lobby flanked by elevators on each side and a list of names indicating the firms that occupied the building. A quick glance told him the third floor was his destination.

Minutes later he was shaking the hand of a man not too much his senior who introduced himself as Tommy Stirling.

"Fancy a coffee? The drinks machine's not bad," Stirling told him.

Cameron shook his head. "No thanks." The idea of coffee in a polystyrene cup didn't appeal. He'd be bound to spill it and make a fool of himself in this plush office with its matching blue carpet and padded chairs.

"Right, then, the Grange's account has only recently come into our hands. It's the sort of bread and butter thing we do all the time, really. There was nothing to show that this was an unusual client until those murders happened."

"The clinic's accounts were all in order, then?"

"Well, the last audit had been done by our predecessors fairly recently so we weren't due to check the books as soon as this. But of course you folk made us look a bit closer."

"And?"

"And there are discrepancies in the accounting. It took a while for me to spot them but I can show you," Stirling handed over a sheaf of papers folded back at a particular page. A turquoise highlighter pen marked several figures in a column.

"What do they indicate?" Cameron wanted to know.

"Unauthorised withdrawals from the main account."

Cameron frowned. "How could that happen?"

"Any withdrawals above a certain amount require two signatures. These only show one."

"Ah," Cameron nodded, understanding what the accountant meant. Against each of the turquoise figures was the name of the person who had taken several large sums of money from the clinic's account. Cameron flicked over the sheets of paper, seeing the same name again and again. It was Mrs Maureen Baillie.

"What exactly does this mean, then?" he asked. "Mrs Baillie is the Director of the clinic."

"She's *one* of the Directors," Stirling replied firmly. "And unless the other Directors are aware of her taking out these sums of money then there's only one conclusion we can come to, I'm afraid."

"What's that?"

"Embezzlement."

"How did you find out?"

"It showed up in the accounts."

Mrs Baillie gave a resigned sigh. "So you know, then?"

"We know that you misappropriated funds for your own use, yes. But we don't exactly know why. Care to enlighten me?"

For the first time since he had met her, Lorimer saw a tremble in the woman's face as if she might actually begin to cry. He could see her swallowing and heard her breaths coming in short gasps as she tried to regain some control.

"I needed the money," she began. "I had debts to repay."

"Uh-huh. And just who were your creditors?"

"Oh," the woman's eyes flew to meet his suddenly. "Just one. A man called Joseph Harrigan." She smiled a bitter little smile. "Perhaps you've heard of him?"

Lorimer had. Harrigan was a notorious bookmaker in Glasgow who had come to the attention of the fraud squad on more than one occasion.

"What on earth were you doing mixed up with someone like that?"

Mrs Baillie straightened herself up and looked

Lorimer straight in the eye. "I gamble," she said.

Lorimer saw the steady way she regarded him as if waiting for some condemnation. She wouldn't get any from him. Other people's weaknesses were not something he despised but pitied.

"Ironic, isn't it?" she continued. "I run a clinic for patients who have various disorders and I can't even help myself."

Lorimer nodded. Those bare rooms at the Grange made sense now. She'd whittled down her possessions as she'd gambled their worth away.

"There is the matter of a legacy in Phyllis Logan's will that I was hoping you would explain to me," he told her.

Suddenly the woman's face changed. Her smile was wistful as she shook her head.

"Ah, yes, poor Phyllis. I did wonder if you would ask me about that."

And then she told him.

Maureen Baillie looked down at the sheet of paper on her desk. She was surprised that her hand was so still, given the turmoil of emotion within. Her resignation as Director of the clinic would take effect from the end of the month in compliance with her terms of employment.

What would become of her after that? Lorimer had told her that there would be a court case pending. But fraud cases could drag on and on. Perhaps she'd have time to cut her losses and simply disappear. But it was her lack of assets that was holding her back, she thought with some bitterness.

The car she drove couldn't be turned into cash as it

was on lease hire, her own house had long since gone, which was her main reason for taking up residence in the Grange. If they ever thought about it, which she doubted, the staff probably believed she was simply being over-conscientious in her duty to the patients.

Harrigan had fleeced her. There was nothing left at all, now that the police had discovered her secret. Her salary would be paid into the bank but that few hundred pounds wasn't going to take her very far. Besides, where was she to go?

Mrs Baillie sat very still, fingering the pearls at her throat. They were all that she had left of her mother. Her face twitched in an ironic smile. Sentiment had proved stronger than her compulsion to gamble.

She could hear the chatter of two of the women as they passed by her room on their way to the television lounge. Her thoughts turned to Angelica who had been here so recently, providing an oasis for them all. And, of course, there was Phyllis to consider. She wondered about Phyllis and that new nurse who was so determined to learn what she could about Multiple Sclerosis. Patients like Phyllis were so vulnerable, she thought. Always prey to infection. How long she could survive was anyone's guess, but she'd seen other cases like hers before and knew that a sudden onset of pneumonia was the thing most likely to dispatch her patient.

Maureen Baillie's fist clenched the paper into a ball.

No. She wouldn't leave right away. She had a duty to patients like Phyllis, even if that duty meant a little bit of suffering.

Chapter Thirty-Nine

They were all set.

Mitchison had been surprisingly co-operative all of a sudden. Maybe it was the lack of DNA evidence, though they'd never really suspected anyone from the team. Lorimer had feigned astonishment when he'd been told of Sir Robert Caldwell, the Chief Constable, proclaiming his desire to follow the criminal profiler's advice. There were wheels within wheels. He knew fine that Solly had mentioned his case to the Professor of Psychology on the very evening when the Prof. was due to have dinner with Strathclyde's finest. He must have taken the hint and bent the Chief Constable's ear. It gave Lorimer some satisfaction to know that the Superintendent was not the only one capable of manipulating people. He wondered just what had been said between Sir Robert and the Professor. Still, it was enough that the Superintendent was giving them the authority to mount this operation without any hindrance.

Maggie had packed him a flask and a box of food. There was enough to feed an army, not just the three men, he'd complained, juggling with plastic carrier bags. But then she'd reminded him that Solly probably wouldn't even think about meals and he'd given in. It might be a long night.

The driver of the British Telecom van was DC Beattie, a lad who'd come into the force around the same time as Niall Cameron. He was dressed in the regulation navy uniform of British Telecom engineers, a mock-up badge clipped to his woollen jersey.

Lorimer and Cameron sat in the back amongst the

paraphernalia of sound engineering and close circuitry, backs against the metal sides of the van with Solomon facing them. Beattie sat up front. Despite the cramped interior of the telecommunications van, Lorimer had a decent view of all the monitors. His eyes wandered over them all but kept returning to those fixed in Phyllis Logan's room. If she were to have an unwelcome visitor they'd be the first to know.

The van was parked facing the crest of the hill that ran down towards Queen's Park, only yards away from the entrance to the Grange's driveway. Lorimer had walked around the area before giving his officers their various positions. There was some advantage in this road being a dead end, he'd realised; whatever vehicle came up this way would have to turn into the driveway or make a slow U-turn behind them before it could accelerate away again.

More than ever Lorimer felt that their killer was somewhere not too far away; perhaps, as Solomon had suggested, he was even inside the clinic already. Beattie was logging every vehicle that came up or turned to leave. So far his list included residents of the surrounding tenement flats as well as known members of staff and previous visitors to the clinic.

Lorimer's eye was caught by a movement from one of the monitors. Pat Crossan, her slim figure hidden beneath the regulation overall, was bending over Phyllis. From what Lorimer could see, the policewoman appeared to be checking the sick woman's pulse. One of Pat's credentials for the job had been her years as a Royal Alexandra nurse. She'd even seen action in the Gulf before coming home and joining the police force.

He saw her straighten up then give a small wink at the camera just to let them know she was aware of their presence. Below her, Phyllis lay inert, her eyes shut. It was impossible to know if she was asleep or not.

"Do you have a list of who's on duty?" Solomon asked, suddenly breaking the silence in the back of the van. He nodded, handing him a copy of the paper that had already been circulated amongst his team. They'd tried to cover every member of staff from the director down. The late shift would continue until ten o' clock, by which time the night staff would have taken over. Before the change of shift the visitors and day case patients would have come and gone. Mrs Baillie was there all day. Not only was she on duty but her off-duty time seemed to be spent more and more in her flat on the top floor of the Grange or wandering in and out of the residents' rooms, according to the under-cover girls.

"Erica takes over in four hours," Solly noted aloud.

"Right, but Pat will still be in the building. She's going to be writing up her essay on the clinic's computer. Or so she's told Mrs Baillie."

"I wonder what she'll really be typing onto the screen?"

Lorimer shrugged. He trusted Pat Crossan to cover her tracks effectively. She'd think of something plausible.

The next hour passed in a haze of boredom as Lorimer switched his attention from monitor to monitor, only calling up the members of his team to check out their positions.

It was a quiet Monday evening in a peaceful

Glasgow suburb when all good residents were out walking their dogs or strolling in the park. There was nothing to suggest that the surroundings contained small pockets of watchful police officers waiting for something sinister to happen. And that was the way it should be, Lorimer thought, looking out from the restricted view they had in the back of the van. He could see the pavement that curved up towards the clinic then turned into its drive. Beyond the dense shrubbery there was nothing else in sight. Above them the sky was full of house martins dipping and diving for insects. Lorimer watched their swooping movements as a relief from studying the monitors. Already it was June. Only a few more weeks remained of the school term, then Maggie would be away on her travels.

Lorimer stretched his long legs out in front of him. Earlier they'd been able to slip out for brief comfort breaks to the pub across the road but now he'd told them to stay put. He was aware of Cameron squirming beside him; cramped muscles no doubt. The monitors flickered as a car passed by, sunlight bouncing off its wing-mirrors.

Phyllis had been watching the woman all day with a growing curiosity. Pat had revealed her identity on her first visit to the room. It was their secret. Nobody else knew that the agency nurses were plainclothes policewomen. It gave Phyllis a small feeling of triumph to be part of this clandestine operation when so much of her existence depended on other people. She had understood the need for the policewoman's presence. Their witness must be protected, Pat Crossan had stressed, especially now that Phyllis had agreed to this.

The paralysed woman told herself that she ought to feel frightened or even excited; after all, she was the bait being dangled to attract the person she thought was the killer. But today she was too exhausted to summon up such emotional energy.

Instead she had merely observed the policewoman's movements, watching her intently until sleep had overtaken her.

Since Lorimer's interview the sick woman had slipped into sleep more and more. Observing her, Pat had wondered at the tenacity of the human thread that held onto life. From time to time she bent over the bed, just to listen to the whisper of her breathing. It could scarcely be heard above the rise and fall of the machinery below the bed that hissed and sighed. She'd been sleeping now for almost an hour. The room was warm although Pat had closed the blinds against the direct sunlight. She wanted Phyllis to have a decent sleep. The poor woman seemed so weary.

A buzzer sounded suddenly so Pat reached up to the red button on the patient's water line to switch off the noise. But Phyllis did not even blink. Below the sheets she was somewhere else, dreaming and drifting as the shadows shifted around the room, oblivious to the fluids being pumped into her body. The policewoman looked at the watch pinned to her uniform. Two more hours and Erica would be here to relieve her. Quietly she left the room, closing the door behind her. She had other things to check; the whereabouts of other members of staff or visitors. And she needed to go to the loo. She wouldn't be away all that long.

Meantime the camera fixed inside the television set

would watch over Phyllis.

As Pat walked briskly along the corridor a figure emerged from the shadows, looking after her.

Then, as silent as a cat, Leigh Quinn slipped into Phyllis's room and sat beside the sleeping woman. His hands strayed towards the vase of flowers on her bedside locker, touching their petals, re-arranging their stems. Then he drew one of them out of the vase and regarded it for a long moment.

Alistair Wilson circled his head slowly, hearing the crunch of fibres around his cervical vertebrae. At least he was out in the open air. Lorimer and the others would be roasting inside that BT van. So far all was quiet. The only communication they'd had was to check out all the visitors to the Grange. There had been no strangers among them, nobody who was out of place. The detective sergeant was sitting with PC Davie Inglis opposite the back entrance to the Grange, the gardening tools at their feet, screened from view by the thick branches of the rhododendrons.

"Reminds me of playing hide and seek at my auntie's garden in Saint Andrews when I was wee," Davie had whispered after they'd scrambled out of sight.

The door to the basement had been left locked, as it normally would be. It was vital not to arouse any suspicions on the part of anyone who might have access to the basement area, Lorimer had insisted. Whoever had murdered Kirsty MacLeod had been able to make their escape this way. But had they? Alistair wasn't so sure about that and he knew Lorimer himself had doubts about the access. Had the door been left open to make it look as if an intruder had broken in? And had the real killer remained in the clinic during the hours that had followed? Whatever theories they might have, there was no way they could fail to keep this exit under close surveillance.

"I need to stretch my legs," Cameron said suddenly.

"Don't we all," grumbled Lorimer.

"No, sir. I mean I really need to stretch my legs," Cameron told him. Lorimer noted the flush around his collar and sighed.

"Okay. But don't be long," he warned. Trips back and forth to the pub were okay for so long. Someone behind the bar might begin to comment if they weren't discreet enough. If the lad really needed to go to the toilet, he couldn't very well stop him, could he? Perhaps Maggie had been a bit over-generous with her refreshments after all.

Cameron clambered over their legs and slid open the van door. The sun had made the metal hot and he winced as he touched it. It was a relief to be out in the air again. He bent down slowly, massaging his calves, then stood up to walk carefully around the van.

Inside, Lorimer craned his neck to watch Cameron walking towards the pub but he was either out of sight or had sprinted across, more desperate than he'd admitted. He tried to catch Solly's eye but the psychologist was engrossed in the papers in front of him. Even in the sweltering heat of the van, the psychologist was trying to keep up with his exam marking.

Sister Angelica was happy. It had been a beautiful day, just like the summers when she was a girl. She'd been telling the other patients in the lounge all about the summer holidays of her youth when the family had spent weeks on the farm in Melrose. She'd walked the Eildon Hills until she'd known every crag of them, she said. Then she'd told them about Lewis and how peaceful it could be in Failte.

The weekly prayer meeting was due to begin soon. There was only one person left to arrive then they could start. She'd lit a fat scented candle and placed it on the table by the window. The breeze stirred its flame beside the muslin curtains, sending the fragrance of sandalwood into the room.

Angelica beamed at them all. It was so heartening to do something for these people who had become her friends. Mondays were quite special for her, now. Her vocation was not over, after all. That was something else she had found out during her stay here.

It happened so suddenly that nobody quite knew how to react. First there was a whooshing sound followed by the table being upset as Angelica lumbered to her feet and one of the girls began to scream. The fire caught hold swiftly, spreading to the wallpaper and sending sparks of tinder onto the soft chairs.

"Out! Everybody! Get out!" Angelica ordered, shooing them all like sheep from the room just as the smoke alarm began its insistent beeping.

They were coughing in the corridor and gasping for air by the time the nun joined them. One man had picked up the fire extinguisher and was heading back into the room, followed by Peter, one of the male nurses. The front door gave its alarmed ring as they all spilled out into the fresh air. Angelica did a swift head-count. They were all there, she told herself. Everyone, that is, except the one person they'd been waiting for. Where was Leigh?

"Something's up. The fire alarm's gone off," a voice came over the radio as Lorimer and Solly crouched in the back of the van. They exchanged glances but Lorimer shook his head.

"Not yet. This could be a false alarm." He switched his mike to talk. "Okay. Let us know the details as soon as you can. We won't make a move unless we have to." His gaze returned to the monitor.

The room where Phyllis Logan lay was bathed in a gentle half-light filtering through the blinds. There was no movement at all; the figure beneath the sheets seemed quite peaceful. There was no sign of the Irishman sitting by her bed.

"D'you think they'll need to call out the fire service?" Solly asked anxiously.

"We'll know soon enough, I suppose," he replied. "Maybe you should back the van up a bit, Beattie," he told the driver. "And what's keeping Cameron?"

As the van shuddered into life the monitors were shaken into blurred lines of grey and white, making observation impossible. The sound of the smoke alarm could be heard faintly from the building.

Lorimer had to know what was happening inside. He tapped out the numbers on Pat's mobile. The ringing went on and on until he gave up in disgust. She was supposed to keep in contact. Where the hell was she? He glanced back at the monitor showing Phyllis's room. Only the patient in her bed could be seen. There was no sign of the undercover officer.

Pat flushed the toilet and unbolted the door. As she

turned towards the basins to give her hands a thorough wash with the liquid soap she was aware of another person coming into the ladies' washroom.

The policewoman only had time to glance at the reflection in the mirror before she felt the sudden pain in her skull then everything went hazy as the sound of a high-pitched bell rang out in her brain. There was nobody to see her limp body being dragged into the cubicle, nobody to witness her nurse's overall being buttoned over another person's clothes.

Lorimer breathed a sigh of relief. The fire seemed to be under control by all accounts and he could see Pat's white-coated figure standing by the window. Any minute now she'd turn towards the camera and give him a reassuring signal.

Only she didn't. As the figure turned to face the screen, Lorimer found himself confronted by a different person altogether.

For an instant he was speechless then he felt the adrenaline rush as he grabbed the radio control.

"Alert all units. Find Pat Crossan. There's a stranger in Phyllis's room. We're going in."

He thrust the doors aside, not waiting for Solly who sat staring at the monitor in a daze of disbelief.

Phyllis woke up, suddenly aware of the shadow above her. But perhaps she was still asleep.

This wasn't the policewoman.

This wasn't meant to be happening.

She tried to scream, but the thin noise that came was quickly stifled by a feather pillow thrust over her mouth.

Now she was underwater, gasping and blowing for air that would not come. A ringing sound began far away then nearer and nearer, filling her ears. Her chest hurt with an unfamiliar pain as if she had been running hard.

Then she heard a cry and suddenly the room was full of whirling shapes as the pillow was pulled away.

Leigh was struggling with another man who had his hands against his throat. She watched, terrified, as they edged towards the wall, the man's fingers pressing into Leigh's neck. There was a thump and both men fell to the ground out of her sight. She stared, open mouthed, as another commotion erupted into the room. Then Lorimer was wrestling with her attacker, pulling his arms away from the bed. She watched as his tall figure grabbed the man from behind. He struggled against the policeman's grip, legs kicking wildly, knocking over the drip stand beside the bed. The crash as it hit the floor reverberated through every nerve in Phyllis's body.

The sound of running feet brought several more people bursting into the doorway, Solly and Mrs Baillie among them.

"Tom!"

Solly came to a sudden standstill. Lorimer had his colleague in a tight grip, the handcuffs already pinioning the man's wrists. The Chief Inspector looked from Solly standing white-faced in the doorway to Tom Coutts. Solly was gazing at the man's face, then his eyes dropped to the killer's shoes.

"*I look towards his feet, but that's a legend,*" he quoted softly. Lorimer saw the slight shake of Solly's head and the brightness behind those horn-rimmed glasses. Trust and betrayal; weren't they always the cruellest wounds?

Tom Coutts twisted once under Lorimer's grasp then, meeting Solly's eyes at last, Lorimer felt him slump in defeat.

"I'm sorry," he whispered. "I'm so sorry."

Nobody spoke for a moment, the sound of whirring machinery the only noise as the two men stared at one another.

Then Leigh Quinn stumbled to his feet. Ignoring the other people in the room he went over to Phyllis and crouched beside her.

"Are you okay, wee lady? Are you okay?" Tears were streaming down the Irishman's face as he stroked Phyllis's hands. "He didn't get you, my dear. You're safe, now," he told her tenderly.

Phyllis watched as they led that man, the man they called Tom, out of the room. She saw Dr Brightman following them, escorting Maureen Baillie gently by the arm. Leigh stood up and the policeman clapped his shoulder. For a moment Leigh flinched but then his expression changed and a grin spread over his face. He gave Phyllis a wave as he turned to go but she knew he'd be back later, sorting her flowers, talking to her about things he was unable to tell another soul in the whole world.

Then there were only the two of them left.

Lorimer came towards the bed.

"I'm so sorry you had to go through all that. Are you all right?"

Phyllis tried to nod but felt her eyes close instead. His voice was gentle.

"It's all over now," he said.

And Phyllis knew that it was.

Chapter Forty

There was a breeze blowing in from the sea, rippling through the new grass as Lorimer stood outside Saint Clement's Rodel. The psalms had been sung with no music, the voices raised in Gaelic song to their Maker, giving Lorimer the feeling that he was hearing words that had been uttered since time began on these islands. He had come alone on the morning plane to Stornoway but now he stood beside Niall Cameron, their heads bowed as the minister intoned the final words of the service. He could see Mhairi MacLeod leaning on her stick, Chrissie by her side as always. The cemetery was so packed with people that he was sure every member of the community must be there to pay their final respects to Kirsty.

At last the minister raised his hand in benediction and a resounding *Amen* came from every mouth.

Lorimer had watched as the simple coffin was lowered into the earth; Kirsty was there at last, laid to rest with her father and mother. There were no flowers. The funeral notice had indicated that anyone who wished might send a donation to the MS Society of Scotland. Everyone knew the nurse's vocation had been to care for such patients and even Lorimer's team had donated a cheque for the charity.

Overhead a buzzard mewed, a sad cry like a lost child's. Lorimer felt Cameron's hand on his arm then saw the mourners turning to leave.

"One minute. I'd like to see Miss MacLeod, if I may," Lorimer told him quietly.

"I'll wait in the car, then."

Lorimer stood aside as one by one they passed him

by. Dougie from the hotel gave him a nod but no smile. When there was only the minister by the grave-side with the two old ladies, Lorimer strode across the clipped turf.

"Miss MacLeod," he offered her his hand.

"Ah," Mhairi MacLeod turned at the sound of his voice, then, seeing who it was, she gave him a sweet smile. "You came!" she said. "I'm so glad."

"Yes."

"She's at peace now, Mister Lorimer. Far from any harm the world can do to her. Safely home with her Saviour," she said. Her words carried such simple conviction that Lorimer felt immediately humbled. Here was an enduring faith that carried on from generation to generation.

"And how are you?" he asked.

"Oh, I'm just biding here till it's my time. Chrissie sees that I have everything I need, don't you dear," she added, turning to the lady in black who was holding her arm.

"Aye. But we should be going now. There will be tea in the hotel if you wish to join us, Chief Inspector," Chrissie told him.

"Thank you, but no. I must get back to Stornoway for the return flight to Glasgow."

"You go ahead, Chrissie. Mister Lorimer and I will take a wee daunder along the path. It's fine," she added seeing the other woman's doubtful expression. "He'll take my arm. Won't you," she added, looking up into Lorimer's eyes.

They did not speak until they reached a green painted bench that faced the sea and Lorimer had helped the old lady onto the seat.

"Well, now. Are you going to tell me all about it or do I have to wait until the rumours and the papers mangle it up?"

Lorimer grinned at her and she returned with a smile of her own and patted his hand. "I may be old but I'm not afraid of the truth. Now, tell me everything that really happened."

"Tom Coutts was a patient at the Grange. He'd been receiving treatment for depression in the wake of his wife's death. Kirsty had been one of Mrs Coutts' nurses during her final illness."

"Yes, I remember Kirsty told me all about her. A right poor soul she was. Couldn't do a thing for herself. Hard on the man, I'm sure."

"Yes," Lorimer replied. He couldn't begin to imagine what kind of life Tom Coutts may have had, trying to care for a wife who had no sight and was completely paralysed. "So hard that he couldn't endure her suffering." Lorimer told her gently. The man's sobs rang in his ears as he recalled his confession; how he had smothered his wife with a pillow. Then a combination of guilt and paranoia had driven him to despair.

"He took her life, then?" Mhairi guessed.

"Yes."

"And did Kirsty know?"

"I thought you might tell me that," Lorimer replied. "The missing pages of her diary corresponded with the dates of Nan Coutts' death and Kirsty's resignation from her job."

"Aye," Mhairi MacLeod sighed. "I knew something was wrong, then, but she never told a soul, Chief Inspector. I promise you that."

"Dr Brightman thinks that those torn pages from

Kirsty's diary simply showed how much she wanted to obliterate the events from her mind. She was never a threat to Coutts. Still, he took fright when he met her again at the Grange. He couldn't rid himself of the belief that Kirsty knew what he had done. So he had to kill her. He was really ill, you know."

"And the other woman? The nurse he killed in her own home?"

"She was on duty the night Kirsty was killed. I think Tom Coutts was afraid she had seen him."

Mhairi MacLeod shook her head sadly. "Such a waste," she sighed. "Such a terrible waste."

Lorimer took her hand in his and felt its warmth. As they sat together in the midday sun the policeman felt strangely comforted by the old lady; her weight of years and greater wisdom a kind of solace to him.

"He copied the methods of another killer," Lorimer began.

"The flower and the praying hands. I remember."

"What puzzled us was how he knew exactly what that other man had done. Right down to the last detail. We hadn't even worked it out at the end," he admitted.

"And how had he found these things out?"

Lorimer shrugged. "Like most things, it was just too easy. Tom Coutts was in and out of the University even during his illness. He expressed an interest in the case. Even helped us with information about the clinic! What we didn't know was that he had been in Dr Brightman's office months before and had found that first forensic report. It was all there. Even down to the position of those praying hands."

"The poor man," she remarked. "To have suffered such guilt!"

Lorimer looked at her in surprise. Here was a large heart indeed that could feel for such a devious killer. Nothing excused the act of murder in his book, and never would.

"And the woman in the clinic? How is she?"

"Safe," Lorimer told her. It was perhaps the best thing he could say about Phyllis Logan. She was safe and well cared for as long as she remained in the clinic.

He recalled Maggie standing at the top of the stairs after he'd returned home, hugging her arms around her body as if she were shivering with the cold. She had asked the same question then promptly burst into tears when he'd told her it was all over.

"Here comes Chrissie. We'd better go," the old lady told him. Lorimer helped her to her feet, handing her the walking stick as Chrissie marched along the path towards them.

"Thank you, Chief Inspector. Thank you for everything," she whispered, leaning across to touch his cheek with her lips.

As the plane circled away from the island, Lorimer wondered if he would ever return. There was something about the place that he found beguiling. In some ways he envied Niall Cameron. It might have been his choice to work in Glasgow, but Lewis was still home. He'd been glad of his DC's company today. It had made him feel less of an outsider. Niall had taken some leave. There were things he had to do, people he needed to see, he'd said. Lorimer suspected one of them might be a girl. His shyness whenever Kirsty's name had been mentioned was merely a reminder of another lassie from home, he thought.

Then he considered Mhairi MacLeod, and her calm

acceptance of all that had happened. If only they could all emulate that old lady's wisdom.

This had affected so many lives. Maureen Baillie might never work again as a nurse, though he had a notion that she would be there until Phyllis Logan passed her final breath. Leigh Quinn was still there, too, watching over Phyllis as he and Sister Angelica had done during that troubled time since Kirsty's death. Their partnership had been more than a bond of faith, they had kept watch over the MS patient, fearing for her life. Would this set Quinn back? Or would the incident give him a renewed confidence? Only time would tell.

His thoughts returned to Mrs Baillie. Who would have thought that the Director had spent so many years as the sick woman's private nurse? She'd been fiercely protective of her relationship with Phyllis. And Solly had been right. Her cold manner had hidden a flawed, but caring, personality. Maybe time would heal her wounds, too.

Time, Lorimer thought. Time. Everything passed eventually. Even this year of Maggie's would wind to a close. He smiled ruefully to himself. She wasn't away yet and here he was trying to wish her back. Solly had said little when he'd told him about his wife's decision, but he'd laid a friendly hand on his shoulder that Lorimer had found oddly comforting. Solly and Rosie were closer than ever these days.

He wished them luck. Rosie was just the balm to soothe any hurt the psychologist was feeling over his colleague's revelations.

Two men were now in custody awaiting their fate. Would their cases ever come to trial, he wondered? Or would their acts be seen as some kind of sickness? Malcolm Docherty's twisted sense of religion was a far cry from the faith he'd just witnessed down there, on that little patch of green that was fast disappearing into cloud.

And Tom Coutts? Solly could console himself that his final profile had not been so far out after all: a highly intelligent man with some sort of personal motive for murder. At least he had succeeded in unwinding the twists of those two threads that had bound their victims together for so long. And the last piece of the puzzle had come from Coutts himself. They'd known the details about the signature had to have come from someone on the team. Forensics had drawn a blank, though. Coutts had simply walked into Solly's room and read the file on Deirdre McCann. And his supposed weekend in Failte had been cleverly timed so that he was the only patient not to have given a DNA sample.

Lorimer looked out at the clouds banking up against the window. Such intricate planning! And yet there was still a chance Coutts would wriggle out of it all as unfit to plead. Well, his destiny was in other hands now, Lorimer knew. But it was a thought that gave him little satisfaction.

Chapter Forty-One

The preliminary hearing had been postponed again. Maureen Baillie knew she should have been pleased but the tension of those last months was finally getting to her. Her post at the Grange would be terminated whenever a suitable candidate was chosen but her fellow directors were being surprisingly slow about finding a replacement. Mrs Baillie had her suspicions that a certain DCI was pulling strings on her behalf. There was no way she'd be reinstated once the case had come to court, but until then her duties continued as normal. Phyllis was still here too, languishing under that cruel disease. She'd been horrified when Lorimer had revealed the extent of the legacy left to her. As Phyllis's nurse for so many long years she had been told to expect a "little something". Shame had made her seek out Maxwell Richards. He'd been quite matter-of-fact about her problem. Now she was determined never to gamble again. No matter what happened.

It was some relief that she had been kept on after the arrest of that man, Coutts, especially when Phyllis was so poorly. The woman needed her, though she might not know it. The Director of the clinic had made it her personal business to have the Multiple Sclerosis patient nursed with extra special care those past few weeks. She knew from experience what that disease could do, remembering her own mother dying far too young, and had vowed that Phyllis should be given as much personal dignity as was possible.

The Chief Inspector had become a regular visitor. Mrs Baillie, who left Phyllis and DCI Lorimer discreetly alone at visiting times, often wondered what he said to her.

It was early morning. Phyllis could hear the blackbirds on the lawn outside her window. Their dawn chorus roused her from a shallow sleep every morning. Even with the blinds shut she knew the sunlight would be making the sky a pearly pink. It had rained last night; she'd heard it against the glass. Now she could imagine the sweet scent of newly cut, wet grass as the sun steamed it dry. Her shoulders felt cold. The bedclothes had slipped off her thin cotton nightdress some time during the night.

There was another new nurse on duty. Phyllis had rather wished that policewoman could have stayed on but of course that was impossible. She was all right, now. Just a knock on the head, Lorimer had told her. The events of that night had left their mark on her, too. Maureen had fussed in and out for days afterwards.

Phyllis tried to breathe deeply and heard the rattle in her chest. She'd been so hot during the night but now her arms were covered in gooseflesh. All she could think of was how tired she felt and how noisy the birds were outside. Maybe she'd slip into a decent sleep again before the nurse came to begin the morning routine. She'd been so weary after Lorimer's visit yesterday. He'd not stayed too long, but he'd told her things about that man, things she didn't really want to hear. It was over now and all she longed for was the blessed oblivion of a deep, deep sleep.

Phyllis closed her eyes as the blackbird on the lawn opened his throat in celebration of another new day.

* * *

"Sure you've got everything you want?" Lorimer asked anxiously.

"I'm sure," Maggie replied, biting the flesh inside her mouth to stop the sudden tremor in her voice. It wouldn't do to let tears spill at this stage.

"Phone me when you get in. Okay?"

"I will. I promise," she said.

Lorimer gave her a hug then Maggie turned away before he could see her face.

The slope up towards Passport Control seemed to go on forever.

"Don't look back," she told herself. "Don't look back."

At the desk, Maggie Lorimer handed over her passport to a woman in uniform. In front of her a queue was forming at the baggage x-ray. Most of them would be holidaymakers off to Florida for a fortnight of sunshine and Disney. She should feel so lucky, shouldn't she? After all, she was going to spend the next ten months in the Sunshine State.

Maggie took back her passport and hesitated, just for a moment, then turned her head to scan the crowds below her. The Costa Coffee seemed full of yuppies with mobile phones. Outside the avenue of shops, people were milling around, their holiday clothes bright splashes of colour against the cool airport interior.

Maggie looked and looked, trying to see her husband among the crowd below.

But he was gone.

Acknowledgements

I would like to thank the following for the help given to me in researching this novel: Jane Anderson, Superintendent Ronnie Beattie of Strathclyde Police, Dr Marjorie Black at the University of Glasgow Department of Forensic Medicine, Alison Cameron, Park Mains High School, Erskine, PC Leslie Duncan of the British Transport Police, the officers of Stornoway Police Station, Lewis, Douglas Harrison of The Multiple Sclerosis Society, Scotland, Suzanne McGruther, Father Michael McMahon, Brenda Mackay, the late Margaret Paton, Procurator Fiscal Depute of the Crown Office and Procurator Fiscal Service, Tony Rennie and, most of all, the late Cathrene Anderson to whom this book is dedicated.

ALSO BY ALEX GRAY

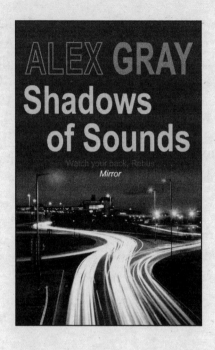

'Glasgow's answer to Ian Rankin'
Good Book Guide

To discover more great crime novels and to place an
order visit our website at
www.allisonandbusby.com
or call us on
020 7580 1080